A WIFE'S *Betrayal*

A NOVEL BY

MISS KP

Life Changing Books
Published by Life Changing Books
P.O. Box 423 Brandywine, MD 20613

Library of Congress Cataloging-in-Publication Data;

www.lifechangingbooks.net
13 Digit: 978-1943174027

Follow Us:

Twitter: www.twitter.com/lcbooks
Facebook: Life Changing Books/lcbooks
Instagram: Lcbooks
Pinterest: Life Changing Books

Dedication

To my sisters, Mia and Jawaun. Thanks for always believing in me and being my biggest cheerleaders. I love you guys more than you will ever know.

Acknowledgements

Well, it's finally done. Book number six. Five years ago who would've thought that I would be here juggling life and still doing what I love, giving you all literature with drama and lessons that you can't get enough of. For those of you that support me, I'mm grateful for you and know that without you, my journey wouldn't have been as successful, so I thank you all!

Rodney, I want to thank you for being such a great support through this tough process. Holding the household down, at times when I have to juggle so much is greatly appreciated. Your support helps to make me successful and I love you til death do us part. Thanks for all you do.

Kameron and Mateo you guys are the purpose of my heartbeat and I thank God for choosing me to be your Mommy. You mean the world to me and I couldn't imagine my life without you two in it. Jordan and Doodie love you guys! Ashley and Wynter I love you to pieces!

Mama (Lita Gray), you are my rock and role model and I love you for all the sacrifices, you've made and as I continue to grow as a woman I enjoy the mother/daughter bond that has turned into a friendship. Daddy (Willis Poole), I love you and am proud to be your baby girl.

Jawaun, Mia (Brent), and Cornell, I love you guys and I enjoy the sibling bond that we share that continues to grow and be strong. Sydni and Javone I love you guys! Baby Jay I love you! Thanks for loving your favorite crazy auntie LOL ;-)

Eve and Jaron, my West family I love you guys, thanks for all your support! Much love to Ava and Alton for always being there.

Tressa (Tony), Leslie (Jeremiah), and Tam (Don) thanks for being such a great circle of role models that help me grow and make me better. I appreciate all the late night talks and love that you give unconditionally.

To my true friends that always support me and hold me down no matter what- Pam, Gill, Shana, Tiffany, Sharawn (Bill), Kym Lee, Dona (Ed), Detrick (Renee), Mike Walker, , Donovan, Toyia and Troy who I want to thank for being a "true" friend. You've accepted my crazy mood swings over the past two decades and I love you for that. Much love to my #OY Boyz- Boobe and Choo, Kenya, Letitia, Shelrese, Indiah, Jai, Ranata, Deon, Kiana, and Latrese. Gervonta "Tank" Davis, love you to death and wishing you nothing but success and a long prosperous, legendary career.

Thanks for your support Abdul (Bliss Nightclub), Taz, Arlene & Lonye. Wassup Deangelo! Tarik Wallace, Pure Lounge, Terrance Brooks, CEO Shake, Bobby Patterson, Chef JR (Kitchen Cray), Raheem Devaughn and the hardest working DJ on the planet, Quicksilva.

Brian (Lash Moi) thanks for keeping my lashes popping and Jermaine (Runway Studios) thanks for keeping my hair on point. Jackie Hicks one of the best photographers in the world, I appreciate you!

To my #PumaLifeFamily- Joy, Karla, Matt, Rob, Randino, Scottie, Ain, Sue, Kelly, Curtis, Neil, and the rest of my buddies!

Thanks to all of my test readers, editors, Viriginia and Leslie, Davita for the great bookcover and my fellow authors for your continuous support!

Get ready for another banger and don't forget to post your feedback on Amazon.com.

Keep up with all things Miss KP-
Instagram @therealmisskp
Twitter/ Facebook/ Periscope @misskpdc
Website: www.TheRealMissKP.com
Also check out all of my novels

The Dirty Divorce
The Dirty Divorce Pt 2
The Dirty Divorce Pt 3
The Dirty Divorce Pt 4
Paparazzi

Much Luv and Hugz!
Miss KP

1 Kennedi

"Baby, I need to feel you inside of me," I whispered in my husband, Malcolm's ear as we entered the gate to our new water-front mansion.

"You know I ain't getting in no wreck but I'm gonna tear that ass up tonight."

Finally, I was gonna have a romantic night alone with my man, without having to tend to my daughter. Our nanny, Nina knew we needed time alone. It was a relief and felt good to have a night off from being Mommy. Finally I had embraced motherhood, which was definitely the new woman I'd become. Lord knows, I'd never given a fuck about any kids before. That was my worthless ass mother, Maricar in me I guess, but I'd definitely changed for the better over the past two years. Our daughter Milan meant the world to me, and she was all a part of the plan so I had to play the role.

Before we could make it up our circular driveway my Tom Ford skirt was around my ankles and my shirt was on the floor, exposing my pierced double D's. I rarely wore under garments these days so access was instantly granted.

"Is this what you want Daddy?" I purred wanting his thickness inside of me.

Throwing the Panamera in park Malcolm unzipped his Balmain jeans and pulled out his extra large pole right there on the spot. Massaging himself, he gave me that look I dreaded.

"Come on, Vee. Can daddy get some head? Your mouth be so wet babe. Bring them juicy lips over here."

"I want you inside of me."

"And…I want that red lipstick all over my dick, so what we doing?"

Leaning over the console disgusted, I moved my long highlighted hair to the side, grabbed his severely burned penis, and started to stroke him slowly. Sucking his dick was a task. I dreaded giving him head and had to be drunk to do it most times. However, in this moment I was sober and it felt like walking on coals or better yet it was like sucking a burnt fucking hot dog. The thought made me cringe. His dick had very little pigment due to the fire two years ago. It was brown and pink and looked like melted plastic around the tip. It was truly a sight for sore eyes. As my mouth filled with water, I was on the verge of throwing up right in his lap.

The night he was burned quickly flashed in my mind…a night that changed his life forever, but my thoughts were interrupted.

"Man wassup. What you waiting on?" he asked irritated.

"Be patient, I just want to look at it and rub it a bit," I lied.

"Man fuck it, that's alright," Malcolm replied in a frustrated tone.

"Don't do that. I was just trying to give a little foreplay."

Making him feel uncomfortable was never my intention. Without wasting another second, I threw his long rod in the back of my throat like it was an oyster I tried to avoid tasting. Sucking, slurping, and gargling all of his love inside my mouth, I put all bad thoughts in the back of my mind and went to work. As if I didn't have a reflex muscle, I sucked him like a chocolate popsicle. While I massaged his sack, he moaned and called out my name.

"Aww shit babe. Damn Vee, this shit feels good. I can't, I can't. I'm about to…"

Just like that he climaxed in my mouth and I swallowed every bit of his milkshake.

"That's all you got, huh?" I teased.

A girl was horny and needed to be fucked porno style. I knew if I talked shit Malcolm would make me pay. That's what I wanted. I wanted my husband to get his pole hard again and take me right in the driveway. It wasn't like the neighbors could see. The closest house was a ½ mile away, and even still I wouldn't care. When I wanted him, it didn't matter where or when. I guess that's what kept our marriage tight.

"You better stop playing before I give you the business."

"Yes, that's what I want you to do."

Malcolm turned his head back and forth. "C'mon Vee not right here. What if somebody drives by?"

I rolled my eyes. I loved my husband but I hated the new man that he'd become. The old Malcolm would've had my ass up in the air right now with no questions asked. The new Malcolm was always scared to make a fucking decision. He always second-guessed his every move, which pissed mc off. I missed his sponta-neous ways.

"Forget it. I'll take care of myself then," I said, turning off the music and moving my seat all the way back.

Sliding my fingers inside of my wet box, I looked him deep in his eyes and placed his hands on my breasts. As I flicked my fin-gers in and out by design so he could hear my wetness, I watched his dick rise again, as if a flag was making its way to the top.

Malcolm smiled. "Look what you did. You done woke my man back up."

"That was the plan, now kiss me."

His smile quickly disappeared. "You know you're gonna have to brush your teeth and gargle first, right?"

"What?" He knew exactly what to say to piss me off.

"Vee, you just sucked my dick and swallowed. You know damn well I ain't kissing you in the mouth after that."

I stared at him for a few seconds in amazement. "Wow. This OCD shit has to stop. For God's sake I'm naked. Who does that? Kiss your…"

Before I could say another word, Malcolm kissed me all over my neck, definitely avoiding my mouth, as he leaned the seat back as far as it would go. Next thing I knew my lcgs were wrapped around his waist and he was deep inside my love.

"Oh shit that feels so good. Yes, fuck your pussy. This your pussy?" I moaned.

"It better be. You better not ever give my pussy away," Malcolm replied as he looked up at me. He wasn't playing and I knew not to play with him.

"Don't fuck the mood up baby and start tripping and shit. Now carry on because you owe me."

Malcolm suddenly stopped mid stroke. "Oh, I owe you, huh?"

Nowadays, with Malcolm's mood swings I never knew what to say to him anymore. He was so fucking sensitive that I always felt myself walking on eggshells before our conversations. The shit was draining.

"Baby, you know I didn't mean it like that," I said, attempting to get him back in the mood.

Without responding, Malcolm pulled his dick from inside of me, then opened the passenger door.

"What are you doing?"

"Get out, Venus." His tone was ice cold.

Whenever he called me that I knew he was pissed. "Are you serious? Now you tripping. Don't you see that it's raining?"

"I don't give a fuck. Get out."

Here we go. This nigga and his flashbacks were getting the fuck on my nerves. How did we go from sugar to shit that quick?

"Malcolm, seriously stop playing."

He gave me an evil glare. "Does it look like I'm playing?"

"Fine…if you want me to get out I will. Hand me my clothes," I demanded mad as shit.

"Hell no. Get out. Just like that. Since you wanna talk shit about me owing you."

As he climbed back to the driver's side of the compact Porsche, I got out of the car, naked. I felt so humiliated. As the rain poured from the sky, I tried my best to hold back my tears. The old me would be ready to turn up and fuck his ass up, but I fought so hard to have this man. I wasn't letting anything ruin what we had built. Looking back at him before closing the door, he looked away unbothered.

Walking away in a daze, I was hurt and had so many emotions running through my head. My bone straight shoulder length bob instantly began to wave up as the summer rain poured all over my naked body.

"Where the hell are you going? It's time for me to pay my debt."

I was so into my feelings I didn't hear Malcolm come behind me. Grabbing me from behind, he started kissing the back of my neck.

"Get off of me!" I pulled away.

"Aww girl stop acting crazy."

Nigga you're the fucking one who's crazy I thought. As badly as I wanted to express my true feelings, I once again had to choose my words wisely. This motherfucka was a ticking time bomb.

"Stop playing, Malcolm. It's raining and I'm standing out here naked!"

"Stop whining."

Suddenly, Malcolm picked me up and carried me into our house. After taking off his shoes, he disarmed the alarm. Still with me in his arms, he held me tight as if he never wanted to let me go. This is what I always wanted. Malcolm to myself. No other bitches, just me, and the love of my life. Malcolm was paid when we met. A huge former entertainment mogul, whose swag is what I fell in love with initially. He was tall, dark, and extremely handsome; a confident man with cold black wavy hair, beautiful brown skin, and a sick wardrobe. Back then, he was beyond vain. Nowadays his looks were not what they used to be. Not only was he totally unrecognizable, but he only had nine fingers, a severely deformed left ear, and the skin on the right side of his face reminded me of Freddy Krueger. His life had changed tremendously, since he almost died in that car fire. Despite all of the material things that I now provided instead of him, I still loved him. I knew I genuinely loved him, because I was still here, fighting for our love.

All my life I never gave a fuck about anything, but it was something about this dude that made me feel safe. He made me feel like I could fall and he would always catch me. Despite how mad he made me, my love for him ran deep.

We made our way up the stairs into our bedroom. Turning the water on in the Jacuzzi and pouring my Lavender scented bubble bath into the water, it was time to relax and unwind. Lighting the candles that surrounded our bathroom, I set the mood, ready for a good round of lovemaking.

"Get the Jacuzzi ready babe, I'll be right back."

"Where you going?" I asked annoyed.

"We just tracked water all over the house. I need to clean it up real quick. I'll be quick, don't worry."

"Oh my God. Really? This cleaning shit is getting on my nerves. What the hell? I'm horny!"

Ignoring me, Malcolm quickly jolted downstairs. Since the fire he'd become a compulsive cleaner. Sometimes cleaning the same spot for hours, which was beyond annoying. His fear of contamination and dirt was stressful, especially the dirty shoe rule. I'd lost count on how many of my shoes he'd thrown away because they were so called contaminated and not allowed in his safe zone. It was almost as if the OCD was the third person in our marriage.

After twenty minutes of waiting and smelling the aroma of bleach, I couldn't take it anymore. Walking to the top of the steps I saw him on his hands and knees scrubbing the same step over and over.

"Baby, come on. It's clean. You've been scrubbing the same step forever!"

"Wait, I gotta get this one spot." He moved the sponge in a circular motion.

"Stop Malcolm! Come fuck me now!" I yelled and stomped back towards the bathroom. Surprisingly, he followed behind. Most times my pouting sessions never worked when he was on a cleaning binge.

"I wasn't gone that long, stop tripping," Malcolm said as he walked into the bathroom irritated like I was in the wrong.

"Look, I don't wanna fight. I just want you. Now come and taste your wife. Make it up to me for making me wait." The thought of his long tongue inside my nest made me wet instantly.

"Maybe after you get in the bath. You're not clean. We've been out all day."

"Are you serious?"

"Damn right I'm serious."

"Well, that shit didn't matter when I was sucking your sweaty burnt up…" As soon as I saw his expression, I stopped mid sentence.

"Oh so that's how you feel. Cool," Malcolm said, turning around. He started out of the bathroom.

"I'm sorry. Please don't leave. I'll get in the Jacuzzi to get clean now. Just promise you'll get in with me," I replied pulling him back.

"Vee you lucky I love you, I ain't never gonna leave you. Promise me you'll never leave me," he said, getting undressed.

"I promise."

As I slowly entered the water I realized it was super hot, but I didn't mind it at all. I knew that the water would tighten me up in all the right places. Laying my head back on my bath pillow I started to reflect on how far I'd come. This time two years ago, I was in a very bad place. I'd been dealt a bad hand in life and didn't know who to trust or love. I had to fight hard against all odds for my husband. That's why I knew our love was meant to be. Finally, I had the life I'd always wanted and no one was ever gonna take this feeling away from me. If I had to move my man from California to the east coast, dodge death, and fuck a couple of people on the side to keep my secrets safe, so be it. The skeletons in my closet were high as the fucking Empire State Building. If Malcolm knew half of the secrets I held onto he would hate me for sure.

Laying back on my bath pillow, I relaxed, waiting on the love of my life to join me.

"You alright?" I asked Malcolm with concern.

"Yeah I'm good."

"You sure. You looked like you were in deep thought."

"Did you mean what you said about my shit?" He could be a little sensitive.

"What?" I knew what he was referring to but decided to play dumb.

"It doesn't matter. Just promise me no matter what, you will love me forever and never leave me?"

"Vee, you're my wife. I'm only getting married once. We are in it for the long haul babe. It's just me and you."

Giving me the forehead kiss, as he looked me deep in my eyes, Malcolm made me feel safe. Taking off his remaining clothes, he made his way to join me in the Jacuzzi. My husband wasn't the same guy he used to be. He was once one of the most powerful men on the west coast who once rocked Gucci and Louie loafers. Now, he could care less about his clothing as long as it didn't cling to his body. I wasn't a fan of the baggy look when I was used to tailored suits but it was something I'd gotten used to. He also suffered from amnesia, which allowed me to mold him into the man I needed him to be. *Who needed that corporate shit anyway?* We were good. Our lifestyle hadn't missed a beat. I didn't care about the burns that covered 65% of his body including his face, which made him less attractive and unrecognizable. Those were war marks. I had my own set of scars, but as long as I did as I was told, my fairytale life would never end.

"Get in here!" I demanded in a sensual tone. I opened and closed my legs to give him a little tease.

Jumping right into the water on top of me he started to panic and scream.

"Owwwwww. Shit. What the fuck?"

I immediately became concerned. "What's wrong?"

"The water is too fucking hot! That's what's wrong. Are you trying to kill me? My skin is melting!"

"Oh my goodness, I'm so sorry."

"You did this on purpose, didn't you!" Malcolm yelled right before jumping out. Within seconds, he went wild, giving me two blows, straight to the face.

Moments later, his hands were around my neck. As he started to choke me, my head went straight under the water. Kicking him in his balls was the only thing that loosened his grip. As I gasped for air, I jumped out of the water as fast as I could. As I coughed uncontrollably, I noticed my husband bent over in pain. This was all my fault. How stupid was I to not adjust the water properly. I'm sure the heat had brought flashbacks of him nearly burning to death in a car fire. Malcom thought he'd been hit by a drunk driver and that his car had caught fire. That was the main reason why he didn't drink, but little did he know, that was far from the truth. Those were memories I tried to keep buried. I'm sure I was labeled insane for giving my husband drugs to keep both of our pasts a secret. But…some shit he just didn't need to remember.

No matter how many medications I fed him to keep his amnesia condition at bay, he was the same ole Malcolm. His exterior might have been hard and tough, but I could never change his core. This is what I had to deal with, and I accepted it.

Malcolm finally looked up at me. I could feel my bottom lip begin to swell.

"Look at your face. I'm sorry. I promised you I would never hit you again. I don't know what makes me do this."

I could feel myself tearing up, but I refused to cry. My life was so difficult right now but I couldn't complain when this was the life I chose. My husband and I both dodged death a couple of times, but as long as I did what I was told, things would remain good. Finally I'd found love, and I was willing to do all I could to keep it, even if it meant betraying my man to keep us both alive. To be honest, I was more like my mother Maricar than I liked to admit. I had so many secrets and continuously had to sell my soul to the devil in order to keep the life I'd sacrificed everything for. I'd come from the gutter to the big leagues, and nothing or no one was going to ruin this for me. It was important that Malcolm and I stayed out of the way and under the radar from everyone, including my family that were less than two hours away, so things would go as planned.

All my life I had been judged for the fucked up things I'd done, but no one understood all the shit I had been through. Hell, I've snitched, killed, robbed, lied, and a host of other stuff. All, just to live the lifestyle I've always wanted. Getting money, being famous, and gaining power always made me feel whole, but that was the old me. Now, I was a new woman, I'd changed. Money was still important, however, in order to live fabulous, I had to live a low-key lifestyle. As long as my secrets stayed buried and all things went as planned, my man would never know all I'd done.

"I love you, Vee," I heard Malcolm say.

"I love you, too and don't worry. We're going to fight to

keep this marriage together. Now come on let's go to bed," I said, reaching my hand out to him.

I loved this man and the family we had. If I had to sustain a few black eyes every now and then to maintain the life we'd built together so be it. As long as our past lives stayed buried, I would continue to live the life as Mrs. Malcolm Fitzgerald.

2 *Kennedi*

What a night, I thought to myself as a single tear raced down my face. Deep down inside I was hurting. Emotionally, physically, and mentally, but I knew my husband didn't mean to hurt me. Sometimes you just had to accept the bullshit to have the glam. On the surface life was great. I had everything a girl could ask for. Looking around the room in my Short Hills, NJ home, I took it all in. The vaulted ceilings, exquisite furniture, expensive paintings that graced my walls, all things I'd become accustomed to over the years. I was used to the best of the best, but something was still missing. *Did I miss the old Malcolm? Did I want him, or the fame and power, he no longer possessed? Was getting my ass whooped worth all of this*? These questions filled my head on a regular.

Getting out of the bed, I prayed my eyes weren't black from Malcolm's one-millionth blackout. It was easy to forgive him because I knew he didn't mean it. He was just sublimely frustrated. As I entered the bathroom, the scent of bleach filled the air. Malcolm had already started his OCD cleaning bullshit throughout the house. He'd been downstairs cleaning the kitchen for three hours.

Turning on the light, I instantly became irritated. Both of my eyes were purple and swollen and my bottom lip was split. Being half Black, half Filipino, my hazel eyes were already slanted, now they were damn near closed. My high cheekbones were bruised and my light skin made it hard to cover the war marks my husband gave me whenever his temper got the best of him. Concealer graced my face on a regular thanks to him.

Turning on the water on my side of the dual vanity, I started tending to my wounds. As my reflection stared back at me, I wasn't pleased with what I saw. I was starting to feel like I'd fallen off. My once 125 lb. frame and flat stomach was no longer. Although my big round ass was still shapely, I'd gained 20 lbs. that I just couldn't lose since I had my daughter.

When Malcolm and I met I was a stripper back in California, and was the baddest chick in the strip club. Body was banging. I needed to get my sexy back. I'd lost myself making everything about him. Taking care of Malcolm and helping him recover from all the medical treatments from the fire had been my life for the past two years. Even having our nanny, Nina on board, still wasn't enough. I'd put my all into trying to hold onto the only thing I'd left in this world that I cared about.

Sometimes I wondered if life would've been better with the old Malcolm. Life seemed easier for some reason as his mistress. He wasn't abusive, but he was married with a family. He was handsome, no burns, charismatic, no black outs. He was a business mogul with power and he took care of me. The new Malcolm was treacherous and mean, but it kinda turned me on. He had more edge, which was the complete opposite of who he used to be. Now as his wife, things had gotten harder and times had changed, but I still wanted it all.

In Malcolm's previous life he was an entertainment business mogul that got caught up in the mafia world. His beef with a very powerful man landed him on a dangerous hit list. I never knew the details of what got him there, but someone tried to kill Malcolm by blowing him up in a car. Malcolm was rescued just in time by firefighters, but somehow with the help of the right people, we were able to get Malcolm back and have the entire world think he was dead. Since I had the right connections, I made shit happen.

Malcolm was a fighter and the average person wouldn't have survived such injuries. He also suffered from retrograde amnesia, which caused pre-existing memories to be pretty much nonexistent. He suffered a head injury in the fire somehow and also lacked oxygen to the brain while trapped inside, thank God. To keep it that way, I fed him medication daily to help keep the old memories and long-term memory loss at bay. Not wanting him to remember who he once was didn't make me a bad person. I was just a bitch determined to keep all she fought hard for. Betraying my husband by having him think we were living off my inheritance from my dead parents was just a little white lie in comparison to all the other secrets I had buried. Who cares if I married him while he was on his hospital deathbed fighting for his life? Who cares if I'd made up the name Venus to keep him from remembering the old me? I was determined to get my man. Malcolm was now all mine. From being his mistress, to his wifey had been a journey, but I earned it. However, I did allow him to keep his old name. For some strange reason I wanted him to keep at least one part of his old life. It even kept me connected to the dominant tycoon he once was. His features were so distorted he didn't look like the old Malcolm anyway so I didn't care. It wasn't like someone would recognize him anyway.

Malcolm's wife and daughter had been murdered because of a debt that Malcolm owed. God rest his daughter and wife's souls, but now I was Mrs. Fitzgerald and we had a family. He didn't remember them anyway. Besides, my daughter Milan and I filled that void. As sick as it might sound, I was glad his daughter and wife were dead. That was the price Malcolm had to pay for whatever went down and I honestly could give two fucks about them being deceased. Besides, it put me in the position to have all I ever wanted, Malcolm. If I had to give sexual pleasures and go on a couple of jobs from time to time for exchange of a $50k monthly allowance from my secret business partner to keep this life, then so be it.

As soon as I attempted to get in the shower I heard loud screams coming from downstairs. It was my 18 month-old daughter, Milan. Racing out of my bathroom and down the stairs, I could see Malcolm's six foot four body sprawled across the floor in the foyer, scrubbing the dark hardwood floor as usual.

"Malcolm! Don't you hear Milan crying?"

"Damn, look at your face? Who you been sparring with, Mayweather?"

"Seriously," I responded irritated. I wasn't in the mood for his jokes right now.

"Calm the fuck down, Venus."

I hated when he called me that shit. Of all the names, I couldn't believe I'd chosen one that was associated with a manly looking tennis player. Luckily he called me Vee for short most of the time.

Quickly, I brushed passed him to find my daughter.

I was beyond angry when I saw Milan in the sunroom with applesauce all throughout her cold black curls, and lying face down on the floor. She must've tried to get out of her high chair and fell. Her mouth was bleeding.

I ran over and picked her up. "It's okay, booski. Mommy's here. Did you fall?"

"Uh-huh," she whimpered between sobs.

"Mommy will make you all better. It's okay."

As I looked into the hazel eyes we both shared, I thanked God she looked like both Malcolm and I. Milan was perfect. She was so advanced to be a one year old. She walked at eight months old, already said a few words, and was so in love with me.

Growing up in and out of foster care and having a mother that wished you were never born, doesn't prepare you for mother-hood. Tending to my baby girl's wounds, my maternal side I thought I'd never possess kicked in. Quickly, I grabbed a paper towel from the kitchen island and started to dab at a small cut I dis-covered on her knee.

"Ma-Ma leg hurt," Milan said with tear-filled eyes. Those words instantly sent me deep into a painful memory…

"Ouch Mommy, my leg hurts," I said, slowing down from a fast paced walk.

"Shut up Kennedi, and come on."

"Mommy where are we going? I don't feel good." I asked, coughing as I wiped my runny nose on the sleeve of my pajamas.

"I'm cold and sleepy Mommy. Why did you get us out of bed," my sister Kasey cried.

"Come you two, hurry up, walk faster! If I don't make it to Billy I won't be able to buy you coats. Y'all not gone make me get black eye again!" Maricar yelled in her annoying ghetto Asian ac-

cent as Kasey and I trailed along in the pouring rain.

There was nothing I liked about that woman. Her scent made me nauseous, her Asian accent was like a screeching chalkboard; even the way she tried to walk like she was sexy drove me insane. The same things that drove me crazy about Maricar, Kasey adored. To Kasey, my mother was God's gift to earth.

Watching her from the cracked door of our bedroom, pump her veins with drugs before performing orgies at least twice a week wasn't enough for Kasey to know she was filth. But I was the smart one, no matter how much Maricar showed Kasey favoritism. I could see right through her bullshit at such a young age.

"Mommy I'm tired of walking," I cried.

"Stop your whining! Fucking kids make me sick. Gotta go out here and make some money. Thanks to Kennedi's ass I can't leave home by yourself. Now come on. All I'm trying to do is make money to keep roof over y'all heads."

"Mommy, why you always making money? You still gonna buy me a doll baby?" Kasey inquired.

"Kasey, Mommy will buy you anything you want if you just walk faster. Now, hurry up before Billy gets mad at me."

"Don't believe her, Kasey, she always tell you that. All she cares about is Billy." I mumbled under my breath, before getting slapped right into a puddle face first. Blood trickled from my knees and bled through my pajamas.

"You don't try and poison my baby against me. That's all you ever do you jealous bitch! Get black ass up now, Kennedi. Little bitch make me sick. You see why I never wanted you! You always fuck up."

"I hope you die! I hate you!" I screamed as I ran the opposite way into the cemetery. I just wanted to get away; far away from that devil. She always tried to play me and Kasey against each other. No matter how much I loved my sister, she let Maricar get in her head. There was no reason why at the tender age of seven, I should've wished that I were never born.

"Kennedi, bring your ass back here. You make me late, I beat your ass!" Maricar yelled as I ran through the cemetery tripping over beer cans. Finally, I hid behind the largest tombstone I could find. It was pitch black and I knew she would never find me. Fear consumed me as I hid shivering from the cold winter's night air. She'd have to find me first before I would volunteer to get an ass whooping. Beating me was nothing new. It was just a matter of how or with what. As the rain fell on my face it masked my tears. I was tired of this life.

I listened intensely to see how close she was. There was so much frustration in her voice.

"Kasey, go find your sister, I'll be back to get you."

"No you're not."

"I will. I promise. You are the one I love Kasey. It was just supposed to be me and you."

"Well then let me go with you. Just leave Kennedi here. She don't love you Mommy, I do. Mommy, please don't leave me. It's nighttime and I'm scared," Kasey cried.

"Kasey stop whining, you're the strong one. You're seven years old, be a big girl! Blame your dumb ass sister! I never wanted two of you anyway! She's to blame for everything! Now, go find her, I have to go!"

"Mommy but I love you, please don't leave me. Please Mommy."

As I peeked from behind the tombstone I watched my sister scream and cry as my mother ran and hopped in a cab. As much as I loved Kasey, her words hurt. She was the only person I cared about; she was all I had. Couldn't she see that Maricar's meeting with Billy was way more important? We were in the way as usual. I never understood why Kasey never saw her for who she really was. She admired everything about her and the way she begged her not to leave us was pathetic.

"Kennedi, Kennedi where are you? Stop hiding I'm scared," Kasey cried out.

"I'm over here." I yelled to her as she followed my voice until she found her way to me.

"Why did you do that Kennedi? She's gonna beat you! You never learn." Kasey looked down at me with tear filled eyes.

"I don't care! I hate her! I hope she never finds us."

There was no doubt I was scared shitless as we laid in the

cemetery waiting for Maricar to come back, but she never did. Lying in the mud as rats ran by our feet, my sister and I held each other until we cried ourselves to sleep.

We were awakened by the cemetery's grounds keeper the next morning. He called the police and they took us home. Of course Maricar lied and acted as if she didn't know we were out of the house. Once the police left and I heard the water boiling I knew I was in trouble. I threatened her that if she burned me again she would go to jail. That was the last straw. Less than a week later Maricar abandoned Kasey and I in a train station and left town.

That was the last we saw of her. Her words stuck in my head all my life.

She never wanted two of us. *It was all my fault. Blame your dumb sister.* Her words were all Kasey recited to me daily. She always felt if I never ran into that graveyard that night, she would've never left us. Kasey never could see that being born to Maricar was a curse. The older I got I understood more than ever why my sister hated me so much. She felt like I took away her life. Little did she know, we never stood a chance at birth. Maricar never wanted babies. All she cared about was making money by selling her body and soul to the streets. She was a whore that haunted me in my sleep and in my thoughts. When I looked in the mirror I saw her. My cheekbones and the shape of my lips were her. My mole and even my hazel eyes were her, and I hated it. She was to blame for my recklessness, my self-destruction. Money was the only thing that made me feel like I was on top. Hell, money couldn't buy me another childhood, but it could definitely buy me a better future. My mother was some shit, therefore so was I. No matter how much I tried, I just couldn't help it. She was that part of me I fought everyday.

Breaking from my daze I looked down at my daughter and wiped her eyes. I loved her with all I had even though Malcolm didn't seem to love her the way she needed him to. Maybe it was my fault he was so hands off with her. Maybe it was an unknown spirit that lived inside of him that caused him to not love her with all he had; especially not the way he used to love his daughter who passed away two years ago. This was my second chance at motherhood and I had to get Malcolm to love Milan the way he once loved the child he lost.

Sometimes I wondered why I went through so much to keep Malcolm, but I honestly had never loved like this before. I loved the family unit that we shared. Being a product of foster care, I never had a family. Having a husband and the security that gave me just felt right and I was willing to do anything to keep it.

Suddenly, the doorbell rang. I knew exactly who it was as I walked out of the kitchen to the foyer with Milan on my hip.

"What took you so long?" I questioned before she could even make it all the way inside.

"I'm not sure how much longer I'm gonna be able to do this. My father is questioning me."

I stared at my nanny. "Look, Nina don't start acting like a scared bitch now. I pay you way too much money for you to be flaking on me now."

"But Kennedi, he could lose his license for prescribing me the meds under all these fake prescriptions," she said, handing me a CVS bag.

"Shhhh lower your voice." I looked back to make sure Malcolm wasn't walking toward us. "You knew what you were getting into when we first started this shit," I whispered.

"It's only half this time. This was all he could do." She looked at Milan and smiled. "Hey, boo boo. Did you have a good time over my house last night?"

Milan smiled in return.

"What happened to her mouth?" Nina questioned with concern.

"Never mind that shit and don't bring her back so early next time." I quickly pulled the bottle out of the bag. "Half?"

"Yes, half," Nina replied with a little base in her voice.

"Why the fuck is it only half? I didn't give your ass half the fucking money!" This time I raised my voice a bit.

"I just told you why. When I first started doing this I was able to get all the different types of medication by telling my dad that most of my patients didn't have healthcare. Of course he thought I was crazy and didn't want to do it, but I begged him for a week to do this for me. He only went along with it because he thought my so-called patients would eventually get healthcare or that he'd only have to do it for a little while. It's been almost two years now Vee so he docsn't want to do it anymore, especially since you demand that I get Benztropine. His pharmacy only had a few pills left this time so that's why you only got half."

After Malcolm was released from the hospital I was informed of several different ways on how to help with his memory loss. Little did they know, I wasn't interested in helping him remember shit. I wanted the opposite…I wanted him to forget everything about his past. After researching, I found a list of drugs that all had memory loss as a side effect. During my experiment, I supplied Malcolm with anti-depressants, anti-anxiety and even anti-seizure medication. All of that seemed to work, but nothing made him more loopy than when I switched to Benztropine, which was a medicine given to people with Parkinson's Disease. When he first started taking it his ass couldn't even remember the days of the week. Now, I believed that his body was becoming immune because he didn't act as crazy after I slipped the pills into his food or morning smoothies.

"Well, your father needs to up the dosage on the next round because this is not enough," I said, looking at the bottle.

Nina seemed frustrated. "Don't you get it? There might not be a next time."

"Bitch, you better find a way to make this happen or you're gonna be a broke ass *ex*-nurse again."

When I said ex Nina lowered her head. I met her at a bar after moving to Short Hills, and it didn't take long to find out that she'd been fired from her job at a hospital as a nurse in East Orange after administering a patient the wrong medicine, an incident her father still knew nothing about. Her name was tarnished in the healthcare field and she'd been out of work for six months when we crossed paths. It didn't take her long to accept my offer of 8K a month to take care of Milan and supply my fake prescription needs. Since she was a former nurse, it made things even better since she also helped out with Malcolm, too. Taking care of a burned victim wasn't easy.

"Nina, all I'ma say is I need this shit, and if you wanna stay fucking employed you need to…"

"Need to what?" Malcolm asked suddenly walking into the foyer.

Both Nina and I looked at each other for answers.

"What are those for?" Malcolm pointed to the pill bottle.

"My birth control pills," I quickly lied. It was dumb but it was also the first thing that flew out of my mouth. Most people knew birth control wasn't packaged this way.

"Good," he responded with an excited grin.

I desperately wanted to respond with a "fuck you" but decided against it. Little did he know, I didn't want another baby fucking my shape up or slowing me down either.

"Whatever, Malcolm." I finally handed Milan over to Nina. "Are you ready for your smoothie? I forgot to make one this morning," I said before walking away with my own devious grin.

3 _Charlotte_

"Umph...Umph...Umph! Oh yeah, ohhh yeah my black Barbie. That's right. Just like that. Feels great doesn't it!"

"Uh yeah," I lied.

"Oh yeah. I'm cumming. Oh yeah."

"Cum Master! Cum for me, please," I begged, rolling my eyes to the back of my head, as Sonny's slender body pounded on top of me with all he had.

Finally! Thank God he was done! It had been the longest three minutes of my life.

Sonny's smile was as bright as the sun. "Woo-hoo that was great!"

"I'm glad you enjoyed yourself," I replied, trying hard to not come across sarcastic.

"I'm about to call down to the staff to have them fetch me a drink. Would you like something my dear?"

"I'm fine," I said, turning over and covering my body with the silk sheets.

No matter how elegant and beautiful my new mansion was, it still wasn't a home. Laying in bed staring at the velour golden drapes that laced my bedroom windows I thought to myself, _how the hell did this happen? What have I gotten myself into_? Those were the questions that stayed on daily repeat in my head.

My life for the past two years was truly the definition of sleeping with the enemy. How did I allow my husband's biggest nemesis to turn my life upside down, and get me to accept his hand in marriage all in one full sweep? As I laid and watched my fiancé give orders to the staff, I gazed at my 6-carat cushion cut diamond. Sonny was hell on wheels and was a man that knew how to conquer anything by any means necessary, including me. His Italian swag was definitely sexy for a man of a particular age, but no matter how hard he tried, I still slept with one eye open.

"Sorry for just rolling over and going to town on you without saying good morning my darling. Did you sleep well?"

"Yes, thanks for the pills."

"No nightmares for almost a month. Impressive, Charlotte. Happy to see we're finally moving in the right direction."

"I guess so," I said before being interrupted by my princess, Gianni as she burst through the doors in tears. I quickly covered my naked body.

"Mommy, Marty almost bit me again. I want to leave this place!"

Right after Gianni ran in, Sonny's vicious pet tiger trucked right behind her drooling at the mouth, exposing his fangs. This was the third time Gianni had a run in with Marty and I was sick and tired of it.

"Sonny, something has to give! You've got to control this damn animal! Who the hell has a tiger as a pet anyway?" I yelled right before Marty let out a huge roar. He was jealous of both Gianni and I but luckily he only attacked on command.

"He would never hurt my two ladies," Sonny replied.

I rolled my eyes unconvinced.

"Just like you love Gianni, I love Marty. He's not going anywhere so you all just have to get along. Now Marty go!" Sonny instructed.

Marty did exactly what he was told and left the bedroom. It was crazy how this man loved that human eating animal. Marty's job was to dispose of anybody Sonny decided to kill or had a problem with. I'm sure I could still smell my dead husband's mistress and love child on his breath. Sonny tortured me and made me watch him feed them both to Marty two years ago. He'd threatened countless times that Gianni and I would be next if I didn't do as I was told, which included being with him.

How things had changed in two years was insane. Sonny

was so in love with me now, I couldn't imagine him hurting me. The one thing that still hadn't changed was Gianni's hate for Sonny. She looked at me confused.

"Mommy, are we ever going to leave this place. I had a dream about daddy last night and he said Sonny killed him. Mommy, he took my daddy away! I miss daddy," she screamed, before jumping up on my bed and straight into my arms.

No matter how much Sonny tried to win Gianni over, she missed her father desperately. Gianni was only four years old when my husband died, but they were thick as thieves. She just didn't understand how to wrap her little six year-old mind around the fact that she would never see her father again.

"Baby it's okay," I said, trying to comfort her.

"But I miss him," she responded.

I rubbed her back. "I know you do sweetheart," I replied.

"Listen Gianni you're going to have to be strong and move on. I'm your dad now. I mean I even bought you your own petting zoo to cheer you up. Hell I've allowed your father's ashes to be in my fucking house for God's sake! What more do you want from me?" Sonny said annoyed. He just didn't get it.

"Really Sonny? Have some respect!" I interjected.

"I don't want anything from you! You're not my daddy!" Gianni yelled out.

Sonny sighed. "Charlotte, help me out here. I've gotten the both of you counseling. Bought you damn near anything you two could ever want…"

"Do you understand how it feels to lose your father?" I said, interrupting him. I spoke as calmly as I could without upsetting my daughter. Sonny knew that this was a sensitive subject, since he was responsible for not only killing my husband, but he was responsible for the death of my father, too.

"Mommy, I just want to go back to California. I hate it here. This house is scary," Gianni added.

It had been two years and Gianni still talked about how scary the house was. I'm not sure if I believed that. She made up every excuse in the book to leave.

"My house is not scary. You have a full carnival on the

grounds, ponies, an aquarium wall unit in your room, diamonds..."

"Sonny stop. Gianni go to your room, let me speak to Sonny for a second. I'll be in there shortly."

Before jumping out of bed, Gianni gave Sonny the look of death then made her way out of the room. As soon as the door to my room closed I went in on him.

"I'm so sick and tired of you thinking that the trauma you have brought on to me and my daughter's lives are just going to be removed by gifts! To be kidnapped, locked in a trunk, and not know if you're going to die, all because of a beef you had with my husband."

"Charlotte shut the fuck up! You're lucky I didn't kill you. You made the choice to live by my rules. If you feel life is so hard for you here, I can make good on my promise."

I shook my head. "There you go threatening me again."

"Besides, you act like Malcolm was so good to you. That asshole had a whole other life with that stripper, and got her pregnant. But you still loved him. If I hadn't killed that white girl and that other baby of his..."

"See, that's what I'm talking about! You want me to love a man that could just kill a woman and her child, all to prove a point. You tortured my husband. Let him burn to death and think his family was dead before taking his life! How do you think I would ever be okay with knowing you caused the pain I see in my daughter's eyes every day?"

Sonny rubbed my arm. "Charlotte, what can I do to make things right? I fell in love with you the first day I saw you. It was a couple years back. I had all intentions on killing you that day, but your beautiful brown skin was so striking I just couldn't go through with the hit. I didn't understand how Malcolm could have such a great wife and not appreciate her."

"Why did you hate him so much? What did Malcolm do that was so horrible to take him away from his family? You have all the money you could ever need, so don't tell me it was about a debt."

Anytime Malcolm's name was brought up it hit a nerve. Getting out of bed Sonny's slim frame paced the floor as he turned red looking like he was about to explode. I couldn't help but stare at his small five inch dick that could never satisfy me. Having sex with him was like watching paint dry. Malcolm may not have been the best husband to me but I missed his dick game like crazy. Finally, he sat down on the fur bench at the end of our bed with his back to me and begun to speak.

"Okay Charlotte. I owe you an explanation! It started off being about principle. You owe me, you pay me…it was that simple. The day I first laid eyes on you was the day I saw Malcolm as the slime he really was. To watch him take advantage of you and love that whore Kennedi just wasn't right. You are a good woman and deserved more than what he could give you. You deserved me. Not your father. Not Malcolm. Just me. At that point, I knew I had to remove all the negative men out of your life, before you could ever be mine. Only mine. I did all of this for you."

"So, you purposely killed my husband and my father for us to be together? You are…"

"In love. You're a beautiful woman, Charlotte. You never could embrace the beauty that I watched from afar. I just wanted to make you happy and love you. Not only you, but Gianni, too."

"You're just saying that. Why should I believe you?"

"If you never listen to another word that I say to you, know that I will show it through my actions. I'm a real man, honored by all. I've been in this game for a long time and have earned the respect I demand. All by action, not words. All I can do is show you what you mean to me."

"Well, prove it. Stop having sex with all of those other women then if that's the case."

"Charlotte, I like to fuck. I like to watch beautiful women fuck. That's just a hobby, like fishing or golf. I thought you enjoyed that I brought out your inner lesbian. Your life has been better since I've been in it so you need to be honest with yourself."

"Okay Sonny you win. I'll will talk to Gianni and make things right with you guys. You're right, life has been better with you. It's just hard to grasp how we got here. I'll do better. I'm sorry."

"That's all I ask my love. That's all I ask."

Sonny had never shown his vulnerable side to me and it felt good. He was right about it all. Malcolm was a horrible husband, but you can't help who you loved. Deep down inside I could tell I'd become Sonny's weakness, and I couldn't lie, it felt good. To be the chosen one in a room full of wannabe's felt damn good for a change. Yes, I was Malcolm's wife, but never his priority. For the first time in my life a man other than my father, made me feel like I mattered.

When I was with Malcolm I was always on edge and could never get all the way into it with him sexually because of his cheating. Now, I was no longer the woman, I used to be. My appearance screamed money. From my long, 22-inch locks of blonde weave that I hated, my designer wardrobe, diamonds, furs, and exotic cars, I was made. My self-confidence was increasing daily. My husband was probably turning over in his grave to see how sexual I'd become. My inner freak had been released. I felt sexy for the first time in forever. I don't know. Maybe it was the threesomes, or being spoiled and getting the attention I always wanted from Malcolm. Whatever it was, I had to stop fighting it and try my best to accept my new life. Forgetting Malcolm would be hard, but Gianni and I both had to find a way to let Sonny in our lives.

Finally, I let Sonny hold me and it was genuine. Just as I drifted into a safe place all hell broke loose.

"Sonny, who the fuck is this bitch? Is she the reason why you stopped sending me money you worthless piece of shit?" A beautiful woman, who appeared to be in her mid 20's tore into our bedroom. Her New Jersey accent was strong.

"Karla, what the fuck are you doing here? When did you get out? Who the hell let you in?" Sonny yelled in his Italian voice.

"I've been out for a while. You would've known that if you would've answered my calls."

"And why would I do that Karla when there's nothing to talk about?"

"Nothing to talk about…are you fucking kidding me? Do you know what I've been through for you!" she spat.

Sonny quickly jumped out of the bed and grabbed her right before she tried to charge at him. He threw her to the floor.

She stared at me for a few seconds. "I bet she doesn't know how fucked up you are? You better beware! When he's done with you, he'll feed you to the wolves, or maybe even kill you. Tell her what you did to me, Sonny! Tell her what you did?" the woman roared.

Before she could say another word, Sonny's top security guard, Bryan rushed the room and grabbed the crazed woman who appeared to be of a Spanish decent...possibly Dominican because of her honey colored skin. With shoulder length jet black hair, her body was completely toned, like she worked out at least three times a week and her peach shaped ass put mine to shame.

Sonny went straight for the top drawer of the nightstand and retrieved his .40 caliber gun. "Put that bitch on her knees, Bryan," he demanded.

"Get your hands off me!" she shouted.

Sonny aimed his gun at her head.

"Sonny, wait...don't do this. Don't kill her!" I yelled.

"I'm not gonna kill her Charlotte, not yet anyway. I'm just gonna make her a little uncomfortable for disrespecting my home."

"Bitch, this coward would never kill me. He knows better! Besides, I know way too much!" she yelled.

"Look, call me bitch one more..."

Before I could say another word, the gun went off.

"Aaaiiiiggghhhh! You son of a bitch! I'm gonna fucking kill you, Sonny! This is the last time you're gonna get away with disrespecting me!"

Sonny had let one loose into Karla's right arm.

"Bryan, get this bitch out of my house! And when I found out who let her in, there's gonna be hell to pay!" Sonny roared.

"Yes, sir," Bryan replied. As he rushed her out of the room, blood dripped all over the marble floor.

I stared at Sonny at what seemed like forever. "Who is she?"

For some reason he wouldn't make eye contact with me. "It doesn't matter. She doesn't matter. I'm just sorry you had to witness that."

"Wow, it looks like you're no different from Malcolm."

He finally looked in my direction. "Don't you ever fucking compare me to him again! Do you understand me, Blackie?" Sonny walked over to me and grabbed my chin as if I'd struck a nerve.

"Get your hands off me and don't ever call me that again," I demanded in a stern tone.

It was bad enough he made me call him master as he fucked me. Deep down inside I was scared shitless, but he couldn't know that. It's not like I really had another choice. I was stuck with Sonny if I wanted to live. I was tired of my life being threatened even if it looked like I wanted to leave. Just that quickly, I'd taken a page out of Miss Karla's book and demanded respect.

Sonny was so bi-polar it was scary. What baffled me was how this woman was the first person I'd ever seen Sonny let disrespect him. Who was this mystery woman and what did she have on him?

4 Kennedi

You must not know bout me, you must not know bout me. I could have another you in a minute, matter fact he'll be here in a minute...

Irreplaceable by Beyonce, blazed through the sound system of my silver Ferrari 612 GTO. As I sung to Queen Bee, I drifted back to my life at that time with my ex-boyfriend, Sharrod. I would sing this song to the top of my lungs to irritate his fat ass. As my blood boiled thinking about him, my phone rang. It was Nina.

"Hello."

"Hi Kennedi, Malcolm just called. I wanted to let you know he asked for me to come over and help with Milan."

"What? Are you serious?"

"I'm afraid so. He sounded frustrated as usual."

"Nina, give me a second and I'll call you right back."

In beast mode I called Malcolm's phone ready for war. I couldn't leave the house for a couple of hours without him always going into panic mode. I needed to go see my grandmother who only lived an hour and thirty minutes away and he couldn't even handle her for a few hours. Even though I loved my baby girl, I could also use the break since I was with her all the time. I was pissed.

"Yeah," he answered annoyed as I listened to Milan scream to the top of her lungs in the background.

"Why the hell is she crying, Malcolm?"

"Look I don't know. She's always crying. I don't know

why you didn't take her with you. She's spoiled as shit and gets on my nerves. I can't even clean the damn house because she wants me to hold her. What side of the family does she get that shit from? I sure hope it's not my side," he stated. "Oh, speaking of family, what happened with you finding my aunt?"

I hated myself for making up a story about a fake aunt in North Carolina. Truth is there was no aunt. Malcolm frequently asked me if he had any other family besides me and Milan. One day after being tired of him questioning me, I told him that he'd told me about an aunt down south named Christine before the accident. Since that day, every so often he asked me to find her. Even though I told him he never told me her last name, Malcolm still didn't care.

"No, I haven't had time," I told him.

"Fuck it, what's the password to the computer again? I keep forgetting it."

"Malcolm, hold Milan, damnit. Why are you letting her cry?" I switched the subject hoping to get his mind off his fake aunt.

"Because I need to clean up that's why."

"Are you serious? The house is spotless!"

"No, it's not. There's this one spot by the dishwasher that won't seem to come clean."

"Malcolm please go comfort, your daughter," I pleaded.

"Look I already told you no."

"Nigga let me tell you something. I got shit to do and…"

Before I could finish my sentence he hung up on me.

"I know the fuck he didn't," I said. "Bi polar asshole."

I was only ten minutes away from my grandmother's house so it didn't make sense to turn back around. I called Nina and asked her to go to the house and help out. I hated having Nina around Malcolm when I wasn't around, but didn't have another choice. Most women wouldn't have a young woman around their husband. Nina was on the slim side, but she was strikingly beautiful with waist long hair that was always parted down the middle and thick eyebrows that were arched perfectly. However, Nina knew I would wipe the floor with her Indian ass if she ever wanted to test her loyalty though. So far she was good at what she did, so I trusted her.

As I turned down Ferry Avenue, my stomach started turning. I hadn't been to Camden, New Jersey since I'd gotten locked up over four years ago. The neighborhood hadn't changed much though. It was still run down with abandoned homes on every block. Most people wouldn't drive a Ferrari through Camden, but they· were used to me stuntin' so they knew not to fuck with my shit around there.

"Wassup Twin, I see you flexin'. You bout that Hollywood life I see," my childhood friend Lil Man greeted me. He was on the corner talking to the dude Brooks who used to like me back in the day. He was from Brooklyn, which is how he got the nickname Brooks and wasn't really well received by my son's father, Sharrod, and his crew. We used to flirt, but never went there because of Sharrod. Brooks nodded out of respect, but held a look of remorse.

"Lil Man, you know I rep Jersey 'til the death of me, how are you?"

"Man, I'm just tryin' to survive out here in these streets. Shit ain't like it used to be since Sharrod been gone."

I went straight into my Chanel boy bag and pulled out some money.

"Well here's a couple of bills for you. Watch my shit, and I got you when I come back out."

"You know ain't nobody fuckin' wit your whip, but I got you," Lil' Man said as he took the money right out of my hand. "You lookin' phat as shit, too."

"Boy, cut it out. You know that ain't for us."

"Man I thought I'd try my hand," he laughed.

"So Kennedi, you ain't speakin', Ma?" he asked in his New York accent.

"Hi Brooks. Bye Brooks."

He laughed. "Yo' ass still sassy. You still look good, too!" he yelled from his white Maserati Gran Turismo. He was still flashy as ever.

He looked good as shit. He was always a looker but damn, I didn't remember him being this sexy.

Here goes nothing, I said, walking up to my grandmother's door. It sounded like a fucking elementary school as I knocked.

"Who is it?" China's grown ass belted.

"It's Kennedi."

"Big Mama, somebody else need to get the door cuz I ain't opening shit for that bitch," China replied. I could hear her walking away.

"Chile, stop being so damn disrespectful, that's still your mutha," my Aunt Lee Lee fussed as she opened the door.

As soon as I walked inside, the funk smacked me dead in the face. It smelled like mothballs, dirt and mildew. Boric acid still was in the corners of the walls just as I remembered as a kid to kill the roaches, and the squealing of mice on the mousetraps still beeped in my ear like an alarm.

"Some things just never change. How the fuck do y'all sit in here with this house smelling like this?"

"Well damn. Look what the wind blew in. You forgot you used to live here, too? Now you driving Farri's and shit you think you betta than errybody."

Lee Lee placed her hands on her once wide hips. Now, they were nothing but a straight board on each side. The crack and hero-ine had definitely gotten the best of her. That bad beauty supply weave didn't help either. It looked like she was trying to force Africa and Brazil to get along. Textures all fucked up and nappy and there was no reason for the ghetto, royal blue pieces that had been added to the matted bob. It was all wrong. She hated me and the feelings were mutual.

"It's called a Ferrari," I corrected Lee Lee just to get under her skin.

"Well whateva. Any-who, I guess somebody gotta be on their death bed for you to come see your kids, huh? What you comin' round here for now? You must think my muva got some-thing for you in her will cuz ain't nobody seen you in two damn years."

"Lee-Lee please don't start no bullshit with me. Do I look like I need anything from anybody in this house? I'm stacked."

"You sure is. Look like you dun stacked up some pounds, what you pregnant?"

I was offended but couldn't let her ass know that. "Ain't nothing over here fat but my ass and my pockets. I'm not on a crack diet like you miss. It's called having a baby and living good. The having a baby part we know you've mastered that, but the living good part, you should try it sometimes. Makes life feel a lot easier."

"Ain't that some shit. So, you playin' house wit' some nigga and a new baby, and not takin' care of your other kids? Why the hell are they stayin' here, worryin' my muva to death when they could've been stayin' with you all this time? I wish Kasey was alive. I would pay to see her whoop your ass."

"Bitch I swear to God, don't speak her name to me," I threatened then got close up in her face.

"You in ya feelings cuz Kasey took your first love. Try me Kennedi, I got a pound of spit waitin' to unload. Fuck wit me," Lee Lee's ghetto ass warned.

"Bitch I dare you. Give me a reason to…"

"Whoa, whoa, whoa. What's going on ladies?" Brooks asked walking up in my grandmother's house like he owned it.

"Brooks mind your business!" I said, cutting my eyes at him. You could definitely tell he worked out by the way he showed off his muscles in his gray tank top and sweat shorts.

"Hey, Big Mama," he said, ignoring me. He gave my grandmother a kiss on the cheek.

"Hey, baby," my grandmother got together enough strength to say hello. She was always fond of Brooks.

"Kennedi you know your grandmother was supposed to be my wife," he said smiling at me with those deep dimples.

His joke even made Big Mama smile.

With Hershey chocolate skin, he almost reminded me of the model Tyson Beckford because of his extremely slanted eyes. His eyes were slanted and when he smiled his eyes damn near looked closed. Brooks was only like 5 foot 10, but could play basketball like a pro back in the day. All the girls loved him in the neighborhood, but he would never mess with any of them, thinking he would get me one day. Unfortunately that never happened.

"Brooks, now you know damn well that bitch ain't shit. You too good of a man for her. Oh yeah, you got my present," Lee Lee inquired.

"Yeah, I got it, and let Earl know that I looked out for both of y'all. Don't be greedy," Brooks said, handing her a small paper bag.

"Still making house calls for these crack-heads? Driving a Maserati, I would think that you were a little more big time than that," I chimed in.

"Come on Ma. This family. Why you wanna give me a hard time? Look, put my number in your phone."

"Hell no, Brooks. She married," Lee Lee interjected.

"Naw, I just want her to keep me up to date about Big Mama. Y'all phone be off and shit. I need to be able to check in on my baby." He looked over at Big Mama, as she smiled with her eyes closed.

Grabbing my phone out of my purse I gave him my phone and he stored his number in it.

"Brooks fuck that whore. She ain't shit. That trick ain't been around here in years," Lee Lee added.

"Alright fam, I'm out," he replied walking out the door as if he'd had enough of our family drama.

"I swear to God Lee-Lee, you gonna make me fuck your ass up! You jealous bitch. You can't battle me, you washed up."

"Now, stop it. Y'all cut it out. I'm not tryin' to live my last days on this earth listening to foolishness," my grandmother whispered with all the energy she had.

I'd never respected her in the past, but seeing her frail body posted up in the living room in a hospital bed did something to me. It took me back to the good days when she first saved us from foster care; the days when she taught me how to play all types of card games. That was before she started to show favoritism towards Kasey, my twin.

"I'm sorry Big Mama. How are you feeling?" I said, greeting my grandmother with a kiss on her forehead. I held onto my bag closely trying not to take any unwanted friends home. Mickey and Minnie were not invited to my mansion and neither were the roaches.

"Your red ass think you the shit. Ain't nobody gonna steal your purse," Lee Lee said, leaning on the living room wall. She seemed extremely irritated.

I ignored her.

"Well, the Cancer is back and they saying it ain't much more they can do. It came back strong this time, baby. Only got a few weeks."

"Is it your insurance? You know I have money. I can pay them to fix it Big Mama," I responded as tears formed in my eyes.

"Ain't no money gonna fix this, baby. I'm afraid it's just too late. If you want to do something for me though, take them kids and make things right with them. They ain't been the same since your sister was killed. They resent you, Kennedi. They think you done kilt her. I keep tellin' dem kids you wouldn't do such a thing to your sister."

"Big Mama. I swear on my father's grave. I didn't kill Kasey."

I was telling the truth. My ex-boyfriend and baby father, Sharrod had accidently killed Kasey because he thought she was me. All those years they were fucking behind my back and for him to be the one to kill her was crazy. Nobody seemed to believe me though. I knew my hatred for my sister ran deep, but I wasn't the one who pulled the trigger. I did however take Sharrod's ass out. Call it self- defense because if I hadn't popped him first, he surely would've put me six feet under. Everyone…including the police thought Sharrod and Kasey were victims of a home invasion and it needed to stay that way.

As my mind drifted off to that night I missed half of what my grandmother said.

"What did you say Big Mama?"

"You heard me right. I said your daughter, China is having sex now and she only fourteen years old. She too fast Kennedi, she too fast. And Chase, Lawd, him and your nephew Rashad, be hanging out all times of night with China, with them boys."

"What did you say about them boys, Big Mama?" my son,

Chase asked.

At that moment, he sashayed around the corner into the living room with some super tight skinny jeans on, a fitted tank top and some fresh retro Jordans. His hair was slicked back in a ponytail with blonde streaks.

"What the hell?" I said in shock.

"Wassup Miss Kennedi? You came to give us some coins?" he said, rubbing his fingers together with his hand on his hip.

I didn't understand. How was my son gay? I always knew my nephew, Rashad was going to be gay. Hell...the entire family peeped that shit early on, but Chase? He was so quiet and timid. Now, he was flaming. I didn't understand how all this happened in a matter of two years.

"Chase. What happened?" Sharrod would've flipped if he saw his son like this.

"What you mean? I'm good. I like boys, they like me. Why you worried about me anyway? You ain't been worried. It's obvious that you don't mess with us. Fakin' like you ain't got no kids. I ain't seen you in forever."

"Who's been in your head Chase? I'm still your mother."

"Mother?" he smiled. "You don't know nothin' bout that. Kasey was a real mother. She loved me and China. She took care of us when you didn't give a shit about us. She made sure we had food when you were off somewhere suckin..."

Before his gay ass could say another word, I smacked the shit out of him. I could no longer take his extra ass attitude.

"Why the fuck did you hit me? You not my mother! Oh watch bitch, it's on. China, Rashad!" Chase yelled as he ran to the backroom.

All of a sudden the bedroom door to the right of the living room opened. Moments later, a brown-skinned man who looked like a dope fiend came out of the room scratching his right arm. He appeared to be at least 50 years old and was extra creepy.

"Damn, who dat is?" he asked, giving my Aunt Lee Lee a kiss on her cheek.

"That's Kennedi, my niece," she replied.

He licked his dark, crusty lips. "Damn, you fine, girl."

Disgusted, I stared at his tall, slender frame that looked as if he hadn't eaten in days. He reminded me of the lead singer, Eddie Kane from *The Five Heartbeats* movie with his wiry hair that was brushed back away from his temples and pointy nose.

"I sure hope she stayin' 'round here for a couple days," he added.

Before I could respond, China walked out of the same room Earl had just come from fixing the zipper on her shorts. She'd grown up so much. She was beautiful. She looked like me, but I could still see my foster father Harry all in her. With bronze tinted skin, high cheekbones, slanted Asian eyes, and a 5'7 frame, she was the human version of a Barbie doll. Her True Religion shorts were damn near up her plump ass, and her cleavage spilled out of her tank top. She didn't look like she was fourteen years old, but more like a grown ass woman with her body that was already developed.

"What the hell were you doing in that room with that man?" I quickly questioned.

"My name Earl," he added.

"Nobody asked you your fucking name," I snapped back before directing my attention back to my daughter. "I said what were you doing in that room with that man, China?"

She chuckled. "First of all, what goes on in this house is none of your business. The last time I saw you, you pointed a gun at me. You wanted to kill me, remember?"

I shook my head. "No, that's not true."

"Oh yes it is. Don't fucking lie. You took the only mother we had away from us and now you come back here like somebody supposed to listen to your bullshit," China replied with pure resentment in her voice.

These kids thought I was the worst mother in the world but they didn't understand. They would never blame Kasey even though it was all her fault. I was always the bad guy when it came to that bitch when she was just as foul. My family had no idea that she'd tricked Malcolm into sleeping with him by acting as if she was me. When that happened, I was determined to get her ass back. To make matters worse, it was even revealed that Kasey and my ex

Sharrod were living a secret life behind my back. I felt betrayed. Locking the kids in the closet that dramatic day two years ago while I went after Kasey might've traumatized them, but I did what I felt was best. I was wrong for putting their lives in danger, but it could've been worse. They're lucky they didn't watch that bitch they loved so much die.

As China continued to talk shit I finally demanded her respect.

"Look, I might not have raised you, but I'm still your mother."

China let out a huge laugh. "Mother, yeah right. I don't have a mother or a father. I'm out here taking care of me and my family, while you busy taking care of your new baby. Yeah Big Mama told us about our new sister when she was born. I wonder who this new baby father is. I'm sure he has money though cuz we all know how you roll."

"What the fuck do you mean you taking care of your family? You're a child yourself, and furthermore what I do is my business. I'm grown. Don't worry about what I got going on. If I wanted to have three more kids, it still wouldn't be your business. Stay in your lane little girl. No matter what you might think of me, *I'm* the one who takes care of this family," I informed. "I may not have been around for a while, but I send money down here every damn month. How the hell you think you got those fresh Jordans on your feet?"

"Please, stop all this arguing," Big Mama chimed in.

"Yeah right. We ain't ever seen no money from you. I do what I can to make sure we good. We don't need shit from you, Kennedi," China continued.

"Big Mama, Aunt Lee Lee, what the hell have y'all done to my kids?" I looked at my aunt. "Lee Lee, you better not be smoking up the fucking money. You and your dope fiend ass dude." I pointed at Earl.

"I ain't doing shit with your money," Lee Lee snapped back.

"Then why the hell doesn't China know that I send money here to take care of them and Big Mama? She needs to know it's my damn money that's keeping the lights on around here. And why the fuck does this house look like this? When's the last time y'all cleaned up? Big Mama is sick. She don't need to be surrounded by fucking filth."

"Then bring your ass around more often and clean it," China added.

I tried my best to ignore her as my blood boiled. "How did my kids get this fucked up? How did y'all let this happen Big Mama?"

"Bitch don't talk to my grandmother like that," China said right before swinging her fist straight toward my face.

Next thing I know we were fighting like two bitches in the street. I had to admit, China was giving me a run for my money, but I refused to let her beat me. As we went blow for blow, we both fell onto the coffee table causing glass to shatter everywhere. Making my way on top of China, I wrapped my hands around her neck and tried to choke the life out of her. I saw Harry. I saw the man who'd molested me and got me pregnant at the tender age of fourteen. I saw the man who started this downward spiral of me becoming such a fucked up person.

"Stop it, Kennedi. Get off my sister!" Chase yelled.

"Earl, help me break it up. They not gonna kill my muva and raise her pressure!" Lee Lee shouted.

"I'm not gettin' in that bullshit," he replied while continuing to watch television.

"Stop it Kennedi! Leave my sister alone trick!" Chase tried to intervene.

His concerns were ignored as I dug my fingers into her skin. Just as China's eyes started to roll back into her head, suddenly a mousetrap came flying straight at my head. I screamed to the top of my lungs. Chase had thrown a mousetrap with a live mouse on it.

Instantly I saw red. Throwing China's body to the floor, I grabbed my shit, and ran to my car to get my gun. I was going to kill everything moving in that house. As soon as I ran to the car a hammer came flying out the door and hit my back windshield.

"Bitch don't bring your ass back around here!" China

yelled.

"I'm going to kill all y'all motherfuckas!" I went straight to my console to get my .357 caliber.

As soon as I they saw my gun they all ran in the house.

Blop, blop, blop…I let loose on that house and didn't give a fuck who got hit. Big Mama was on her death bed anyway!

5 Charlotte

"Oh, shit," I whispered as I twisted and turned my new lipstick shaped dildo in and out of my wet box.

Finally I climaxed and my body fell limp as I leaned against the shower wall. *I needed that shit,* I said to myself grabbing my loofa sponge. I poured shower gel into it until it lathered. Despite the fact that Sonny was a sex addict, he still couldn't manage to satisfy me in bed for some reason. It was something I'd been struggling with since we got together. I even tried to visualize Malcolm when we had sex or my celebrity crush, Omari Hardwick but nothing seemed to work.

As the water splashed from all angles of the multiple faucets, I inhaled the vanilla fragrance from my body and took a deep sigh. I thought about my plans for today and smiled. It was going to be a great day. Morning brunch with Sonny and then Gianni and I had planned a mommy, daughter day at the zoo. I was looking forward to some alone time with my baby girl.

Getting out of the shower I went to the mirror and admired the new Charlotte. I was a bad bitch with D-cup voluptuous breasts, a flat tummy tucked stomach, and long blonde hair extensions. The hair color was the only thing I didn't care for, but it was something that Sonny insisted on. My husband, Malcolm was definitely turning over right now. Sonny was to thank for all of the updates to my new body. He'd gotten one of the top plastic surgeons in New York to perform the work and I must admit, the results were well worth the pain. All those years of being married to Malcolm I was always Miss Plain Jane, and now here I was looking like someone from *The Real Housewives of New Jersey*. Clearly, I was used to having money, being as though I was born with a silver spoon, but now I actually looked like money. My family owned a multi-million dollar construction business and my grandfather made sure my inheritance was stacked. Yes, I had money, but it was something about being with Sonny that made me feel not only wealthy, but rich. It wasn't just about the ambiance of the house, or the diamonds and furs. It was the status, the lifestyle that made me feel like I was a kept woman. For the first time, I was finally at the center of attention in my marriage and it felt good…damn good.

After drying off, I entered my bedroom and saw a beautiful white-fringed Herve Leger dress, and white D-Squared platform strappy sandals, lying across the bed.

"Oh hey darling, get dressed, I have a wonderful plan this morning for you and Gianni," Sonny said overly excited as he entered our bedroom.

"Umm, Sonny. I had a mommy-daughter day planned with Gianni, so can…"

"Charlotte, my beautiful black Barbie, trust me, you guys will have your day. I just want your morning. Francesca is getting Gianni ready now. It would mean a lot to me if you got dressed in this stunning ensemble here, and meet me outside on the terrace."

I sighed.

"Trust me, it'll be worth your while."

"Okay. Give me some time…at least an hour."

"Sooner is better," Sonny responded in a demanding tone and exited the room.

After getting dressed I approached the mirror with confidence and blew myself a kiss. Once I put on a final coat of bronzer on my t-zones I was ready. My hair was laid with a beautiful messy side fishtail. There was no doubt Sonny had amazing taste, because I looked like a million bucks. Now clearly I wasn't going to the zoo in this outfit, so I decided to get to the terrace to see what Sonny was up to.

Really Sonny? I thought to myself as I started down the staircase. *Who the hell puts a bowtie on a tiger?*

I stared at Marty sitting at the bottom of the stairs in the

5foyer yawning exposing his discolored fangs. As soon as I got to the last step he got up as if he was escorting me to the terrace. The closer I got, I could hear music playing. Once I approached the terrace I was in complete shock. All the staff members were lined up, dressed in white. As soon as I entered the room, a jazz quartet suddenly began playing a very familiar tune. My mouth dropped when *Here Comes the Bride* filled the room. Gianni stood beside Sonny in the most amazing organza white dress with a rose headband draped around her wild curls. No matter how beautiful Gianni looked, her facial expression was startling. It looked as though she was going to break down at any moment. Seconds later, Francesca our nanny handed me a bouquet of white tiger lillies and smiled.

"You look beautiful," she said.

As bad as I wanted to accept the compliment, I couldn't. It honestly felt like my mouth was wired shut and my feet where stuck to the floor.

Sonny held his hand out. "Come to me my beautiful black Barbie."

Once again I looked at Gianni who now had tears in her eyes. At that moment, I wanted to turn around and walk away. Something told me that this was all a bad idea. Of course I loved Sonny and I loved the way he'd stepped up to the plate and taken care of me and my baby girl after Malcolm died, but something still didn't feel right. My stomach was in complete knots.

"Charlotte, I'm waiting," Sonny ordered. The look he gave indicated that he wasn't going to say it a third time.

With extreme hesitation, I slowly made my way down the rose petal filled aisle. Sonny smiled proudly as he stood next to a balding white priest. I didn't know how he pulled all this off, but I wasn't happy. This wasn't the kind of surprise I had in mind. Putting on a brave face for my daughter, I approached my fiancé and took his hand, right before giving my baby girl a kiss on her cheek.

"Honey, I couldn't wait another moment. I love you and I don't want to let another day go by without you being my wife." Sonny stared deep into my eyes as Gianni pinched my leg trying to get my attention.

"Mommy. Mommy," she whispered.

Ignoring her I went along with Sonny's program.

As the priest rambled my face went blank. This was really happening. I was marrying my husband's sworn enemy and there was no turning back.

"Charlotte, Charlotte," Sonny called out.

"Oh, I'm sorry. I do," I said in a daze. The priest mumbled some more and then it was official.

"I now pronounce you husband and wife, you may now kiss your beautiful bride," the priest announced.

Just like that, Sonny was my husband, kissing me as if no one else mattered.

After Sonny finished ramming his tongue down my throat, the priest handed us the marriage certificate. A part of me didn't want to sign it, knowing if I didn't I had one last chance to back out. However, when Sonny handed me the pen, once again he gave me a look that said I didn't have any other options.

"You have a very beautiful bride, Sonny," the priest said. Once he signed his name it made everything official.

Sonny smiled with so much pride. "Thank you. I picked a good one this time."

This time, I thought. I quickly wondered if he'd ever been married before and if so how many times.

With all of the commotion and congratulations from the staff I didn't realize Gianni had taken off.

"Sonny, where is Gianni?"

"I'm not sure. Go find her. I'm sure she's upset so you should go tend to her and meet me back out here. I would like for her to join us for brunch."

Making my way back into the house which felt more like a castle, I had a feeling where she might've gone. Opening the French doors to the butler's pantry where she sometimes liked to hide, I looked but she wasn't there. I even checked to see if Gianni was hiding on the elevator, but she wasn't there either. Just before checking to see if she'd left the main house and had gone to the guest quarters where Francesca and the rest of the staff lived, I thought to check the library where my late husband's soul rested. As soon as I walked into the small library where Sonny kept tons of books he never read, I saw her looking up at the brass urn that held her father's ashes.

"Daddy, how could this happen? Why did you leave me here with these people? I miss you daddy." Gianni burst into tears as she sat there on her knees looking like an angel. Through her sobs she still didn't see me watching her and started to pray.

Dear God,

Please bring my daddy back to me. I miss him and I need him. Please take me away from this place to my daddy. God, I love my mommy, but I don't think she loves me any more. Please help her see Sonny is a bad man.

Amen.

My heart sunk to the heels of my feet. My daughter was in so much pain and for the first time in a long time I felt helpless. It felt like there was nothing I could do to remove her pain.

"Gianni, baby mommy does love you. Why would you think something like that? I love you more than anything in this world," I stated as tears streamed down my face. I stared down at my broken daughter.

"Well why did you marry him mommy? He's mean."

I walked over to her. "Sweetheart he's not mean. You'll see. Just give him a chance."

"I don't want to! I want my daddy! I hate being here. You don't keep your promises and you love him. You don't love me anymore." There was an overwhelming amount of sadness in her voice that damn near crushed me.

"I do love you, Gianni and I always keep my promises baby," I said, wiping tears from my eyes.

"But you said we were going to the zoo today."

"Hey, what's going on in here? Why are you two crying? Today is supposed to be a happy day," Sonny interrupted.

"Give us a minute, Sonny."

"Well, Charlotte, that's not going to happen. We are a family now, so we need to discuss things as a family."

"I don't want to talk to you about anything. I miss my daddy and you…"

"Now look Gianni, I'm sick and tired of these spoiled charades you keep pulling. Today is a special day for me and your mother."

"I don't care!" Gianni screamed.

"Charlotte, you have no control over this child! I'm sick and tired of the disrespect!"

"I want my daddy!" Gianni wailed.

"Come here baby," I said, consoling my daughter. I held her tightly in my arms.

"Listen, I've allowed your father to sit in my damn house and you still don't appreciate me!" Sonny's voice echoed through our 20,000 square foot home. He was sweating as his five foot eight frame towered over my daughter.

"Sonny please calm down," I urged him.

"No, fuck this. Since you want your father so bad, here you go." Sonny walked over to the urn, grabbed it, and dumped the ashes all over the floor.

"Nooo, daddy!" Gianni screamed.

"Sonny, what the hell are you doing? How could you?" I asked.

"You both want that loser so bad and now you have him," he said, throwing the urn down. He walked out of the room in a complete rage.

"Come on baby," I said, picking Gianni up and carrying her to her room. She was completely distraught and sobbing uncontrollably.

What have I done, was all I could think of as I laid across Gianni's Swarvoski encrusted pink satin blanket. After crying ourselves to sleep, we finally woke up and decided it was best to go to the zoo to make Gianni feel better. I quickly slipped on a Puma workout suit and sneakers and tried to get the hell out of the house while Sonny was gone.

"Mrs. Sabatino," Alfred the doorman called.

"Alfred, please call me Charlotte."

"Mr. Sabatino has ordered if you are to leave, you can only be escorted by Rafael."

"Umm, Alfred I think I will drive."

"Mrs. Saba...I mean sorry, Miss Charlotte please do not disobey Mr. Sabatino. He was very upset when he left," Alfred stated very concerned.

"Okay, can you let Rafael know, I'm ready to go."

"He's already waiting for you outside in the car. I heard you ladies coming downstairs." He looked at Gianni. "And princess, no more tears, Miss Francesca swept your dad's ashes up and is out right now getting you a new urn so no worries."

"Say thank you Gianni."

"Thank you," she whispered. Gianni was actually very fond of Alfred. He was at least seventy years old and had a very calming spirit. He was Italian as well.

As soon as Alfred opened the door, Rafael was sitting in the tinted Escalade ready to escort us to the zoo. As we rode in silence Gianni held onto me so tight. She was already dealing with so much and I didn't need Sonny to make things worse, which he'd managed to accomplish. I made a vow to talk to him as soon as I returned so we could be on the same page going forward. Something like this could never happen again.

As soon as we pulled up to the zoo Gianni lit up as if the horrific incident had never happened.

"Mommy we're here!" she said with so much excitement. "We're here!"

"I know baby."

"I love the zoo! Let's go!"

Her smile immediately reminded me of Malcolm.

As Rafael helped Gianni out of the car, suddenly a loud screech sounded and a black Suburban pulled up directly beside us. Before I had time to react, a barrage of gunshots rang out.

"Oh no! Oh no!" I screamed.

6 Kennedi

"Yes, bend over just like that! Shake that ass baby!"

Ass phat, yeah I know, you gettin' cash, throw some mo', Nicki Minaj's voice blasted through the alarm clock radio as I twerked to the beat.

"Like this," I said, bending over and making my butt cheeks clap.

The seductive dance move immediately took me back to my short stint as a stripper. Watching his ass squirm around in handcuffs made me laugh deep down inside. If only he knew what I had in store for him.

"Damn, take these cuffs off of me. I'm trying to fuck your fine phat ass. That red thong peepin' in and out got my dick hard as shit," Tommy replied.

"You like these juicy tits baby," I said, juggling my breast all in his face, teasing him.

"Hell yeah. Come on, Brittney, I need that pussy now," he said, calling me one of my alias names.

"Just like I need my fucking money," a deep Jersey accent said from behind me.

Finally, I thought to myself as I walked over to the hotel room floor and picked up my clothes. My work was done.

"Man, what the fuck," my target replied in shock. "Bitch you set me up! My man know who I'm with, he gonna kill your ass," Tommy spat.

"Nigga whatever. Your man probably already dead," I responded without a care in the world right before I let out a big wad of spit right in his face. This was business as usual for me, little did he know. He was nothing but a mark.

Tommy's face filled with anger. "Bitch!"

Before he could get another word out, a pistol went straight across his face. Blood went everywhere.

"Well, Brittney thanks for informing him about his dead man."

"No problem partner," I flirted.

"So gangster," he flirted back in that sexy accent that I loved. He was fine as shit and was a boss. I usually didn't do white men, but his old ass could get it anytime he needed. Especially if he kept my lifestyle popping the way he did.

We made such a good team and he knew it. Jobs like this kept the bills paid, since Malcolm's career was over. Shit, Malcolm thought *Venus* was a rich brat whose parents died in a car accident and left me millions. Little did he know, the moves my partner kept me on, made sure we lived our rich lifestyle.

Watching my partner in crime get physical with that smart mouth ass Tommy, made me laugh to myself, especially as he went down the list of everybody he killed.

"Okay so your man is dead, so is your mother, your second child's baby mother, did I leave out anyone," he looked over and asked the big dark skinned dude who accompanied him.

"Trey did I forget anyone?" he asked one of his security goons that only frequented our capers. Apparently Sonny had goons for different jobs. I only saw Trey during our hits so I could only assume he was the best at this certain job.

"Umm, you forgot his teenage son, what's his name Tommy Jr.?" Trey added.

"Oh yeah, he had to go, too. Just way too much mouth."

"Dog! You kilt my fam! All over a mill. Shit I'll give you your money man, damn," Tommy cried as blood dripped from his nose.

"So, you think you're going to keep supplying people and making all this money in the streets and I'm not supposed to get paid. I even expanded your territory. It's like a smack in my face. Your generation, I tell you. No loyalty, no respect. It's a shit show," my partner stated.

"Man, I'm going to get you your money! How you gonna get paid if you kill me. My wife got the bread at the house," Tommy pleaded.

"Oh, I already got my money after I fucked your girl. Might've put a baby in her. No, just kidding, I used protection. She's still alive though. I just have her stashed until I see what I want to do with her."

"Motherfucka you betta not have touched my wife!" Tommy snapped.

"See what I don't understand is that you were about to fuck Brittney, but you don't think it's cool for me to fuck your wife? If you were home with her instead of being here, maybe you would've survived all this, or maybe not."

A clean shot right in the middle of Tommy's forehead. He was dead, just like that. I'd seen this man kill so many people, I never knew if and when it was going to happen. It was like he could be having a conversation with the target one minute and then kill them whenever the mood seemed fit. You could never brace yourself. It was like he was emotionless. I wondered if there was anybody he cared about.

"Great work as usual Kennedi."

"No problem, daddy," I flirted with his fine old ass. He was so thorough and that shit turned me on when he handled his business.

"Now Trey, get the clean up crew in here and add his body with the others. You know what to do," he instructed. "Kennedi, let's go upstairs to the penthouse suite."

After adjusting my Hermes belt, I was dressed and ready to go. As we approached the elevators, his phone rang.

"Hello. What? I'm on my way now," he said, pushing the down arrow instead of up. All I could think of was, nobody better not be fucking up my 50 g's for this job. I needed my money now.

"Kennedi, I'll make sure you get the rest of your money. I have an emergency. An extreme emergency. Shit take this for now just in case you need something right away. It's like ten stacks."

"Is everything okay?" We both walked into the elevator as I

fanned through the stack of hundreds making sure my ten thousand was there. He never shorted me. Just a bad habit. Tossing the money in my bright blue Birkin bag I went in fake concern mode.

"No, but thanks for asking and thanks for helping me up there."

"You never have to thank me. I owe you my life."

He put on his Porsche shades as if he was covering his emotions. It also seemed as if he couldn't get out of the elevator fast enough. I guess he did care about something or someone, because whatever that call was about had him extremely upset.

Just as I was getting in my car to leave the hotel, my phone rang.

"What Lee Lee? You think you can just call me after you and your wack-ass boyfriend let them stupid kids jump me," I answered ready for battle.

"Kennedi, Big Mama dead," she informed me with no emotion.

"What do you mean, she's dead?" I asked in shock.

"My muva is dead, and I was callin' you to…"

"What happened? When did she die?" My heart started to pound. Guilt filled my heart. Damn, how did I let them bastards get me off my game when I could've been using that time to spend with my grandmother.

"Cancer, what you think? She died yesterday mornin'."

"And your dumb ass is just calling me!"

"Stop fakin' like you care, Kennedi. Look if you really care, then we need you to help pay for the funeral."

"So, is that the only reason why you're calling me? Are you fucking serious right now? You couldn't call me yesterday, but you can call me when money is involved?" Tears poured from my face as I jumped on the Atlantic City Expressway and headed straight to Camden.

"Well, if you ain't givin' up no paper, then you ain't comin'."

"What the fuck did you just say? Are you threatening me?"

"If you take it that way."

"What is your broke ass gonna do if I don't pay?"

"Fuck you, Kennedi! The last time your crazy ass was here you busted off on us damn near givin' your grandmuva you care so much about a fuckin' heart attack. Those are the last memories she got of you."

"First of all, you ain't gonna stop me from seeing my grandmother before she go in the ground. If you really want to know, I made peace and talked to her a few hours after I left. I apologized for shooting up the house. I guess your creepy ass boyfriend Earl ain't tell you I called, huh?"

"I'ma fuck you up, Earl! You ain't tell me Kennedi called here. I told all y'all motherfuckas in this house don't let that bitch talk to my muva!" Lee Lee yelled as if I wasn't on the phone.

"Bitch, some conversations need to be had in person. I'ma check your ass real soon!"

My blood boiled. I couldn't wait to fuck Aunt Lee Lee up. I was tired of her damn mouth. The good thing was, Atlantic City wasn't that far from Camden. Taking off my Gucci shades, I let off a horrific scream. I had mixed emotions. Big Mama was really gone. I was heartbroken. All I could think about was her telling me to come see her more, and I didn't. I was so disrespectful to her while she was here on Earth, and I felt bad about it. The only thing I could do to make it up was to send her off in style. After all I'd done, I owed her that much.

It was times like these when I wish I had someone to talk to. Since Malcolm didn't know who I really was, he had no idea what I was going through. In his mind, he and Milan were all the family I had. I felt so alone.

As I got off the exit headed toward Big Mama's house I was ready for all I had to deal with. I put my .357 at my waist and pulled my t-shirt out of my jeans so that it was covered. As soon as I parked, some of the neighborhood kids ran up to my car.

"Aye!" I yelled, "get y'all hands off my window!"

"Can I get a dollar?" one of the kids yelled out when I opened the door. I was pissed at the fact that his lil' ass was coughing all in my face.

"Come on y'all," I said, walking them all to the ice cream truck. I knew if I didn't do something the little motherfuckas would possibly fuck up my car and I couldn't have that, especially since I didn't see Lil' Man around.

"Oh my. Little Kennedi all grown up."

"Hey, Mr. Gunner. How you been?"

"Sweetheart, just trying to enjoy life. I see you're doing well. What kind of car is that young lady?"

"It's a Ferrari."

"You're staying out of trouble Miss Lady, right? You know that fast life ain't where it's at no more. You see your sister and that baby father of yours had to learn the hard way, oh and where are my manners, I'm so sorry about your grandmother, baby. Been her neighbor for quite some time now, so I'm sure gonna miss her." He shook his head. "She was such a sweet woman; always had a smile on her face when she saw me."

"Thanks Mr.Gunner." Still feeling emotional, I reached into my pocket, pulled out three crisp $100 bills, then over to him. "I know I've never said this before but just wanted to say how much I appreciate you feeding me when I was a kid, when no one else could. Buy you something nice okay."

"Kennedi, now come back here, you know I can't accept this."

Ignoring him I walked off and made my way toward the truck. After making sure all the kids were straight, I made my way back to my grandmother's house ready for war. The door was open so I walked right in. The hospital bed that Big Mama was laying in the last time I was there was gone. The house was actually clean. I couldn't believe it. Trying to hold back the tears, I called out.

"Who in here?"

A familiar smell was coming from the kitchen. Instantly I felt ill, as my stomach bubbled. It couldn't be. As I walked into the kitchen my heart sunk.

"Well hello, Kennedi."

It couldn't be. Grabbing my gun from my waist I aimed. Finally, I would have the chance to handle some unfinished business.

7 Charlotte

"Get these cameras out of here, no cameras!" Sonny yelled as we left the hospital.

"Mommy I'm scared," Gianni said as she nodded off for the second time. Her pain medication had her in and out.

"It's okay, baby," I said, consoling my daughter while being ushered into the SUV.

Gianni was going to be fine, thank God. The bullet had only grazed her arm, but she was still an emotional wreck. We both were. I was so angry with Sonny I couldn't see straight. There were so many questions, and I had so many mixed emotions. As Sonny gave orders to this person and that person sending threats to make sure the news outlets didn't show pictures of Gianni and I, my heart ached. I rode in silence the entire way home trying to devise a plan to get out of this God forsaken marriage somehow. Not even twenty-four hours of being married to this man and my daughter's life was already at risk. I wasn't sure how much of this gangsta lifestyle I could take.

As soon as we pulled through the gates the staff was waiting in a panic.

"Gianni, are you okay?" Francesca asked with concern as she helped us out of the car.

Once we got in the house I had Francesca take Gianni to her room so I could have a conversation with Sonny. I entered his office in beast mode.

"So, did you do this? This has your name written all over it. What type of sick fuck are you to have us shot at? It's not enough that you killed her father, my husband!"

In attack mode I charged at him trying to claw his eyes out. Rafael was nowhere in sight to stop me. After getting in a couple of scratches to Sonny's face, he grabbed me and held me tight in his arms as we both fell to the floor. I just laid there and cried. Tossing me to the side Sonny was pissed and acted as if he really wanted to hit me.

"Charlotte, don't you disrespect me or my house like that again!"

"*Your* house? I thought we were married. Shouldn't this be our house now?"

"Lower your voice, now!" he ordered.

"Answer my question Sonny, did you have us shot at?"

"Are you kidding me? If I want to send a message I make it clear that it's from me. I don't hide behind cowardly ass drive bys. It's not my style."

"So, who would want to kill me and my daughter, Sonny? I need answers," I demanded between sobs.

"The only thing I need to tell you is that it will be handled. That's all you need to know. Now, get out of my office."

"I'm not leaving here until you…"

"Get out!" he roared. His face was red as fire.

"I'm leaving you. I can't do this!"

The look he gave me was frightening. "The only way you will ever leave me is in a body bag. Now get the fuck out before I lose my temper."

His words were chilling. At that point I knew Sonny meant what he said. Upset and frustrated, I ran to the stables to clear my mind. I had to get myself together before I faced my daughter. As I entered, the head of security, Rafael was in there. Once I walked in, he closed the gate to Sonny's horse, Big Mack, who was trained to race. Rafael often rode him on his free time and was always brushing his beautiful, chocolate brown coat. I hadn't been to any races but from what I heard, Big Mack was pretty good at winning. I guess Sonny wanted yet another stream of income and thought Big Mack was about to be the next damn Seabiscuit. Rafael seemed very fond of the horse, and I might've been interrupting their bonding time, but I didn't care. I needed to get away from Sonny.

Rafael sat down on a bed of hay. "Hey, Charlotte, what are you doing out here? Are you okay?" Rafael asked as he took off his gloves off and wiped the sweat from his brow.

He didn't have a shirt on and his whiskey colored skin glistened with sweat. Standing at least 6'3, with broad shoulders, and sultry eyes, he was so damn sexy. It wasn't often that I saw a twenty something year old body in the flesh, so for a quick moment, I was distracted. After staring at him like an idiot, I finally answered.

"No, I'm not okay. This has been the worst day of my life," I said before sitting on the hay opposite of him.

"Yeah, I heard about Gianni. I'm sorry about that. I feel so bad about not protecting you better today."

"Rafael, it's not your fault. I don't know if I can take this any longer though. My daughter could've died today," I stated angrily.

"Charlotte, but she didn't. You've gotta look at it that way."

"That's easier said than done."

"Listen, I know it's probably tough being with a man like Sonny, but you're blessed to have the life that you have. Hell, any life can be tough sometimes and it throws you mierda, but you…"

"Umm, what's mierda?"

"Sorry that means 'shit' in Spanish."

I smiled a bit. "Oh."

"You gotta roll with the punches. I don't want you to be fearful. I failed for not protecting you guys today, but I owe Sonny. He's made a better life for both me, and my family," Rafael continued.

"So, what's your story? You never told me, how you ended up here."

"Well, I usually don't discuss that with anyone."

"Okay, so I'll tell you my story, and then you tell me yours. Deal?" I asked.

"Deal," he said, exposing his perfect set of white teeth and deep dimples.

"Okay so Sonny hated my husband for a debt that he owed from a bad business deal. My husband and Sonny's nephew Frankie were best friends from college…"

"You mean the one who offed himself, the one who was fucking Sonny's last wife," he interrupted.

"Yes. So my husband was actually there when it happened. I think that's why Sonny was so hell bent on making my husband's life hell, to get back at his dead nephew. Anyway, for months Sonny tortured my husband giving him deadlines to pay back both him and Frankie's bill. I even gave my husband money to pay Sonny and he didn't. One day Sonny got in touch with me and asked if I would be willing to leave my husband for him. I thought he was crazy and blew him off. I never told my husband about the call."

"Why not? He might've been able to help."

"The day I went to my husband's downtown L.A. penthouse to tell him, I found him in bed with one of his mistresses with his head between her legs."

Rafael scrunched up this face. "Ouch."

"Yes, ouch is right. The pain of actually seeing him cheat and be so intimate with another woman hurt me to the core. I was different back then Rafael. I was weak. My mom was battling Cancer and died. I was just going through so much."

"I'm sorry to hear that."

"Well, Sonny didn't care too much about that. One of the messages he sent to my husband was an explosion that killed my father at my mother's repast. I buried both my parents within a week and dealt with constant betrayal from my husband with his mistresses. I had another weak moment right before I knew it was time to file for divorce. Gianni and I were leaving town due to Sonny being after my husband. I was going to stay with my cousins in Chicago until my husband could join us there. Just when I was considering making things work, we were approached by another one of my husband's mistresses at the airport. She confronted him about a son that he wasn't taking care of."

"I knew it was over. I just jumped out of the car with Gianni and before we made it to security Gianni had wondered off.

She was trying to get back to her father. He was her world. She didn't know the man he really was. I panicked and went searching for her. I went into the ladies room and that's all I remember before waking up in the back of a SUV."

"What?"

"Sonny had abducted both me and my daughter to use us as bait for my husband."

"So, I'm confused. You guys seem so in love."

"Rafael, I didn't have a choice. He tortured my husband making him think Gianni and I were both dead, right before killing my husband blowing him up in a car. It hurts me how my husband and I ended things. The last time I saw him was at the airport. Marty probably had him for breakfast."

"How do you know about Marty and..."

"And what? How he is a garbage disposal for dead bodies. I'll tell you how? Sonny tortured me and had me watch Marty eat my husband's white mistress Cherry and her son. See, that day at the airport he got them, too."

"He made you watch?" Rafael asked.

"Why do you seem surprised? He let me know, if I didn't move to New Jersey and be with him, Gianni and I would be next."

"I'm sorry to hear all this Charlotte. You're such a nice lady."

"Don't call me a lady, like I'm old. I'm only 32. How old are you?"

"I'm 22," he laughed.

"So, what's your story, I pretty much just laid out all my dirty laundry," I laughed.

"Well, it's short and simple. My father ran an escort service back in the Dominican Republic. When people came to visit from the U.S., my father provided women to them. He only dealt with people of a certain status. Sonny visited one day, and obtained my father's services. From there they became partners. He offered my dad a way to make even more money faster with his connections and contacts. This was all before I was even born. When I was eight years old, my father committed suicide. Sonny still kept in contact with my mother, but eventually moved us to the states for a better life."

"Oh my gosh. Why did he kill himself?"

"I don't know. My mother won't talk about it."

"So, how many of you are there?"

"Well, I have an older sister that now lives in L.A., she's 28. She and my mother still runs the family business back home. They travel back and forth. Anyway, I moved to the states when I was eighteen, graduated college in Upstate New York, and now I'm here."

"Wait…so you have a degree and you work security for Sonny. I don't get it."

"Well, my degree is in Internet security, so I do way more than you see. I'm compensated well," he laughed.

"Oh, I'm sure. So, what's next for you?"

"I'm good with what I'm doing." Rafael got up as if I made him suddenly uncomfortable.

"Please don't go. I enjoy talking to you. You make me feel human again in this superficial bullshit. I just want out."

Suddenly, tears started to flow and I could no longer hold them back. Sonny having this much control over me, was taking a toll on my mind.

"Please don't cry Charlotte, it's gonna be okay," Rafael said as he walked over and held me close in his muscular arms. He felt right. I felt safe.

"How? I'm stuck with him. My daughter hates me. She hates Sonny. Everything is just so wrong."

"So why did you marry him?"

"I felt like I had to…like I didn't have a choice. Everything is a dictatorship around here."

"I don't feel like that. Sonny doesn't treat me like that. I'm my own man. Maybe if you stand up to him a little more, maybe things will change," Rafael said, releasing me from his embrace.

"I just tried to stand up to him. I told him that I was leaving him, and do you know what he said?"

"I'm afraid to ask."

"He said the only way I was leaving him was in a body bag," I told him as I started to cry again. I felt like I was in a no win situation.

"Hey, stop that crying," Rafael said, lifting my chin with his pointer finger.

We just stared at each other. I was lost in his brown eyes and all of a sudden I lost my balance and fell back on a bed of hay and took Rafael down with me.

"Ouch! Shit!" I yelled and immediately grabbed my ankle trying to play it off.

"What's wrong, are you okay?" Rafael asked as he kneeled in front of me and placed his foot between my legs.

"Owww," I faked.

"Does this hurt?"

"A little. I'm so embarrassed," I laughed a bit.

"You don't have to be embarrassed I just want to make sure you're okay."

"I know you want to laugh."

As soon as I said that Rafael let out a little laugh exposing that gorgeous smile. As I stared mesmerized again, there was a loud noise. Suddenly, the stable door creaked open and my heart sunk with fear.

8 Kennedi

"What the hell are you doing here?" I asked with my gun pointed at the person I hated more than anyone in the world.

"I'm here to pay my respects. Now, put that gun down and come give your mother some love," she said unbothered. Her deep raspy voice still sounded the same.

I guess she thought I didn't have the heart to shoot her ass. If that was the case, she was right. I couldn't shoot her before getting all the answers that I deserved.

"Why are you here? Why now? You choose now to come back? You haven't been here in fifteen years! You fucking bitch. You left me. Why did you come back?" I asked with so much anger. It felt as though my mother had opened a wound and thrown salt in it.

"Kennedi stop it! I'm not the bad person you think I am. I have…"

"Bitch don't tell me you've changed. All of the pain that I went through in my life is all your fault! I need answers Maricar!"

"Kennedi I've been through some shit, too! I was locked up for those eight years. I got out two and a half years ago. Just in time to bury my precious Kasey. Fuck, if you wouldn't have missed your sister's funeral then you would've known I came back."

"Fuck you and fuck Kasey! You left me for dead and that's unforgiveable."

"Look Kennedi. I'm gonna need for you to let all that shit go. The past is just that…the past. I did what I had to for you girls.

It was for the best."

"Wow…you selfish bitch. You left us in a fucking train station. I was raped because of you."

"Kennedi, you think you're so much better than me. What do you think is happening to your daughter, China right now? You left her just like I left you."

I didn't have a comeback because for once she was right.

"So since you're the mother of the year, did you know that your daughter was caught sucking that old man Earl's dick last night?"

My eyes widened.

"Yeah, while there was a house full of damn people up in here giving their condolences, your daughter was giving somebody head in the back room. I had to bust that damn Earl upside his head," Maricar informed. "You see you're more like me than you want to admit, Kennedi."

"Where the fuck is he? I'll kill him!" I yelled then looked around.

"Oh, he went to the store with Lee Lee. She didn't care. Just like you really don't. Let me ask you something. The man who raped you…do you see his face when you look at China?" She didn't wait for a response. "Well, if you do then I've been there. I always felt like you girls were the reason my life went to shit. Do you know how hard it was being on my own with two bi-racial babies? My family basically disowned me because I had babies by a black man," she informed.

"So that was our fault? Your family also probably disowned you because you were a crack head. Nobody told you to be in the streets and get knocked up by a black dude. That was your fucking choice."

"You're right, but maybe if I'd only had one child, life wouldn't have been so hard."

"So, is that why you loved Kasey more than me? Do you wish I was never born?"

"It was your fucking mouth Kennedi. It's like a knife. Kasey was warm….caring. You were always so fucking rough. Should've been a boy. That's why that boyfriend of yours fell in love with her I hear."

"Well damn, this shit might be better than putting a bullet in you," I could feel the blood rushing to my head. I was heated. She'd definitely struck a nerve and I was determined to hurt her.

"What the hell are you talking about?" Maricar questioned.

"How should I tell you this?" I laughed and had a seat at the table opposite of my Pilipino mother.

I put my gun back in my waist. Even though she had a petite frame, she'd aged over the past fifteen years. She now had dark circles under her eyes and a bad case of crow's feet on her pale skin. Hair pulled back in a long ponytail, Maricar had on over exaggerated eyelashes and earrings with her name on them like she was still in her twenties. She was probably fucking somebody young. Looking at her discolored teeth, I wondered if she still smoked a pack of Marlboro Lights per day. I also wondered if the cigarettes had anything to do with her deep voice.

I couldn't wait to erase that stupid smirk off of her face. If she felt an ounce of pain by me, it would make me feel a little vindication.

"Let me guess, you didn't come to your sister's funeral because her and Sharrod were together right?" she jabbed.

"Oh it's cool they were together. It's even better that they're still together now. I loved the face he made when he finished her off," I laughed.

"What do you mean?" Maricar yelled in her Filipino accent she tried so desperately to hide. When she got emotional, she couldn't cover it up.

"I watched Sharrod empty a bullet straight to her head. He killed her and I got the opportunity to watch him do what I should've done a long time ago. She deserved to die after betraying me the way she did."

"You're a liar! A fucking liar! He would never kill her. The kids told me how he loved my daughter."

Maricar stood up and started to pace the floor looking crazy. Her thin body sashayed back and forth, and I loved every bit of it.

I got up and stood straight in her face and looked her deep

in her slanted eyes.

"Your precious daughter D-I-E-D, for being in the wrong place at the wrong T-I-M-E. Things happen the way they're supposed to, *Mommy*."

Just like that she slapped me with all she had. I didn't hesitate to react though. Drawing the gun from my waist, I put it straight in her mouth.

"Now look here bitch. You think you gonna fuck my life up and then come back here and act like you ain't done shit wrong."

"Get that gun out my fucking mouth," she mumbled.

"Suck it you whore…just like you used to suck those crack pipes. Hell you probably still do. You're a whore just like Kasey."

"You killed Kasey! Tell her. Tell her the truth!" China yelled when she walked in the house.

"Shut up China. I didn't kill her!"

"You did. I know you did. Now you gonna take my grandmother away from me, too! If you shoot her I swear I'll make sure you go back to jail where you belong."

"China fuck you! Worry about why you busy sucking Earl's nasty ass dick you whore!" I yelled.

Slowly pulling the gun from Maricar's mouth, I placed it up against her high cheekbone.

"You killed my precious daughter. Sharrod loved her. These kids told me. They told me how you left them for Kasey to take care of," she said.

"Bitch you don't know shit! Do you know how many nights I played mommy to your daughter when she couldn't sleep at night? I got molested for years from my foster father, just so he wouldn't do the same to Kasey. I fucking raised your daughter. She was the weak one. She betrayed me by screwing my boyfriend behind my back and I'm the bad guy! Fuck all y'all."

"What's going on in here?" some young dope boy asked. He walked like he was running shit.

"It's okay Proctor. She's harmless. Let's just go," Maricar responded. He must've been her little boy toy.

All of a sudden an officer walked up to the door trying to look in the screen door.

"What's going on in here? Somebody called complaining…"

His words fell deaf on my ears. I don't think I'd ever been this upset in my life. I was tired of being compared to that bitch Kasey. Just because I was the outspoken twin, the realest one, I was always hated. The thought of killing Maricar right there entered my mind. Just as I raised the gun and pointed it at her, police ran in with their weapons pulled out.

"Drop the gun. Drop it now!" the white officer demanded. With all that had happened in the media with Sandra Bland and all the other victims of police brutality I dropped the gun and placed my hands in the air.

"Arrest that bitch!" China yelled out.

"You have the right to remain silent…"

As the officer read me my rights a flash of Milan entered my mind. How was I going to get out of this one? My daughter needed me. I couldn't leave her out here to be raised by Malcolm. He was too crazy to raise her alone. What was I going to tell him? He could never know about my life outside of him. That could spark a memory or something. I couldn't afford losing him.

As China and Maricar taunted me, I was carried out of the house in cuffs. I decided to leave them with some choice words though.

"I'll be out of jail within an hour. Trust me, I got connections."

"It's Friday evening. You'll be in jail for the weekend. Have fun," Maricar teased.

"And bitch when I get out, I'll make sure it's my business to take this fine ass chocolate man right from under your nose. I'm sure your old ass ain't fucking him right anyway. What's your name again, Proctor? We're fucking, sir. Next time I see you, I'll show you what a real woman is."

"Let's go and close your mouth," the officer demanded.

Biting my lip, and lowering my eyes I know I'd made his dick hard. The way he looked at me let me know I had him. He was cute too and looked like he had swag and money. I had no idea what he was doing with Maricar's ancient ass.

"That's your brother you stupid bitch!" Maricar yelled out of the door as the police placed me into the squad car.

I was in a state of shock. I had a brother. All these years she left me and Kasey. She was out here raising another child with someone else.

That trifling bitch, I thought.

9 Kennedi

After being booked in jail, I was put in a cell with a stripper looking chick who stared at me from the time I'd been brought in. Although she had a cut going down the side of her face, she was very pretty and her body was thicker than a fudge brownie. Even though we'd already changed into a pair of ugly ass orange scrubs, you could still see how phat she was in all the right places. Even the guards kept walking past our cell taking a quick peek. While she stared at me all I could think about was what I was going to tell Malcolm when I got out. He was certainly gonna get in my ass for not coming home.

"Hey wassup, pretty," she finally worked up the courage to say then sat beside me.

"Hey," I responded in a dry tone.

"What you in here for?"

"Trying to kill my mother, how about you?" I chuckled.

"Damn, gangster. I thought you might've been in here for some dumb shit like a speeding ticket, but you hardcore. You a pretty thug ain't you?"

I couldn't help but laugh again.

"Well, I'm a dancer and I got into it with some bitches in the club. They were hating as usual.

I knew you were a stripper, I thought.

"I'm Mocha, what's your name?"

"Kennedi."

She held out her hand that was in desperate need of a manicure. "Nice to meet you, Kennedi."

"Nice to meet you, too, Mocha. That's not your real name, right?" Although her bright blue polish was chipped, her hands were baby soft.

"Naw, that's my stage name. I'm so used to giving that shit out to thirsty ass niggas it's a habit. My real name is Keira. Hell, I don't even know how I came up with Mocha being that I'm a red bone."

We both laughed. Not only was she a red bone but she even had a few faint freckles on her nose. Her sandy colored weave was on point though and complimented her hazelnut eyes.

"I used to dance some years back out in Cali, so I know all about hating ass bitches. I had to fight a couple of times. I was the 'it chick' in the club and they couldn't take me. The crazy thing was, I was new at it. You better not let them bitches fuck with your money."

"They fuck with me on purpose sometimes knowing I'm gonna get stuck down here for the weekend. I'm from Philly but the club owners out here in Jersey love for me to come and perform. I don't know why I fall for this shit. Sometimes I feel something has to give. I've been dancing since I was sixteen."

"Damn."

"Yeah, it's been about ten years now. The money good, but I'm getting tired. How did you get out?"

"The good thing was I only did it for a couple of months. I met the right dude and never had to go back."

"That's a good look. Shit I need to get out of here. It's a couple of ball players coming through Philly this weekend and I need that bread."

"I'm not staying in here the entire weekend either, I can't." I thought about Malcolm and how he would lose it if he had to take care of Milan for the entire weekend alone. I needed to make a call to get the hell out of here.

"Well girl if you got some type of connect to get outta here, hook a sista up."

"I'll see what I can do. Guard! Can I make my call?" I yelled.

"Girl they gonna ignore the hell out of you. They always do

that shit." She stared at me for a few seconds. "Damn girl, you fine as shit. You mixed ain't you?" Mocha got closer and closer. I knew what time it was, but I played dumb, just to see how far she would go.

"Unfortunately. The Philippine part is my dumb ass egg donor, and my father was black."

"Was?"

"Yeah, he died when I was young. Don't remember him much. Guard! I'm fucking pissed. I need to get home. He's going to kill me!" I yelled out again.

"Who, your dude?"

"My husband."

"Damn, I thought I had a chance."

I smiled once again. I really was flattered.

"You seem real cool. I would love to just taste you if I could. You don't have to do nothing. You been with a girl before," she let out a nervous laugh.

"Why you ask me that?"

"I don't know one girl that dance who has never been with a girl before."

I hesitated a minute before answering. "Yeah, I've been with one before."

"I knew it!" Mocha smiled, showing off her tongue ring.

"Well, I was locked up for a couple of years, so that's where I had my first experience."

"What were you in for?" Mocha asked like she was sitting back eating popcorn and watching a movie. I was never this trusting of someone so soon, but for some reason I felt comfortable talking to her.

"My child's father was in the streets, and got caught up with his shit, so I went in."

"Damn, that's why I try not to fuck with street niggas no more. That shit played out like a cassette tape for real. It's too many dudes out here getting legit money, especially them white dudes. I got a few snow bunnies who come to see me. They tip good, too."

"I know right. Definitely learned my lesson, but the legit

dudes be tight as shit though, unless they from the streets."

"You right," she laughed.

"My dude now though, I love him. He changed my life. He saved me from the streets, well kind of," I laughed thinking about the move I was just on earlier.

"I don't want to hear about your dude. Tell me about when you were with the girl," Mocha replied.

"It's simple. The bitch faked like she loved me. I fell in love with her. She used me, and betrayed me. I don't trust nobody and I let her in. Never again, end of story."

"Don't let that bitch fuck up you missing out on some good head." At that moment, Mocha started rubbing my legs and I immediately felt turned on. She knew I wanted her no matter how much I was fighting it. I guess she could feel it.

"Girl stop," I said, pushing her hand away.

Mocha was just about to make another move when I was saved by the bell. An officer finally came to the rescue.

"You got one call Miss, and Miss Rogers you've already made your call so don't ask for another one," a short, stubby female officer said as she opened the cell to let me out.

"Yeah…yeah I know," Mocha mumbled.

I knew who would get me out of this and make it all go away. The phone rang three times and finally my partner answered. I knew he would accept the call.

"What's going on Kennedi? Why are you in jail?"

"Nothing like that. Domestic shit. Can you get me out of here?"

"Your husband?"

"No, my mother?"

"Your mother? I thought…"

"It's a long story. Can you get me out of here? I can't leave my daughter with him."

"Let me see what I can do, what favors I can call in."

"I need this to go away. He can't find out. He thinks my mother is dead and I have no family."

"He won't. I'll get you out of there."

"My car is still outside my grandmother's house. I need

you to make arrangements for that as well."

"No problem, just make sure I get the address before we hang up."

"Oh, and one more thing. I need you to get my cellie out, too."

"Look, you're pushing it. Let's worry about you for now."

"Thanks, I owe you."

"Nonsense. You don't owe anybody. I'll make some calls."

A couple of hours went by as I listened to Mocha talk me to death and finally I fell asleep in mid conversation. Around 6:30 a.m. the next morning, I woke up with reality hitting me that I was still in jail. Before I could panic though, the stubby officer was back at our cell pulling out her keys. From the way she looked at me, I knew I was about to get out. I got excited.

"Miss Fitzgerald, you must have some friends in high places to get you out on a weekend. You're free to go."

My smile was wide. "It's Mrs. actually."

"You're good to go, too Miss Rogers," the officer said to Mocha who just woke up.

"Are you serious?" she asked.

"Mocha let's go. You can ask questions and thank me later," I said, walking out.

Even though it was Saturday morning, we were still released. We were also notified that all charges had been dropped, so to say that my partner came through was an understatement. Mocha wouldn't stop hugging and thanking me enough as we changed back into our street clothes and walked outside. I couldn't wait to take a shower to wash the jail stench off of me. As soon as the doors opened, I saw my car waiting outside just like he promised. I could tell Maricar or China had taken revenge out on me by all the scratches on the driver's side door, but for once I didn't care. Small shit like a coat of paint was nothing to being locked up. What was odd though was the young dude that was sitting on the hood.

I quickly walked over to him. "Umm, who are you, and why are you on my car?"

"Who I am is irrelevant. Maybe you should say thank you for me coming to bail you out. Your partner told me to give you this envelope and call him tomorrow," he said, just before walking over to a black SUV on the opposite side of the street.

"Girl he fine as shit," Mocha said almost drooling at the mouth. However, she was right because dude was drop dead gorgeous and sexy as shit.

"So you just gonna walk off and not let me know who you are?" Sonny's normal goon, Trey didn't have shit on this dude.

"We're in the same business. You know we don't do that," he responded.

"What?" I asked, trying to flirt, but he wasn't buying it.

"See you the next time you need me," he said, jumping into the SUV and pulling off.

"Girl, what type of shit you got going on?" Mocha's nosey ass tried to pry. "I mean, look at your fuckin' car."

"Nothing. Look, are you good because I need to rush home to my daughter?" I stared at her awful pink diamond encrusted leotard and thigh high boots. I didn't recall being that tacky as a stripper.

"Well, I can call somebody to get me, but I don't have no money on me."

"Oh damn my bad. Hold up let me see what I got in my glove compartment."

After searching for some cash, it dawned on me to check the manila envelope. It was tons of cash in there. That's what I loved about him. He would just give me bonus cash from time to time for no reason. After hitting her off with $300.00, Mocha and I exchanged numbers then I quickly pulled off. I had to hurry home to Milan.

As soon as I got on the turnpike my stomach was upset. I had butterflies and didn't know what I was going to tell Malcolm about not coming home the night before.

Hitting the remote control on my visor exactly one hour later, I opened the gates. Looking at my Rolex, I saw it was almost nine a.m., so I hoped Malcolm and Milan were still asleep. Maybe I could just sneak in and sleep in Milan's room. Disarming the alarm from my cell phone so I wouldn't wake anyone, I finally got out of the car and snuck inside. My plan was to sneak past my bedroom and into Milan's however, when I got upstairs and ran past my room, I caught a glimpse of a female silhouette laying with her back facing me. She was in my bed.

I stopped immediately and turned around. *What the fuck? I'm gonna kill this motherfucka,* I whispered to myself as I walked back into my room and snatched the bitch off my bed. She hit the floor with a loud thump.

"Kennedi, what are you doing?" Nina yelled right before waking up Milan. She quickly stood up.

"What the fuck are you doing in my bed, and I know damn well you don't have on my husband's fucking t-shirt. Where are your scrubs?" I asked firmly as Milan looked up at me half asleep.

"Well, since you decided to take a mini-vacation and not come home last night Malcolm called me back after I got off, in a panic. You can't leave him with her, Vee. He's not ready. When I came back, he was a wreck."

"So, you spent the night with my husband? Was that your way of comforting him? You are taking your job way to…"

"Vee please stop. I don't want Malcolm, he's not my type and further more I don't do married men. Besides, he cleaned all night long and never came upstairs. The only reason why I have on his t-shirt is because Milan has been throwing up all morning and threw up all over my scrubs. I've been laying down trying to put her back to sleep and…"

"No need to explain. I'm sorry Nina. I just had a really fucked up couple of days. Where's Malcolm?"

"He's downstairs in the theater room. He's not well, Vee. You might want to rethink the medication and…"

"Look I know what my husband needs. Did you give him his medication yesterday?"

"Yes."

"What about this morning?"

"No, not yet but…"

"Don't worry I'll handle it," I said, cutting her off. I went downstairs to see what Malcolm was up to. I knew he was upset with me.

As I tiptoed downstairs I geared up ready for World War III. Once I came inside, I saw that the projector was on in the theater room. He loved to record the nightly news on the DVR so I was sure he was watching a replay of that.

The six-year old little girl who was grazed by a bullet earlier today at the Camp May County Zoo, has been released from the hospital and is now recovering at home with her family.

Wow a little girl was shot at the zoo, that's fucked up, I thought to myself as the news reporter continued.

I didn't even bother looking at the screen as the news was always so damn depressing. I quickly tuned her out as I walked closer to him. The guilt of me leaving him all alone the night before was starting to get the best of me. The closer I got to him the more my heart sunk. I was scared because I didn't feel like fighting. I prayed to God he would understand and believe the lie I had in store. The closer I got to Malcolm I could see the chair rocking back and forth and could hear him saying something repeatedly.

"Shar, Shar, Shar, Shar, Shar..." he mumbled, looking straight ahead. As I got closer I noticed he had my Glock sitting on his lap.

My eyes enlarged. "Malcolm," I called out. "Malcolm!"

Breaking from his daze he looked straight through me. I felt very uneasy, as if I came to a gunfight unarmed. Trying to back out of the room to get to another gun, he stopped me.

"Venus! Sit the fuck down!"

"Malcolm, why do you have a gun?"

"It's time that you learn not to fuck with me," he said, pointing the gun.

The look in his eyes was filled with so much pain. Damn, was he mad I hadn't been home and what the hell was he mumbling? I'd fought too hard and dealt with way too much shit to go out like this.

10 Charlotte

"Charlotte, Sonny said for you to come back upstairs," Rafael informed me as he looked away.

He'd become a little distant after Big Mack's trainer, Ramone came into the stables the other day and nearly scared us have to death. I'm sure both of us thought it was Sonny and quickly feared for our lives but quickly breathed a sigh of relief when only Ramone walked inside. Although we weren't doing anything, if Sonny had caught us in such an intimate setting, we would both be dead.

"Damn, I just came to get a bottle of water," I said, shaking my head as I opened up the refrigerator. I really wasn't thirsty but it was the only thing I could think of to get away from Sonny for a second.

A part of me was a little embarrassed because I knew that Rafael was aware of what Sonny and I were doing. Our upstairs playroom was where Sonny and I entertained his female friends. There were all types of sexual contraptions in the room. Whips, chains, ropes, swings, handcuffs, breast clamps, gag rings, stripper poles…you name it…Sonny had it in that room. There was even a pool table that was utilized as a bed many times.

"Well, let me know when you're ready to leave and pick Gianni up from camp. She has to be picked up by 3:30, right?"

"Yeah." When Rafael turned to walk away, I stopped him. "Do you want to talk about the other day?"

He nodded his head. "Not really, but I just want to say I'm

sorry. I shouldn't have been near you like that."

I walked over to him and grabbed his hand. "You don't have to apologize. It's not like you forced me to be in the stables with you."

It looked like he wanted to kiss me. "How's your ankle," he whispered.

I giggled. "It's fine."

As Francesca suddenly made her way into the kitchen I quickly dropped his hand. "Just let me know about Gianni," Rafael said before walking away.

Only four days had passed since the shooting and Sonny was determined for Gianni to get out of the house. I begged him not to send her to camp, but he insisted that she get back to her normal life. She looked so sad while leaving that morning, but I knew if I tried to intervene, Sonny would eventually get his way so I quickly gave in. It made me feel better once I talked to her during lunch and it sounded as if she was having fun so I decided not to make a big deal out of it.

As soon as I walked back into the playroom they were at it again. Instead of joining in, I took a seat in the velvet red chaise lounge. Staring out of the window, I picked up my flat champagne from earlier and continued to drink. They knew I wasn't ready yet.

"Come on, have some," Megan said as she snorted down more coke into her nostrils.

No matter how much Sonny begged me to join her, I wasn't doing any drugs. I left that up to Megan and some red headed girl she'd brought along this time. Megan was a regular in the play-room but I'd never seen the mysterious red head. As I sipped more champagne, I watched them party without me.

Megan and the red head fondled each other and stared at me while Sonny pleasured himself. Now it was time to take a shot of Patron to ease my jitters. I'd done this all before, but I was just tired of it all.

"Come on Charlotte, you still have too many clothes on." Megan was high and drunk and ready to have her way with me. She knew how to please me for sure and the more I drank the more I became ready for her, too.

"You tell her," Sonny instigated as he stroked his little dick.

I knew what was about to happen so I finished that glass of champagne, then quickly downed two more. As Megan suddenly sashayed over to me in her lace bodysuit, the red head continued to get high sniffing more coke and tossing back her drink. She was sexy, very busty like Sonny liked.

"Can I kiss you Charlotte?" Megan questioned.

"You have to ask," I replied.

"Can I kiss her, daddy?" Megan asked Sonny in a child like tone that he loved.

"Yes," he responded, stroking his dick a little harder.

"Your girl just came to get high, huh," I asked as Megan flipped her brunette hair to the side and started to unbutton my shirtdress then softly kissed my neck.

"Hey. Get yourself together. You have a job to do," Megan said as she got up and went over to the wall to get a whip.

"That's right Megan. Let her know. Come on you dame! Take your fucking clothes off, so Megan can show you how to act," Sonny ordered.

Smack! Smack!

"Get on your knees bitch," Megan ordered as she spanked the red head.

"Ahhhahhhahhaa," the red head laughed. She enjoyed being spanked as her back welted with red marks all over her creamy white skin. She was so high I'm sure she didn't feel much of anything.

"Come over here and please me while the girls do their thing. You're too high to do anything else," Sonny demanded. She was a mess.

I watched the red head bend over and suck my husband's dick as he played with her ass. Within seconds, Megan was back ready to attend to my needs and by that time I was drunk and horny.

"Why are you so tense Charlotte? Loosen up," she stated.

"Loosen me up then," I responded.

As Megan laid me back she was between my legs again, this time her face was buried as she sucked my clit and fingered my pussy in and out.

"Megan, that's right suck it. Suck my wetness," I moaned.

All of a sudden I felt a vibrator enter me from nowhere. It was huge. Just what I needed as she continued to flick my clit with her tongue. Megan raised my leg up so she could get to my spot and pushed the dildo further inside. She knew just the way I liked it.

"Holy shit, Megan you're so nasty."

"Just the way you like it. You missed me Charlotte?"

"Yes, I missed your pretty ass."

I sat up and kissed her. It felt like it was just me and Megan in the room. At that moment I needed companionship and I didn't feel like there was another soul around.

Pushing me back down on my back, she spread my legs all the way back and went to town rubbing her hand all over my treasure. Holding back both of my thighs with her upper body, she placed her big nipples in my ass and titty fucked me.

"Yes, just like that, baby," I moaned.

"Does it feel good?"

I closed my eyes. "Yes."

Placing her finger in my ass she was back at it, sucking my clit again.

"Yes, stick it in there. It feels good."

"I want to suck this tight pussy some more," she said in between slurps until I climaxed all over her face.

"Shit, I'm cumming. I'm cumming," I replied as my body jerked forcefully.

When I finally opened my eyes Sonny was right there kissing me. I wasn't feeling him though and immediately became irritated. I was still pissed about him threatening me. I guess he thought us having Megan over would make me forgive him, but not this time. After giving up a few fake pecks, I suddenly thought about Gianni. I hopped up and put my dress back on.

"Where are you going?" Sonny asked as if he was going to supply me with round two.

"I have to pick Gianni up from camp."

"I'll have Rafael fetch her."

"No, you won't. I'm gonna pick up my own daughter."

"Well Rafael will drive you."

"It's crazy how many cars sit outside and how often I don't get to drive any of them. The shit is crazy," I slurred a bit as I slipped on my Gucci flip-flops. "I promise I'll be right back. Stay here with Megan and keep her company."

"Stop being upset with me and be safe," Sonny finally gave in before kissing me on the forehead.

"I will. You guys have fun," I said, giving them permission to carry on without me.

As soon as I came out of the playroom and made my way to the foyer Rafael was there waiting.

"Shit, I'm late picking up Gianni. It's 3:45," I stated looking at my ceramic Chanel watch. "I need to get to her." I stumbled a little.

"No you won't! I'm driving. You've been drinking," he said helping me out the front door and into the truck.

"I feel dizzy," I said, putting my Chrome Heart sunglasses on then leaning the passenger seat back.

"Here, drink this." Rafael handed me the Fiji water bottle with so much disappointment in his eyes.

"Charlotte, do you know you...never mind."

"What?"

"Nothing. I just. Nothing. I need to mind my business."

"What Rafael?"

"No seriously. I don't want to overstep my boundaries."

"What are you talking," I slurred.

"You're drunk."

"I'm not."

"You are, and I'm disappointed!"

I pointed to myself. "In me?"

"Yes. I just think you forget how beautiful you are sometimes. I mean, I'm not here to judge you, but you can't do things like..."

"What have threesomes? Do you know how it feels to be with a man you don't love and don't have a choice? I deserved to be pleased. If I have to fuck women sometimes to have an orgasm from time to time, then so be it. I have needs Rafael. Don't judge me."

"I'm not judging you and I never want you to think that."

"Then why are you looking at me with disgust? You're making me feel like shit right now."

"I'm sorry if I made you feel that way. You're just such a sweet person and I don't like to see you like this. Here, drink the water. You have to get yourself together before you see Gianni. You don't want her to see you like this, right?"

"Right," I said, turning the water bottle up. As my stomach started to turn I knew what was about to happen as bile filled my gut.

"Pull over quick!"

Luckily Rafael reacted with lightening speed and pulled over just in time as I swung the car door up and threw up in the grass on the side of the highway.

"Can you hand me some wet wipes?"

"Here you go?"

"Don't look at me like that, I'm sorry." I burst into tears.

"What's wrong Charlotte? Please don't cry."

"I don't mean to keep putting all my problems on you. I'm just going through so much right now and sometimes I don't know if I'm coming or going. I know Sonny isn't right for me, but I don't have a choice. You know how crazy he is! I just feel stuck. No matter how much of a cheater my first husband was, I never felt so empty, and alone."

"You're not alone Charlotte. Trust me," Rafael said, putting his hand on my mine. "I got you."

By the time we pulled in to the parking lot of Gianni's camp, we were over an hour late. I threw a piece of Orbit gum in my mouth and hopped out of the truck in a panic. I knew my daughter was going to be highly upset with me. I felt so guilty. Here I was having sex with women while my daughter waited for me to pick her up. I felt like an unfit parent.

Quickly making my way down the hall to the office I gathered my thoughts together on how I was going to explain to Gianni why I was so late. Opening the door to the office, I entered with an apology.

"Hello. I'm so sorry I'm late. I'm Gianni Fitzgerald's mom, and I'm here to pick her up."

"Oh. Um, well there aren't any more kids here. They've all been picked up I'm sure but let me double check," one of the camp leaders said.

After checking the clipboard, she looked nervous right before picking up the phone to make a call.

"Hi yes, Mr. James, Gianni's mom is here to pick her up, but I have record that she has already been picked up. Is that correct? Okay, that's what I thought." She ended her call. "Ma'am, she was picked up thirty minutes ago."

My heartbeat started to increase. "What do you mean she was picked up? By who?"

The woman looked at her clipboard again. "She was signed out by her mother, Charlotte."

"That can't be right! I'm her mother!" I screamed and pounded on my chest. "I'm her mother, Charlotte! That person wasn't her mother!"

Running out to the truck in a panic I rummaged through my purse to find my cell phone to call Sonny.

"What's wrong?" Rafael asked concerned.

"It's Gianni. She's not here!"

"What?" he replied in shock.

"Hello," Sonny answered.

"Did you have someone pick Gianni up?" I asked.

"No. I didn't. Charlotte, what's wrong? I thought you went to pick her up."

"Oh my God! My daughter is gone. Someone has my baby Sonny! She's gone!" I cried in disbelief.

11 Kennedi

"Where the fuck have you been?" Malcolm was furious and erratic. For the first time, I was scared of him and what he might do.

"Why do you have a gun?"

"Do you think you can just keep lying to me and think it's gonna be all good?"

"What are you talking about? Lying to you about what? You need to put the gun down before someone gets hurt," I said, afraid that he might've remembered something. At the end of the day I wasn't admitting to shit.

"You keep lying to me. What have you been doing? You been listening to your father again. I knew it." He got up and started walking towards me with the gun pointed at my chest.

"Malcolm, stop it! My father is dead. Put the gun down," I said, backing up.

"Did you find my aunt? Is that where you were?"

"No, Malcolm I didn't."

"Then where were you?" he yelled.

All of a sudden Nina walked up behind me.

"Malcolm, what are you doing with that gun? What's going on," she asked in a calm tone.

"Nina, she's a liar. I don't know what she's doing. She lied to me."

"Malcolm, baby, what did I lie to you about?"

"Everything. You lied about everything."

"Malcolm, listen to me, give me the gun," Nina said as she

walked up to him without an once of fear.

I stood and watched how quickly she was able to calm him down. Just like that he lowered the gun and gave it to her. I didn't know if I should be thankful to her or smack the shit out of her. It hurt to see that another woman could be a calm place for my husband. I was starting to rethink if this was all worth it. I loved Malcolm, but him threatening my life was on another level. *Was it the medication? Was it legit?* My mind started to wonder, was this bitch Nina doing some shit to jog his memory when I wasn't around. Now it was time to activate the cameras and get to the bottom of this shit.

"I've been nothing but good to you! How could you point a fucking gun at me?" Now I was pissed.

As soon as Nina retrieved the gun from Malcolm, he sat back down in the chair and I instantly went into beast mode. I needed to let them both know not to fuck with me.

"Nina, give me the gun," I demanded.

"How about I just take it with me and get it out…"

"Bitch, give me the fucking gun now," I replied in a stern voice.

"Please don't do anything crazy, Vee," Nina said while handing it to me.

As soon as it was safely in my hand, I went fucking ham on Malcolm.

Smack! The sound of the gun landing against Malcolm's face was loud.

"What the fuck?" Malcom said, holding his mouth.

"Nigga, don't you ever in your fucking life hold a gun up to me unless you gonna use it," I threatened.

"Vee, stop!" Nina pleaded.

"Bitch, mind your business! This is *my* husband, and he will not disrespect me in my house."

Nina pointed. "You're crazy. Look at him, he's bleeding."

"I don't give a fuck. Do you know how many black eyes I've gotten from this man? He's not going to keep on abusing me. Threatening me. I don't deserve this. If it wasn't for me, his ass would be dead."

"What the fuck is that supposed to mean, Vee?" Malcolm questioned. For some reason those words caught his attention. I had to watch what I said these days because little things were starting to give him flashbacks. I didn't need him remembering shit.

"It means what I said."

"Venus, stay the fuck away from me, until you can tell me why the fuck you were out all night and didn't come home," Malcolm said as he left out of the room with Nina in tow.

"Nigga, I got locked up alright!" I yelled.

"Yeah right. Let me know when you want to come clean!" he yelled back.

What the fuck is that supposed to mean, I thought. Did Malcolm know something he wasn't supposed to?

"And Nina your ass needs to go the fuck home!" I yelled out again.

Three hours later, everything in my house had calmed down. After kicking Nina out, feeding Milan and putting her down for a nap, I took a much needed shower. I hid all of my guns from Malcolm before that of course, then went into one of our guest rooms for some rest. I had a long emotional weekend and just needed to sleep. When my phone went off, ten minutes later I wasn't so sure if I was gonna get any sleep.

Got a job for you. Hit me when you can, the text read.

Cool, I typed back.

This one pays double. This one is personal.

I got you. No doubt.

That's the type of shit I loved to hear. Pays double. As I deleted the texts, and started to unwind once again, I heard the door open.

"Vee, you up?"

Ignoring Malcolm, I faked like I was sleep. I could feel him getting in the bed with me.

"Look, you not really sleep so it's all good, just listen to me. I know you would never cheat on me, so I wasn't thinking that. It's just hard taking care of Gianni by myself so I get so stressed out."

I shot up in the bed. It was the first time in two years that he'd remembered his former daughter's name. It was the first time he'd remembered anything about his past.

"What did you just say?"

"I said it's hard taking care of Milan by myself so I get stressed out," he responded.

I couldn't lie. That shit got me shook. *Was he really starting to remember*? I had to come up with a plan, sooner than later.

"Listen, I know it's not easy being with me. I love you and I'm sorry for making things hard for you. I just wish I had an outlet sometimes. Some other friends or family to talk to. I wish my mother was still around. I just feel so alone at times. That's why I want you to find my aunt so bad."

"I know, baby but even though your mother is gone that doesn't mean you can't talk to her." Out of all the lies I'd told, this time what he said was actually the truth. Malcolm's mother really was dead.

I stared at him before responding. I saw past the burns and scars. For a moment, I could see his old face. I imagined life before all the bullshit. When we would lay like this in the penthouse years back…when he wasn't mine. *Why did I have him once he was all fucked up? Why couldn't I have had him when he was that nigga?* When he had the status, the fame, and the money. Now no one knew he was alive. I had the key to making him the man he used to be and here he was apologizing to me.

"What's wrong? Why are you looking at me like that?" Malcolm asked. He touched his face. "I know I'm ugly. You don't have to stare."

"Don't be silly…you're not ugly. I'm staring because I love you. I'm sorry, too. Let's just erase the past and start over. I know you don't remember what we were back in the day, but we were happy. We never fought. We made Milan out of love. Let's get back to that," I lied, knowing damn well we just met three years ago, and I was once his mistress. He didn't remember anything from the past years…so who cared.

"I agree. No more fighting."

"Sorry for hitting you," I laughed.

"My face hurts like shit," he said, rubbing his hand over his chin. "I already got scars and now you wanna add more."

I kissed his scar. I had really fucked him up.

"I'm sorry. I promise I won't hit you with a gun again, but promise you won't point a gun at me after I spent the night in jail all night."

"So you really were in jail?"

"Yeah. I was at the gas station and got into it with some girls. The police took us all to jail actually. I called you but you didn't answer." It was the quickest lie I could come up with.

"What the fuck? Are you serious? How did you get out?"

"You know I got the gift of gab. That don't matter. All you need to know is that all I could think about was getting home to my family. I don't want to talk about this any more. I just want you to hold me."

"I can do that. I'd do anything for you," Malcolm said, putting his arms around my waist and pulling me closer.

"Love you, husband."

"Love you more, wife."

The next day it felt good knowing Malcolm and I were in a better place. Hopefully he was serious about not wanting to fight with me anymore. Who the hell wanted drama in their life anyway? Shit, I was all about getting to the money. I had moves to make, so I had to put my pride aside, and apologize to Nina for my behavior the day before. Besides, I needed her. She took care of my family when I wasn't home so I had to quickly make amends.

After putting my wifey and mommy crown on, spending some quality time in the pool earlier in the day, and then ordering dinner, I got prepared for my night. After I got out of the shower my phone rang. It was Mocha.

"Hello."

"Hey girl, what you doing tonight?"

"I got some business to take care of, what's up with you?"

"Well, the owner of the club is making me the featured dancer tonight and I want you to come by."

"That's a good look. Text me the address and I'll be there."

"Cool. Don't be late. I go on at ten o'clock. Hold on, I'm texting you the address right now."

"Damn girl, that's in a couple of hours. Your text just came through. I'll be there."

"You better," she laughed.

As soon as I hung up, I texted my new target from my business phone and told him where to meet me. It was probably best if he came at eleven, to at least give me some time to enjoy myself a little. After checking in with my partner and getting all the details down to a photo of my target, I was ready to get dressed. Once I walked through my colorized closet, that my husband organized everyday voluntarily, I stopped at the black section, and thought it was best to wear something sexy and simple. I still had a couple of pounds to lose but it was nothing my waist trainer couldn't tame. My Herve leggings and tank top held everything in place and fit my curves to a tee. My Givenchy shark bait heels were comfortable and perfect for what I had to do tonight. Once getting dressed, I went into the bathroom and sat at my vanity to apply light makeup. As soon as I looked up, I saw my husband staring at me through the mirror.

"Where you going sexy?"

"Hey babe. Where's Milan," I asked changing the subject.

"She's downstairs with Nina. Where you off to?"

"I have a business meeting to discuss possibly opening a boutique. You know how I love fashion. I told you that at dinner." I lied through my teeth.

"Why are you going so late?"

"Well, it's kind of like a girl's night out slash, business dinner."

"Cool, do your thing. I think it's cool to invest." You know I was thinking it would be good for me to start doing my own thing. I mean I know your parents left you money and we are good, but I'm getting better and better and want to start stepping up and taking care of my family. I'm a man. I don't want to live off you forever."

"Babe, we are good. I don't need you to do anything but

keep fucking me good," I said, grabbing on the seat of his pants trying to skip the subject. I couldn't risk him going out into the world starting a business, and someone realizing who he really was.

"Well, if you help me get started then…"

"Okay let's discuss this later. I love you," I said, standing up dismissing his idea without trying to deflate his dreams.

He was starting to sound like the old Malcolm and it scared me. I gave him a kiss and grabbed my Valentino cross body bag. As I walked down the stairs Nina and Milan were coming up the steps.

"Okay Nina, I'm leaving. Milan, give Mommy a kiss."

"Bye-bye," Milan said as I gave her a hug and a kiss.

"Nina, give Malcolm a sedative after I leave. I can't come in tonight and have another episode."

"Why are you doing this to him? What are you hiding, Vee?"

"Nina, do I pay you to ask me these types of questions?" She removed Milan's hands as she pulled her hair. "No."

"That's what I thought. Besides, you need to trust me. I'm protecting him."

"If you say so," she replied then took Milan up the steps.

I knew she hated what I was doing to Malcolm but I didn't pay her for her fucking concern so she would soon be replaced if she didn't stay in her lane.

The ride was only an hour. Philly wasn't that far. The entire ride I listened to Raheem Devaughn. His music was so soothing and kept my mind in the right place. Pulling up to the club, I drove up to the valet and gave the guy an extra $100 to keep my car out front. Just in case something popped off I needed to make sure I kept my keys.

As soon as I got out of my Ferrari all eyes were on me. I was five minutes late so by the time I came in Mocha was just about to come out. As soon as I got my VIP band and was escorted to my table, Mocha was being announced.

"Coming to the stage is the lady of the night, Miss Mochaaaaa!"

All I gotta do is put my mind to this shit, cancel out my ex I put a line through that bitch. I like all my esses with two lines through that shit...

Mocha did her thing as Drake spit his lyrics on the 'My Way' remix. Hell, she was almost as good as me. Money flew everywhere as Mocha did acrobatic stunts, splits, and some more Cirque du Soleil shit. The females were even tipping. But of course I had to show up and show out. Fuck getting ones, I threw a stack of hundreds all over her ass, and walked back to my table looking like money. Of course when I did, all the other strippers ran over to me like flies, but I quickly sent their hungry asses away. I was only interested in one girl tonight.

After security got all her money together in a trash bag she came over to me smiling from ear to ear with her sexy ass.

"Girl you killed it." I got up to give her a kiss and a hug.

"Thanks for coming out and bringing that paper. You shitted on everybody up in here. The club owner is gonna love you," she replied. "Let's have a shot or something."

"Girl, I bought all these bottles, we can sip, but I can't get twisted. I got some major shit going on right now."

"Oh, I thought you came to turn up with me," Mocha said as she poured herself a glass of Ace of Spade.

"Girl, you called me all late. I got some shit to take care of, so I thought I would kill two birds with one stone, as a matter of fact, go make your rounds and I'll holler at you once I'm done discussing business."

"Oh you dismissing me," she laughed.

"No boo. I'll let you know once I'm done."

"I can't wait to find out what kind of business you got going on. Shit, I might need to get put on," Mocha said before walking off in her bright yellow thong set.

As I spotted my new mark looking lost, like a fish out of water, I motioned him over to my table. He was dressed in a suit like we were eating at Mastro's or something. He was probably the only Hispanic man in the building. He was actually fine as hell. Shit, I prayed to God my partner didn't want to kill him. I could see me fucking the shit out of him. Right before he got to the table,

I'd already slipped the ecstasy in a drink I'd poured for him.

"Well hello sir, how are you?"

"I'm good now. So, this is how you like to start your night, huh? A little strip club action."

"Yeah, it makes me horny. It gets me nice and wet."

He smiled. "Well, that's a good thing. I like it wet."

"I'm sure you do, let's make a toast," I said, handing him his glass.

"What are we toasting to?"

"To good pussy and money."

This time he laughed. "I'll definitely toast to that."

After listening to him talk about how much shit he had, his sexiness went out the window. He was corny as shit. Once the ecstasy kicked all the way in and he was nice and drunk, I had Mocha help me take my target to my car.

"Hey babe, where are the keys to your car?" I asked after he got in my passenger seat. "I'll make sure my girl brings it to you in the morning."

"You sure," he answered.

"Of course. I'm fucking you all night and we not gonna be back in time before the club closes." I felt him up making him rock hard. *The shit men do for pussy*, I thought as he gave the keys up with no more questions asked.

"Alright girl I'll call you later, let me make sure he gets home okay. In the meantime, here are the keys to his Bentley. You can drive it home."

"Girl, are you serious?" Mocha asked.

"Yeah, I'll call you in the morning," I said, as I hopped in my car and pulled off.

I texted my partner to let him know we were on our way to the spot. The drugs definitely kicked in because Mister Touchy Feely was grabbing my tits and pussy every five seconds.

When I got closer to North Philly, I turned off of Germantown Avenue and ran over the brick that was placed right where my partner said it would be.

"Shit. I got a fucking flat."

"Damn, in this neighborhood. What the fuck?" he slurred

with his eyes rolling in the back of his head. The drugs were definitely kicking in.

"You know what? Fuck it. Let's do it right now. I can't wait any longer."

"So where do you want the dick? In the car?" he asked, then rubbed his crouch.

I pointed to an abandoned house. "Let's go in there."

"What? Are you serious? Naw…hell no I'm not feeling that."

As my mark hesitated, I knew I had to work harder to get him in that damn house.

"Don't you want to fuck me?"

"Yeah I do, but why not in a hotel like we planned?"

"Because this is what I want, and when I get what I want, I give a man all that he needs." At that moment, I bent over and put my mouth in the seat of his pants.

"Look, I know it sounds a little sick, but I've always fantasized about a man ramming his big cock inside my wet tight pussy in an old abandoned house. I would love to see how your dick would feel in my tight ass." I teased, then softly kissed him on his neck.

Seconds later, I grabbed his dick that was hard as a brick. The drugs were now in full effect and I knew he wanted me bad.

"Okay, fuck it…but let's not stay too long." His dick was probably about to explode.

I sashayed in front of the target leading him up the steps as he stumbled a bit.

"I can't wait to get up in that pussy, girl."

"I can't wait either, baby."

Once we walked inside the house a dim light came on causing a rat to run across the room. I was so fucking grossed out, but had to maintain my composure. My partner was already inside and had everything set up, ready to go.

"Wait…what's this about?"

My target was obviously confused at the fact that there were two men sitting down at the table when we walked further inside. I guess he'd sobered up a bit. Suddenly, my partner came out behind him and put a 9mm straight to his dome.

"Nicholas let's talk," he said, pushing him in a chair as his goon, Trey handcuffed his hands in his lap.

"What's going on? Man, I told you I had nothing to do with that shit. So, you had this bitch set me up?" Nicholas questioned.

"Umm yes, he did. By the way, this motherfucka talks too much," I said as one of the men handed me over a large manila envelope.

"Okay sweetheart, I got it from here," my partner said as if I was being dismissed.

"Now, back to you. Where is she? I'm gonna cut off one finger at a time until you tell me."

"I wouldn't dare hurt her. I wouldn't do that."

"Okay I'm leaving. Call me later," I informed.

Ignoring me, the first finger was cut off like it was nothing. Once Nicholas screamed to the top of his lungs, I knew that was my cue. As I left out of the door Nicholas' last scream stopped me dead in my tracks.

"I don't have Gianni. I don't know where she is!"

12 Charlotte

"Come on, Charlotte. You haven't eaten anything in two days and just drinking water isn't enough."

"I don't want anything to eat. I just want my daughter."

"You have to come out of this room. A nice warm bath will make you feel better. You've been in Gianni's room for days."

I'm sure I didn't smell so great since I hadn't taken a shower in forty-eight hours. With puffy, bloodshot eyes and wild, uncombed hair, a part of me was embarrassed for Rafael to see me this way, but I couldn't be worried about winning a fucking beauty contest right now.

"Rafael, you don't understand. I've been through this before. I know how Sonny operates. I know he took my daughter. Why hasn't he come home since this shit went down? We haven't seen him. He's trying to teach me a lesson."

"Oh no, don't say that. I've known Sonny for a long time. He wouldn't do that to Gianni. If anything, he's out somewhere trying to find her."

"I know what I have to do. Just leave me alone. Give me some time alone," I demanded.

"Sure, but if you need me, I won't be far. I'll be in the hallway."

Rafael gave me a comforting smile before turning around and walking out of the door. As soon as he left, I crawled into Gianni's bed and cried like a baby. I missed her so much and had no idea if she was dead or alive. She was all I had. Without my parents and my husband, Gianni was all I had left. I couldn't lose her.

Sonny would die or go to prison before I let him get away with taking my daughter.

The more I laid on the bed with my mind and heart racing, I decided it was time to do what I thought was best. Dragging my weak body to the dresser, I got my cell phone out of my purse, and did exactly what Sonny told me not to.

"911, what's your emergency?"

"My daughter is missing and I need the police to come help me find her," I slurred. I was tired and weak.

After answering a million questions, there was a loud knock at the door. It had only been fifteen minutes but it felt like an eternity.

"Charlotte, I know you didn't call the police," Rafael whispered as he bust through the door in a panic.

"Yes, I called them. Sonny promised he would find her and it's been days since she's been gone, so I took matters in my own hands."

"He's going to lose it! Charlotte, you never call the police, for all..."

"I don't give a fuck about any of that. Gianni's kidnappers could be in fucking Mexico with her by now. I need an Amber Alert issued so my daughter can be returned home safely," I said before going downstairs to greet the police.

"Hello, Mrs. Fitzgerald," a cocky officer greeted. I could tell all his ass did was lift weights.

I stared at the other officer with the military buzz cut and wondered if they all went to the same fucked up barber.

"Officer, I need your help. Can you bring my daughter home to me?" I didn't have time for the formalities.

"Can we go somewhere so we can ask you some questions," the officer asked.

Before I could respond, Sonny walked in the door in an uproar in the same Burberry polo and khaki shorts he had on when he left days ago.

"Who the hell called the cops? Why are there police officers in my home?" he roared.

"I did," I stated boldly. "They're here to help me find my

baby. You haven't been home in days and I need my daughter to come home."

"Both of you, get the hell out of my house!" Sonny yelled.

"Sir, we've been called about the disappearance of a little girl. We need to issue an Amber Alert as soon as possible since it's been two days now."

"Officer, let's talk. Please come outside. Both of you," Sonny demanded.

"Sure," the cocky officer replied before him and his partner made their way to the front door.

I could tell Sonny was pissed at me as he shot daggers in my direction then quickly followed them out. However, at the moment I could care less. I wanted my child back home safely and was willing to do whatever it took to make that happen.

I paced the floor back and forth anticipating their return. Five minutes later, Sonny came back in the house alone, without the cops. After he closed the door, he excused any staff that was around and ordered me to his office.

"Where did they go? Where did the police go Sonny?" I asked while we walked to this office. He didn't answer though. Instead, he closed the door behind me.

"Sonny, answer me. I need them to…"

Before I could say another word, he slapped me so hard I flew across the room into the bookcase. As he walked over toward me, I tried to crawl away but was entirely too weak. He grabbed me off the floor in seconds.

"You black bitch…don't you ever call the fucking police to my house!" He placed his hand around my throat and pressed firmly. "There's nothing a cop can do for you that I can't do anyway. Do you understand me?" He removed his hand just before I was out of breath.

"No, I don't, where did they go? Why did they leave?" I coughed a few times as tears formed in my eyes.

"You dumb bitch. I'm the fucking King of the East Coast. There's no one with more power than me. I fucking sent those pigs away and they won't be coming back. Now they think you're crazy," he said, grabbing me close to his chest by my shirt.

"Now you're gonna kill me like you killed my father and my husband. Did you kill my daughter, too?"

"I've been out here for days killing people that might be innocent just to get your daughter back. No matter what you might think of me, I'm not a damn monster!"

"So, what are you then? Sonny, I don't have anything else to live for. You've taken it all from me!"

Suddenly, there was a knock at the door.

"Go away!" Sonny yelled.

"Sir, please open the door. There's someone here to see you," Francesca's muffled voice answered.

"Who the hell is it?" Sonny questioned.

"It's Ernestine. She says it's important. It's about…"

"Send her in," Sonny quickly interrupted like he didn't want me to know what Francesca was going to reveal. He looked at me, then pointed to the bookcase. "Charlotte, go upstairs that way, not through the hallway."

"Why…why are you taking fucking visitors at a time like this?"

"Please do as I say. If you fuck this up, it can ruin our chances of getting Gianni back," he replied in a sincere tone.

I didn't know how to react to his sudden change of character but decided to go along with the program. "Okay Sonny, but please promise me you will get my baby back," I said, leaving the room through a secret door that looked like an actual bookcase. It was some James Bond shit that was rarely used.

"Send her in Francesca!" Sonny ordered but didn't answer me.

Little did he know, instead of going upstairs I left a small crack in the door and prepared myself to eavesdrop. He was in such a rush to entertain this woman that he didn't even check to see if I'd really obeyed his orders.

"Well hello Sonny," a woman's voice called out.

"Hello Ernestine. Where the fuck is your daughter?"

"Oh Sonny, you've created such a damn mess. You've created an animal in my daughter. She's determined to make you pay for all you've done, and now she's out of control. You need to make things right with her."

I peeked out the small crack at the loud, boisterous woman. She was tall with a sharp chin and a long charcoal black ponytail that swung along her shoulders. She appeared to be older, at least forty, but her body was still shaped like a rap video model with Double D breasts and an oversized ass.

"Ernestine, I know what she's done, so let her know she has twenty-four hours, or I'm not gonna play nice. That goes for her brother she loves so much, too. Did she forget that I can reach out and touch him at any moment?"

"Now you're threatening my son, don't fuck with me Sonny. All over a child that's not even yours."

"It's about respect. She's fucking with me, and…"

"Well, you should've never crossed my daughter! When those tables turn it's vicious ain't it? Karma is a bitch."

"Are you here to help me find this little girl or talk about mistakes I made in the past?" Sonny questioned.

"Well, Sonny, I could care less about Karla kidnapping the little girl. If that's her way of getting back at you for sending her to prison, then so be it? Why does she keep saying that you set her up though? Are you still gonna hold out on that information after all these years?"

"I didn't send her to prison and she knows it! I would never work with the police and you know it. I thought you knew me."

"Look Sonny, I just don't want her vendetta against you to fuck my money up. I have a lucrative business that loses money daily when people are in their feelings. Why did you have to shoot her the last time she was here?"

"Because she came in my fucking bedroom trying to start some shit with me and Charlotte. Plus it seemed like she was trying to expose me about some shit, so I had to shut her up."

"This shit has to stop...now!"

I fucking knew it, I thought. My eyes widened and I started to panic at the thought of Sonny knowing who'd done something to my baby girl.

Sonny chuckled. "I like when you get all bossy. You're still feisty as shit. It reminds me of old times."

"Fuck you Sonny! You were wrong. We both know how you like to dispose of your women," she fired back.

"If you're referring to my ex-wife, then that bitch deserved to die. Besides, I love Charlotte and Gianni. I've changed."

"Motherfucker, you haven't changed. I know what you're up to, and that poor Charlotte has no clue. I know more than you think Sonny. I know who's on your payroll and trust me, if you touch my son, I will blow up your spot. Literally," she threatened.

"Are you done you old hag?"

"Yes, I am,"

"Great, then get the fuck out."

"Gladly."

What type of sick fuck was Sonny? I thought to myself as I quickly made my way up the back stairs.

My late husband had once tried to tell me how ruthless Sonny was when he once witnessed him killing his nephew, but to hear him speak about killing his ex-wife as if it was business as usual was hard to hear. It killed me to keep my mouth closed now that I knew the truth, but for once I had to be smart. My daughter was missing and it was all because of that bitch. Karla. I wanted to fucking strangle her with my bare hands. I couldn't let Sonny know what I'd heard though. I had to devise a plan. At least now I knew my baby was alive, but now I needed someone to help me and I knew just the right person who could. My heart was heavy as tears streamed from my eyes. I was pissed at myself for putting my daughter in this type of environment. Malcolm might've been a deadbeat husband, but he loved his daughter to death and would've never put her in any danger. I felt guilty. Gianni had already been through enough and she deserved better. I had to come up with a way out.

⌇

After taking a long hot bath, I slipped on a tank top and tube skirt and came downstairs to get a bottle of water and a banana. Feeling nauseas, I had to get something in my system before passing out. After Sonny announced to everyone he had to make a run I went out to the stable to clear my head. Once I opened the stable doors I ran into Rafael.

"So, here we are again," I said, looking down.

"Great minds think alike I guess," Rafael said with a charming smile. "You seem to be in better spirits. Any luck on Gianni yet?"

"No, but I have to give it to God. I prayed and now I feel little better." I really liked Rafael, but didn't trust him enough to share what I'd overheard earlier. "So, what are you doing out here?"

"Sonny is getting another horse next week so I'm just out here getting the stable prepared."

"You know he has staff for this type of stuff, right?"

"Yeah I know, but I like being out here with Big Mack. He's a great horse. It's actually therapeutic."

"You seem a little off. Are you okay?"

"Just have a lot on my mind."

"Anything you want to talk about?"

Rafael shook his head. "No, you have enough on your plate right now."

"You're right, Rafael. No matter how I try to be strong, I can't help but to wonder if Gianni is okay."

As Rafael walked closer to me, he held my hands and looked deep into my eyes.

"Charlotte. Don't worry. Gianni is fine."

"I believe you."

"Good because she's gonna be home soon."

"You make me feel safe, Rafael."

"That's my job."

"No, it's like you care more than that. You treat me more than just the bosses' wife."

He stared at me again, then licked his lips which instantly made me moist.

"That's because I do care. I care a lot about you, Charlotte. I hope you don't take this the wrong way but Sonny is one lucky man."

I blushed. "I wish he knew that. I wish he was more like you. I wish…"

"Ssshhh…don't say another word," Rafael said, placing his finger on my lips.

No longer could I fight the feelings I'd been trying to ignore. All of a sudden we locked lips. He kissed me so passionately. Falling back on the bed of hay, we kissed like two high school kids. Blood rushed to my clit and I was so wet as we continued to kiss fervently. I wanted Rafael inside of me bad. As he pulled my skirt up, I reached down in his shorts and was immediately pleased at what I felt. He was large and in charge down there. He wasn't suffering from the little dick syndrome like Sonny. Now, I needed him even more. He pulled my thong to the side and attempted to enter my body. His penis was so big. After lifting my legs a little wider and adding a bit more force, he finally entered my tight pussy. As I moaned and ran my hands across his broad shoulders, moments later I found myself on top of Rafael riding his big dick as if it didn't hurt. His Love by Killian fragrance had my box throbbing. As he thrust in and out of my wetness, I begged and begged.

"Rafael, please don't stop fucking me. Please don't stop."

"You're a lady Charlotte. I would never fuck you. This is making love. Now turn over."

Right after he smacked my ass and dusted off the hay, we were back at it. Grabbing my waist, his thickness tore into me, and it hurt so good.

"That's right, take all of it Charlotte. Does it feel good to you baby, huh?"

"It feels great. So great!"

"When's the last time a man made you cum?"

"It's been years," I answered in between moans.

"Have you ever squirted?"

"No…never," I whispered.

"Squirt for me."

"I don't know how."

"Get back on top," he instructed. After pulling out, he laid on his back.

His dick stood at attention. As I looked at him beneath me he felt perfect. My young stallion was going to be mine. He was about to teach me some shit and I was more than ready to learn.

As I carefully sat down on his extra large pole he started with his lesson.

"I'm going to hit places that have never been hit before, you ready?"

"Yes."

"When I hit that spot, don't tense up just let it happen. Just when you feel it cumming, tighten your muscles, comprende'?"

"Comprende'."

As Rafael thrust his hips in a circular motion, I rode him just like the stallion in the stable. His sex was epic.

"Oh Rafael. I feel it."

"Let it go baby. Right now, let me have my way with you. Let it go."

Just like that, the wetness flowed.

"Am I peeing?"

"No baby, you're squirting, and you're shaking. Are you okay," he laughed.

"I'm more than okay," I said, laying his chest exhausted.

"No, get up. Now, I'm going to make you cum."

Laying me on my back he spread my legs apart and started sucking my clit and licking my pussy. As I fucked his face, he made me feel things no one had ever made me feel before. Not even a woman. Lately that was my only sexual pleasure that made me feel satisfied.

As soon as I felt like I was about to climax he stopped.

"Oh my gosh. Why did you stop?"

"Now you know I can make you cum with my tongue, but I want to make you feel what I'm really capable of. You deserve for me to make you cum like this."

Climbing on top of me, Rafael entered me once again. As my wetness smacked, his thrusts became harder. We moaned together.

"Tighten your pussy. Yeah, just like that."

"Oh shit, Rafael."

"Keep tightening it. Just like that. Cum for me."

"I'm cumming. I'm cumming."

"Me too…oh shit," he said, just before pulling out.

Moments later, his body began jerking uncontrollably.

As we laid in silence, I knew what was going through both of our heads. *What had we just started*? As good as he felt to me, I needed him again and again. Who would've ever thought I could be a student to a twenty-two year old. I'd always looked at him as a boy, but now I knew he was a grown ass man.

"So, did you enjoy yourself?" I asked.

As Rafael closed his eyes and sighed, I instantly became nervous. Waiting for a response seemed to take forever, until finally he spoke.

"What have we done? This cannot happen again."

My heart sunk.

13 Kennedi

As I twirled my fork in my CPK BBQ chicken salad my mind raced. I was confused. There was no way that Malcolm's daughter Gianni was alive. Not to mention, I knew Sonny would never betray me like that. I knew he wouldn't lie to me about something so big. Maybe Gianni was some girl he was dealing with me. For the past couple of days the shit had me shook, though. I struggled with confronting Sonny or digging a little deeper to see what I could find out. *Maybe I'm just being paranoid. I mean it's not like there's only one Gianni in the world. If Sonny had never given me a reason not to trust him, then it's no need to start now. It was just a coincidence*, I tried to convince myself.

"It's hot as shit out here! Fuck! I don't know why you wanted to sit out here on this patio anyway. This umbrella ain't enough shade," Malcolm said, breaking me away from my thoughts. "Plus, the food is nasty."

I guess so, I thought. I'd crushed up a few pills before we left home and sprinkled the powder onto his food when he went to the restroom.

"Milan likes to sit outside, that's why. Furthermore, if you didn't have on an oversized long sleeved shirt out here in 90-degree weather, then maybe you wouldn't be as hot. I know you don't come out much, but take a look around. Most people wear shorts and tees in the summer time."

"Don't be fucking disrespectful. You know I have to protect my skin."

"That's what your ointment is for."

"Shit, I'm hot. My skin is burning. Do you have my ointment?"

"Sorry sir. I can't keep up with your shit and Milan's."

"Are you serious? Let me call Nina and see if she can bring me some," Malcolm said, picking up his iPhone 6 plus.

I gave him a look of death. "If you call that bitch and ask her for anything it's gonna be a problem."

"Oh, so I hit a nerve," Malcolm replied. "Are you mad because Nina takes better care of your family than you do? I mean you're always busy running the streets taking meetings and shit even though nothing ever comes out of it."

"Let me tell you one motherfucking thing. I'm the one who makes all this shit possible for you. The surgeries, the medicine, the fancy cars, the big house, foreign clothing on your back, so don't get it twisted, boo. *I* pay that bitch Nina, so she should do what the fuck I say. If I want her to tend to y'all, then that's what the fuck she's gonna do."

Malcolm was right he did strike a nerve. It didn't help that the other night when I came home I checked his phone and saw that he'd been talking to Nina for over an hour at one o'clock in the morning. If she left my house at 11:00 p.m. there was absolutely nothing they needed to talk about that time of night. If he was fucking her, I had to get proof, before I just jumped out there.

"French fry, Mommy," Milan said, holding up her food.

She was such a pretty girl. We didn't go out to often, but when we did, I made sure my daughter stepped out in style. She looked adorable in her white Gucci dress and sandals. Today I did her hair in two curly ponytails with red and blue ribbons that matched the trimmings of her dress. Anyone who walked passed our table complimented on how beautiful she was.

"Daddy, apples?"

"Yes, those are apples Milan," Malcolm replied uninterested. He picked up his phone and laughed as if he'd received a funny text message.

I hated how he was so detached with her. It made me cringe. Years ago he was so in love with his daughter, Gianni and it pissed me off how he was so hot and cold with Milan.

"What's so funny?" I questioned when he laughed for the second time.

Malcolm put his phone on the table. "Nothing. You ordering desert?" he asked, skipping the subject.

Snatching his phone off the table, I instantly went in jealous wife mode.

When Malcolm smirked, it immediately reminded me of his old cocky personality.

"Are you gonna cause a scene?"

"No, but I want to know what the fuck you think is so funny?"

As I pushed his code, 0-8-1-0, just like I thought, it was a text from Nina. As I touched the message I noticed it was a video of Nina feeding Milan, and Milan throwing macaroni and cheese at Malcolm. They looked like one happy family. It crushed me to see Malcolm laughing with Nina having such a good time with my daughter. I'd never see him laugh and play with Milan before. My feelings were hurt.

Throwing his phone at him, I put my Tom Ford shades on to hide my pain. Just then, my phone rang. It was Mocha. I wanted so badly to ignore her, but I'd been doing that ever since she helped me by taking my mark's car that night so I knew I had to answer sooner or later.

"Hello."

"Hey girl, what's up? Where have you been? I've been callin' forever."

"Oh sorry. I've been super busy lately."

"Well, are you going to ever come pick this car up? I don't want my son's father to get suspicious. He's starting to act like he got some sense again these days and I don't have time for him to think I got a nigga with paper. He thinks the car belongs to my lil' cousin's man, who's involved in a bit of illegal activity if you now what I mean. He thinks I'm just holding the car until they get back from vacation tomorrow night, so I need you to come get that shit before then. As soon as he thinks I might be lying then the money might stop and I…"

"Okay, okay. Let me get on top of that. Thanks for calling. I'll let you know the outcome," I said, cutting her long-winded ass up.

"Call me back, girl seriously."

"I will," I replied just before hanging up the phone.

"What was that about?"

"Why? Didn't you just blatantly ignore me when I asked what you were laughing at?" I didn't wait for him to respond. "Yeah, you did so don't ask me shit about my phone calls."

"Vee, stop tripping. Who was that?"

"It was a prospect for a new nanny," I said just to fuck with him. Malcolm and Nina were getting way too close, so I wanted him to know I could put an end to him and his new best friend's relationship with a snap of my finger. After all I'd done to get Malcolm, there was no way I was going to let anybody come in between us.

"A new nanny. Why? Are you mad that Nina working at that private hospital part time now? Vee, she needs to get back at what she loves to do. I mean, she went to school and got a degree for goodness sakes. All she wants to do is work two jobs to better herself. We aren't suffering with her working less hours…"

"Malcolm shut the fuck up! The way you defend her makes my skin crawl."

He looked around as several people looked in our direction. "So, you're just gonna embarrass me like that?"

Motherfucka have you looked in the mirror? Your skin is an embarrassment, I thought but didn't have the nerve to say.

"I'll be back. I'm going to the restroom."

"Take Milan with you."

"Fuck no! You watch her for once," I spat, getting up from the table.

As I made my way to the bathroom to call Sonny about the car, all I could think of was how I was going to stop this train wreck that I'd created. If Nina and Malcolm weren't fucking yet, they soon would be. I had to start fucking Malcolm again every chance I got. I had just been so consumed with so much shit. I needed Nina, but that bitch wasn't going to take my husband.

"Shit, no answer," I said, ending the call.

I hadn't heard from Sonny since my last job and that concerned me. My fingers couldn't move fast enough as I sent him a text.

Give me a call ASAP. It's important!

I hoped that would get his attention. Making my way through the aisle of tables and back toward the patio, I was instantly stopped in my tracks as a beautiful Dominican woman was at my table talking to my husband. She looked like money. From the diamond bangles, to the $20,000 Birkin bag in her right hand, I could tell she was paid. In her other hand was a little girl. With her back to me I couldn't see her face. There was also a little boy in tow as well. Watching from afar Malcolm's white long sleeved button up shirt had been splattered with strawberry lemonade so I'd quickly figured out what happened. However, this mystery woman typing information into her phone had me confused.

As soon as Malcolm saw me coming he knew he had some explaining to do. I didn't understand why the fuck he was exchanging information with this bitch.

"I'm sorry for spilling juice all over your clothes. I shouldn't have been running," I heard the little girl say.

"It's okay honey. It's hot out here anyway," Malcolm said, taking off his shades and wiping them with a napkin.

"What happened to your face?" the little girl asked.

"Hey, that's rude. Don't ask anyone questions like that. Where are your manners?" the woman questioned.

"She's fine. I was in a fire…"

Before Malcolm could say another word, I interrupted wondering what the hell was going on. That was the main reason why we didn't go out often. I couldn't risk anyone talking to him and recognizing him.

"What happened?" I asked trying my best to hide the fact that I was pissed. As I placed my sunglasses on my head I cut my eyes at the woman and directed my attention to Malcolm.

"Karla, this is my wife, Vee, and you've already met my little girl, Milan."

"Nice to meet you, Karla," I said, giving her a what the

fuck are you talking to my husband about face. Looking at her arm in a sling, I couldn't help but wonder if she had domestic problems. Most grown women didn't walk about with injuries like that.

"Nice to meet you, too. This is Cruz and Gianni," the woman responded as I took my seat.

As soon as I looked up my suspicions were no longer, it was really her, Gianni. As I caught eye contact with my husband's daughter, my heart sunk...deep. I was speechless and that wasn't often.

"Hey, are you okay, Vee? It looks like you just saw a ghost," Malcolm said with a huge smile.

My tongue felt paralyzed. I couldn't speak. How could this be? How could she be alive?

"Vee, seriously are you okay?" Malcolm questioned with concern.

I took a drink of water. It felt like I was about to pass out. "I'm...I'm fine. It's just hot out here and I'm starting to feel bad." I stole a quick look at Gianni again, then looked at Karla. "Are you her mother?" I asked without thinking.

"No, just a friend of her mom. Well, let us get going. I apologize again for Gianni bumping into your table. Say you're sorry, Gianni," Karla instructed.

"I'm sorry, sir."

"Awww it's okay. It was an accident."

At that moment, Gianni reached out and gave Malcolm a huge hug. Their embrace lingered as if they both felt some type of connection. Even Milan looked at the two of them and smiled.

As Malcolm interacted with Gianni, my thoughts went into overdrive. *How can this be? How can she be alive? She's supposed to be dead. If she's alive, then what about Charlotte?*

"You're so sweet. Now, you be a good girl, okay?" Malcolm said.

"Okay Gianni. You can't hug strangers, especially men," Karla said, interrupting Gianni in a protective manner. Seconds later, she grabbed Gianni from Malcolm's embrace.

"I'm sorry Miss Karla," Gianni said as the little boy Cruz looked off not interested in anything that was going on.

Ignoring Karla, Malcolm continued conversation with Gianni. "How old are you young lady?"

"Six years old, sir."

"Okay, we need to go," Karla stated.

"You don't have to keep calling me sir. Call me Malcolm."

"That was my…"

"We need to go," I said, cutting Gianni off as my heart
raced. I grabbed Milan out of the high chair and placed her in the
stroller.

"Okay Malcolm. I have your information and I promise to
take care of your cleaning bill," Karla said.

"I told you that's not necessary, but since you insisted, no
problem," Malcolm laughed, mesmerized by Karla's beauty.

"Umm, Karla, that's your name right?"

She looked at me. "Yes."

"We don't need you take care of the cleaning bill. Great
gesture, but we can afford to do so ourselves."

"Okay. Well, you folks have a great day," Karla added.

"Thanks," Malcolm said with a massive smile on his face.
He was damn near drooling as he watched Karla's ass while she
walked away.

Gianni kept looking back with a look of confusion.

Throwing a hundred dollar bill on the table, I yelled to Malcolm, "Let's go!"

Quickly placing my handbag in the bottom of Milan's Phil
and Ted Buggy stroller, I pushed my daughter away maneuvering
through the tables. I needed answers.

As Malcolm placed Milan in her car seat, he gave her a soft
kiss on her forehead. "I love you baby girl."

I believe that was the first time I'd ever heard him tell
Milan he loved her. When he got in the car, Malcolm smiled at me
and held my hand as I pulled out of the Short Hills Mall parking
lot. My heart had to be sitting on my big toe by now. I was confused and anxious.

"That little girl was so pretty, wasn't she?"

It took me forever to reply. "Yup."

"I bet Milan will look just like her when she grows up.

They kind of favored don't you think."

"Nope...not to me."

"I mean, when she hugged me, I felt something. I don't know what it meant, but I felt emotional; like I wanted to cry or something."

"You just need some meds that's all," I said, turning the radio up.

They were playing Keri Hilson's song, 'Get Your Money Up', which was coincidently the song I danced to when Malcolm and I met. My skeleton's were falling out of my closet one by one. I changed the station immediately.

Moments later, I grabbed my phone and texted Sonny once again.

911!!!!!!! Call me. It's an emergency. It's about Gianni.

14 Charlotte

My mind raced as I laid in bed thinking about where Gianni could be. My emotions were all over the place, especially since Sonny still hadn't mentioned anything to me about knowing who took my daughter. My plan so far had been to wait until he told me the truth because I knew he would only lie if I confronted him. My patience for that plan had run out though because I wanted to spit in his fucking face every time he was in my presence. I'd even been sleeping on the couch ever since I'd overheard his conversation to avoid him touching any part of my body. Of course he thought my distance was because of Gianni and that was true, but my hatred for him was deeper than that now.

Missing Gianni and having sex with Rafael also had my head spinning. Rafael was my only confidante at the time and I couldn't help but wonder if sleeping with him was a mistake. He'd become distant in the past couple of days so I didn't know what to think. I needed him, as my friend and his cold shoulder approach had me worried. Jumping out of bed, I was ready to confront him so I slipped on some workout clothes I had on the floor by my bed. He was my ticket to helping me get my daughter back and I needed answers. I had to know where we stood.

Irritated at the sound of Sonny's voice belting from his office, my heart sunk. As soon as one of the security guards, Bryan spotted me, he closed the door like he didn't want me to hear what Sonny was up to. I was used to Sonny's secretive behavior, so normally that wouldn't have bothered me. However, since Gianni still wasn't home I needed to know what the closed door meeting was about. Still on a mission to find Rafael I played my curiosity off for now and went to the kitchen to grab my morning smoothie that the chef prepared for me daily. After walking through every room possible, Rafael was nowhere to be found.

Maybe he's off today, I thought even though Sonny's goons were on call twenty-four seven.

I then decided to go eavesdrop on Sonny. Running up the steps, I walked into our master bathroom and up to the door beside Sonny's sink. I then punched in the four digit code that only Sonny and I had access to. If the average person walked into the bathroom, I'm sure they thought it was a linen closet or something. Seconds later, the door opened revealing the back staircase that led to Sonny's office. Closing the door behind me, I quietly walked down the stairs heading to the fake bookcase. I sat there quietly and listened as I sipped my smoothie. When I realized Sonny had the person on speakerphone, I now understood why Bryan had closed the door earlier.

"All I need to know is, how the hell did you guys let her get the little girl? Who the fuck allowed this?" Sonny belted.

"Well, wouldn't you be pissed if you thought someone set you up? Why does she keep saying that, Sonny? I really hope that she's not telling the truth because that would be beyond fucked up. I mean her allegations against you, Sonny, that would be even low for you," the woman said in a calm voice.

"I don't have time for this bullshit. Time is money."

"Sometimes it's not what you do, it's how you do it. You knew all that shit Karla had gone through. Being a mother at sixteen was just the beginning. If what she went to prison for is the truth then I would never forgive you for that. That shit would be dirty, and would hurt me to the core. I can barely stomach dealing with Karla because of all that's happened, but she's still my daughter. You've done both me and Karla wrong. I can see you taking your anger and frustration out on me but not Karla.

"Well, Karla needed to be taught a lesson. She wasn't the only one in pain. No matter what you might think, I'm human. She was just too careless. Shit, and I know you aren't still complaining.

You've been compensated quite handsomely for all that I put you through. I mean you've made me a lot of money, but have cost me a lot as well."

"So now you're going to bring up me setting a part of your house on fire? What the fuck did you expect me to do after what you did? I could've killed you Sonny, but I let you live."

Sonny laughed loudly. "Kill me...in your dreams bitch. No, I let *you* live. Do you know what I could've done to your entire family after that shit? I could've made you watch as I slowly tortured your son."

Ernestine was quiet for once.

"You better be glad I had a change of heart and let you back into the organization."

"You probably let me back in because of your guilty conscious," she stated.

"Maybe...maybe not."

"Let's not forget that I came back because I decided to forgive you."

"Bitch you didn't have a choice. Where were you gonna work? McDonalds?" Sonny laughed again.

"Look, I've tried to move past all of that shit. I have a real man now and the only drama I have in my life, is you."

"A real man? That punk was sucking dick in the pen. You're married to a down low pussy. I bet you strap on with that little pansy."

Ernestine laughed. "Did I hit a nerve Mr. Sabatino?"

"Absolutely not. But don't get it twisted. I could have you if I wanted you."

"Listen, I'm almost forty-five years old and I'm at a point in my life where I just want to get money, get fucked good, and live. The only place you fit in that equation now is getting money and now your drama is starting to interfere with that."

"Whatever," Sonny answered.

"It's true. You're not focused. Now that Karla has your precious Gianni though, what's plan B?"

"Ernestine, I'm really trying to avoid using my last resort, so you better get in touch with your daughter quickly. I've gotten a text that can ruin everything I put into motion for the past two years."

"What plan?" she questioned.

"That doesn't matter. I just need to know where you think Karla could be?"

"I don't know where she is. I've been calling her like crazy just like you and she will not answer my calls. This shit is all your fault to begin with, Sonny. You never told me why you wanted me to take Gianni from her camp in the first place."

My heart was beating so fast it almost came out my chest as the details of what happened began to unfold. Biting down on my lip in order to keep myself from saying anything, I instantly tasted blood. It took everything in me to remain silent.

"Bryan!" Sonny called out.

"Yeah, boss," I could hear Bryan respond a few seconds later.

"I just wanna make sure Charlotte is not anywhere within ear shot," Sonny stated.

"She walked by several minutes ago, but I haven't seen her since," Bryan said.

"Okay, well make sure she doesn't come anywhere near that door."

"10-4, boss."

"It's not my fault you dumb cunt. It's your fault! You're the one who let your deranged ass daughter take Gianni from you! Hell you're the one who let off those gun shots at the zoo when that wasn't the plan! You were supposed to kidnap her that day, but you fucked up!" Sonny spat as soon as the door closed. "You can forget about that other fifteen grand I was gonna pay you after the job was done. You fucked up so there goes your money."

"Don't fucking act like you're innocent in all this bullshit. Why the hell did you have me take her in the first place?"

"I wanted to save the day. I figured if I had you kidnap Gianni and I got her back, then…"

"Then what dumb ass?"

"Then maybe I would win them both over. They'd feel in debt to me," Sonny admitted.

"You're sicker than I thought. I gave you the benefit of the doubt thinking that this had something to do with killing Charlotte's husband, but this is crazy," Ernestine informed. "It sounds like to me that you're trying to win over your newest project. This shit is getting old and I'm getting tired of it. You are so pussy-whipped and here I'm helping you get closer to the next young trick. You're pathetic," she said with disgust.

"Are you jealous? No better yet, are you jealous and bitter?" You're still in love with me, aren't you?"

"Sonny, don't be ridiculous. Love you, hell, I barely even trust you."

"Admit it! You're jealous of my beautiful Black Barbie!"

"Sonny you're delusional! Who wants to be with someone you can't trust. You single handedly destroyed my family. We were doing well before my husband ever went into business with you. My love for you vanished many moons ago. The day you sent my daughter to prison even though you were in the wrong, is the day I no longer looked at you as someone I loved, but someone who fucked up not only my life, but both of my children's lives."

"Get over yourself Ernestine! I've made those kids' lives better. Your husband could never provide for them the way I did. Don't make yourself out to be such an angel. You have your own secrets and skeletons. Let's not forget how I can ruin that angelic image your kids have of you. Be careful and tread light."

"There you go with your threats. You really have me fucked up. I'm smarter and stronger than you think. If trying to turn my children against me makes you feel better Sonny than so be it! I came to this country over twenty years ago and since I've been in the states, I've had to deal with a bunch of bullshit. I'm immune to your shit at this point Sonny…"

I'd had enough. More importantly, I'd kept my mouth closed long enough. I was tired of motherfuckers thinking I was a weak. First Malcolm…now Sonny, but that shit was about to stop. I needed to prove to everybody who decided to cross me that I was tired of playing games. Fucking with me was one thing, but messing with my seed was an entirely different story.

With my blood boiling, I quietly made my way up the back

stairs, then went straight to my closet and grabbed the first gun I saw. The gold handcrafted revolver Sonny had bought me a couple of months ago would do the trick. I was going to show his ass once and for all how my gun range practice would finally paid off. Sonny was going to die today. I was going to see to it that he paid for taking my daughter.

I put the revolver in the waist of my pants before creeping back down the back stairs. I was frantic, angry, and a nervous wreck all at the same time. *How could he do this to my baby*, was the only thing that played in my head. This bastard was a monster. What sane person would purposely kidnap an innocent child to prove something? I hated Sonny and he was going to pay.

Waiting for the right moment, I tried to open the fake door, but it was locked. To make matters worse, I almost dropped the gun out of my hand, which made a loud thump.

"Who's there?" Sonny called out. "Hey, Ernestine get on top of that shit immediately and we'll chat later, I gotta go," he said, as his voice got closer to me.

As soon as he unlocked and opened the fake door I was waiting with the gun in my hand. I didn't know what to expect. I didn't know if he was going to be armed, too. I didn't know if I was about to die, but it didn't matter because I was going all in no matter what.

"Charlotte what the hell are you doing back there? Put that gun down," Sonny said, walking away. He didn't seem the least bit phased.

"Turn around you sick fuck," I said, letting off one gunshot in the air to let him know it wasn't a game.

"Woman what the fuck is your problem," Sonny replied as both Rafael and Bryan ran in the room with their guns drawn.

"Charlotte put the gun down!" Rafael ordered as if I wasn't just squirting all over him a couple of days ago.

"Fuck that! He had my daughter kidnapped by that sick bitch, Ernestine. Now, her fucking daughter Karla has her. I'm going to kill him Rafael. I'm not fucking around!" I yelled with the gun aimed at Sonny's chest. "Put your hands up you bastard!"

"Bryan leave the room and watch the door for any other

staff because this might get ugly," Sonny instructed.

"No problem, boss," Bryan said before turning around and closing the door.

As Sonny put his hands up he laughed. "Damn, Charlotte, I didn't know you had this fire in you."

"Is it true what she's saying Sonny? My mother took Gianni?" Rafael asked, still pointing his gun at me.

"Charlotte has no idea what she's talking about. Now sweetheart put down the gun. You have this all wrong. Let's talk this all out."

"No, Sonny. I know what the fuck I heard and…wait a minute, your mother?" My heartbeat started to race. "Wait so you were behind this shit, too?" I looked at Rafael for a quick second. "You knew your sister kidnapped my daughter all this time and you faked like you cared! You pretended to…"

"Charlotte, put the gun down now!" Rafael yelled still pointing the gun at me like he was trying to shut me up.

"Rafael, put your gun down. She's not going to shoot me," Sonny chimed in. "She doesn't have the heart."

"Like hell," I said, firing another shot.

Rafael ducked. "What the fuck?"

"You missed bitch. Now stop fucking playing and put the gun down." I could tell Sonny's patience was evaporating.

"So, you continuously torture me, lie to me, and deceive me, and now I'm a bitch. Now you're the victim?"

"Stop your fucking whining!" Sonny instructed.

"I heard everything Ernestine said. You're the reason why Karla took Gianni. You're the reason why she's so mad. You sent her to prison! You wanted to get rid of her for some reason!"

"Is this all true?" Rafael asked confused. It was the first time he'd lowered his gun. His face showed confusion and pain.

"Tell him the truth Sonny! I know what I heard."

Sonny never said a word.

I walked a little closer to him…this time aiming the gun at his head. "Tell him!"

Sonny still hesitated for a moment. "Yeah, it's true but it had to be done."

Rafael looked devastated.

"Now do you see why I have to kill him, Rafael?" I asked.

"Charlotte, just stop it! You're not built for this. Anyway how are you going to get Gianni back with me dead? Use your brain, idiot," Sonny added. He turned his direction to Rafael. "Why the fuck is your gun not pointed at her? You're supposed to protect me at all times. Don't forget who you work for?"

"Rafael, since Karla is your sister, can you help me get my daughter back?"

"Charlotte, Karla doesn't listen to anyone. Just put the gun down before you make things worse." Rafael lowered his head looking defeated.

"You know what, neither of you care. My daughter was probably killed. She's probably dead already. Maybe I should just kill myself and then everything will be okay." Pointing the gun at my head, my hands shook wildly. I was frantic as tears streamed down my face. My body was covered with sweat.

"Charlotte, please don't! I love you," Sonny said.

For some sick reason I knew he was telling the truth.

"If you love me, then bring my daughter home. I'm a mess. I don't know if she is dead or alive and I can't think straight. I need to go find her. What's Karla's address?"

"Do you think it's that easy? If she was at home sitting in her living room, playing Old Maid with Gianni, we wouldn't be having this conversation!" Sonny belted.

"I'm leaving!" I shouted.

Sonny shook his head. "You're not going anywhere!"

He hated not having control. With the gun in my hand and no weapon in his grasp, me taking away his power was frustrating him more and more. I had to find a way to escape. I needed to get my daughter back. My body shook like the temperature was twenty below zero as I contemplated my next move. I knew what I had to do. Aiming the gun back at Sonny I tried to make my exit.

"Charlotte if you leave this fucking house, it's gonna be big trouble for you," Sonny threatened.

"You either let me go, or die," I shot back.

Sonny laughed. "You're not built for this, Charlotte."

"Rafael, give me your keys," I demanded.

"Charlotte, don't you want to get your daughter back? That's where your focus should be right now," Rafael stated. He was tripping if he thought I wanted to hear anything he had to say.

"Now! On the desk!" I yelled.

"Rafael, let her go. She won't get far," Sonny stated.

As soon as Rafael put the keys on the desk, I backed out of the room. "Don't try to follow me!"

With no shoes on I made it out of the house in the summer rain. I didn't care. I jumped in the Suburban, locked the doors, and started the car, as my body continued to shake. I was so nervous but my instincts told me I was making the right decision. As I tore down the driveway to the gate, I hit the remote to open it, and escaped. I had no destination. No phone. No money. Just a full tank of gas and my faith that I was going to get my daughter back. As the rain poured harder and harder I said a prayer,

Father God, I know I haven't spoken to you in a while, but I need you.

I need my daughter. She is my heartbeat. She's my life. She's all I have.

Without her, I'm nothing. Father, send me a sign that my daughter is okay.

Please bring her back home to me. Amen.

As I tore through the windy roads to make it to the main street I cried like a baby. Banging on the steering wheel, tears continued to flow. I was a mess, tired and fatigued. Just as I wiped my eyes, a deer ran out in front of the car. Trying to dodge him, I swerved which instantly made me lose control. My life flashed before my eyes as the truck flipped a couple of times before everything went dark.

15 Kennedi

There was so much going through my mind. I didn't know if I was coming or going. How could my mother and aunt have my grandmother cremated after all the money I'd sent them to ensure she was put away nice. I'd promised Big Mama that she would be buried in style and now she had to sit inside a fucking urn in the hood. I thought I was gonna be able to see her one last time, but that didn't happen. To avoid the drama I arrived at the funeral right before it started, and bailed on the repast. My money was good enough to pay the expenses of the funeral, but not enough to even include me in the obituary. If Maricar and my aunt were out to hurt me, they'd surely succeeded. As I pulled up to my house my cell phone rang.

"Hello."

"Girl, your ass is damn near impossible to get in contact with. I still ain't figure out what you want me to do about this car?"

"I'm so sorry, Mocha. I've been all over the place lately."

"You sound horrible. You okay? I haven't talked to you since Saturday."

"I just got home from my grandmother's funeral and I'm so exhausted."

"I thought she died like two weeks ago?"

"She did, but of course them trifling ass family members of mine kept fucking the money up which prolonged everything. Can you believe they cremated her?" I cried, no longer able to hold back my tears. I was in so much pain.

"Oh my goodness! Do you need me to drive up there? Let's

have dinner, drinks, something?"

"I'll be alright. It's just frustrating that everyone always expects me to be strong, but what about me," I said in between sobs, "I'm human and have a breaking point. No one gives a fuck and that's frustrating!"

"I care. You're a good person. Shit, you've been there for me when you barely knew me. I can't imagine the shit you've probably have done for people you really care about. Look, just go in the house, take a long hot bath, and if you feel like company, give me a call."

"Okay, thanks for listening. I'll be alright."

"Don't forget about this car either. I could always drive it to your house."

"Okay, I'll call you."

What made Mocha think she was coming to my house had me cracking up inside and actually made me feel a little better. It was actually like she'd told me a joke or something. She was cool, but with all the bullshit I had going on, she definitely didn't need to know where I lived. As I got my YSL heels from the backseat, I went in the house. It was now time to face the other issue that had been on my mind, Gianni being alive. I still hadn't heard from Sonny, which had me worried.

Sonny call me ASAP. You did me wrong. I thought we were partners. I thought I could trust you, I texted.

Since Sonny was so erratic I was careful with how I communicated with him, but at this point I didn't care. I needed answers. I'd texted and called him so many times and he still hadn't responded, which wasn't like him. I still hadn't gotten the rest of my money from the last move we'd made. He always paid me on time. Had he cut me off? Was he done with me? These were all the questions that filled my head. I couldn't sleep, and barely ate. Gianni being alive could ruin everything that I'd built with Malcolm. Hopefully I just had Gianni to worry about, if Charlotte was alive, then that would be an even bigger problem. I would no longer legally be Mrs. Fitzgerald, she would be. I couldn't lose Malcolm. Sonny needed to call me back.

As soon as I walked inside the house, the smell of bleach

punched me in the face. As I walked through the foyer and down
the hallway, I could see Malcolm in the kitchen. He was at it again,
cleaning shit.

"Hey, Vee, where you been?"

"Had some errands to run."

"In a tight ass black dress. What kind of damn errand was
that?"

"Meetings, errands. Where's Gianni, I mean Milan?" By
trying to avoid the question, I'd fucked up by saying Gianni's
name. *Shit*.

"She's asleep. I see that little girl is on your mind, too, huh?
All I keep thinking about is how sad she looked when they walked
away. She had so much pain in her eyes."

"Malcolm, stop being dramatic. You met that little girl for
five minutes and now you can't stop thinking about her? You
sound like a damn pedophile."

"Vee, really? You just don't understand me sometimes."

"Nina does though, right?"

Malcolm sighed.

"No, seriously. You don't even touch me anymore. When
was the last time we made love?"

"How can we when it seems like your mind is a thousand
miles away these days. Either you're not here, zoned out or we're
arguing."

"Enough with all this talking. Meet me in our bedroom in
five minutes. It's about time I give you a treat," I said, giving him a
quick kiss on the cheek and a sexy look.

Malcolm finally stopped scrubbing the counter. Smacking
me on my ass, he replied, "Get that pussy nice and clean, and I'll
make you regret thinking anything negative about me. I'm gonna
make you remember that I only have eyes for my wife."

"I like the sound of that."

As I walked up the stairs it dawned on me, I needed to
mind fuck my husband, like I did when I was his mistress. Maybe
fucking him everyday was the answer to keep his mind off that
bitch, Nina. Now I even had to get Gianni out of his mind too, so
that was double the amount of blow jobs coming his way.

Quickly running up the steps, I got undressed and turned on the shower and made sure the temperature was just right. Lord knows I wasn't in the mood for Malcolm to flip out again. I put the music on my iPhone on shuffle and placed the volume on max. As I got in the water, I took a deep breath. Running my sponge all over my body, I closed my eyes and let the water just take me to another place. All I could think about was my grandmother as 'No More Tears' by Anita Baker blasted through my Harmon speakers. *Big Mama loved that song,* I thought as I suddenly broke down and cried. Moments later, Malcolm joined me. As he embraced me with concern, I buried my face in his chest and sobbed.

"Vee, what's wrong? I've never seen you like this?" He was right. I barely showed vulnerability.

"I just don't want to lose you. I love you and I feel you don't love me anymore," I lied.

"Baby, I love you and I told you I'm doing this marriage thing once. It's me and you forever. Now hand me that washcloth so I can wipe your nose."

"Really Malcolm?" I laughed.

He didn't laugh though. After wiping my nose as he'd planned, I guess he finally felt comfortable enough to make a move. Leaning down, he kissed me with so much passion. It felt like I was kissing the man I fell for years ago. This kiss was different. Maybe the old Malcolm resurfacing wasn't a bad idea. I felt safe. His kiss felt genuine. Pushing my back against the shower wall, he got on his knees and kissed my inner thigh before sucking all of the juices out of my pussy. As I reached an orgasm he pulled out of me.

"Malcolm I need you. Make love to me. Right now."

"Bend over," he whispered.

Climbing onto the bench in our shower, I bent over and let my husband enter my wetness. His extra large pole thrust in and out of me until we both climaxed together. I fell on the bench and laid on my back and stared at him. He was perfect. I didn't care about his scars or the fact that he wasn't as handsome anymore. All I cared about was the man behind all of his war marks.

"Kiss me."

"I have to…"

Before he could say another word I stood up on the bench, grabbed my husband and made him kiss me.

"I wanted to taste my pussy."

He smiled. "Girl, you're crazy."

After washing up we got out of the shower and got in bed for a quick afternoon nap before Milan woke up.

"It feels so good laying in your arms. I love you, Malcolm."

"I love you, too, Vee."

Just as we both started to drift into a slight slumber the doorbell rung five times in a row.

"Who the fuck is that?" I asked irritated as I got up to slip something on.

"It might be Nina?" Malcolm said trying to hurry up and slip on his boxers and sweatpants.

"Not ringing my doorbell like she don't have any sense. Besides, I thought she told us she had to work at the hospital today?"

"Yeah, that's true but maybe she got off early or something. Lay down, I'll see who it is."

Just when I thought I'd made headway with Malcolm, there he was breaking his neck to get down the steps to see if it was Nina. Nobody else came to our house, so I guess he was right. Grabbing the remote to my sound system I turned the music off and listened closely to hear what they said. Jumping out of bed, I walked out the room and listened from the top of the stairs.

"Is Kennedi Kramer available?"

"Um, you have the wrong house, there's no…"

"Are you sure?"

I immediately knew her deep voice.

"Yes, I am ma'am. It's just me and my wife V…"

Before Malcolm could say another word I quickly interrupted. I couldn't believe that bitch had the audacity to come to my home.

"Babe, I got it. Close the door while I slip on something."

"Just one minute ma'am," I heard him say.

Doing as he was told Malcolm closed the door with a puzzled look. I ran back into the room and slipped on the first thing I saw which was a pair of yoga pants, a tank top and some Chanel flip flops. I then ran down stairs.

"Who is that?" Malcom asked as I reached the bottom step.

"Remember the lady who I met with about the boutique, well that's her. I don't know how she found out where we lived though. It has to be some type of mix up. I'll clear it up now."

Just as I was about to open the door, I heard Milan crying.

"Please get Milan, babe," I said, needing him to go away.

"No problem," he replied before running upstairs.

When I opened the door I was ready for war.

"What the fuck are you doing here?"

"You never seemed to be in a good mood when you see me."

"How the fuck did you find out where I lived, Maricar? Besides, shouldn't you still be entertaining the people who came to Big Mama's funeral?"

"How'd you like the service? Wasn't the obituary, nice?"

I could already tell this bitch was here to play games, and I wasn't in mood.

"How did you find me?" I asked again.

"Well, the night you went to jail, I decided to break into your car and get your registration so I could have your address just in case I needed it."

"Okay, so now what? You are not welcome here." I turned around to make sure Malcolm wasn't coming.

"So, you're not going to introduce me to your little boyfriend?"

"Husband." I corrected.

"I can't meet my son-in-law? Let me in."

"Bitch, why are you here?" I whispered.

"Babe, you good?" Malcolm called from the top of the stairs with Milan in his arm.

"Mommy!" Milan yelled.

"I deserve to meet my grandchild. Speaking of grandchildren, that's the purpose of my visit. Who the hell supposed to take care of your kids while you up in this big house with your new family."

"Please don't do this to me. Finally my life is going well. Don't ruin this for me," I pleaded.

Maricar let out a deep, husky laugh like she had phlegm in her throat. "Oh, so your man don't know about your kids huh? Shit, you more like me than I thought."

"Please Maricar."

"Babe, your phone keeps ringing," Malcolm said as he entered the foyer with Milan on his hip and my phone in his hand. Quickly looking down, I saw Sonny's number, but couldn't answer. His ass had terrible fucking timing. By the time I looked back up, Maricar had made her way into my house, pushing past me.

"Is this my grandbaby? Hi I'm Maricar Kennedi's mother, but you can call me Ma. Let me see this child, looking just like your Mema." As Maricar reached for Milan, I pushed her back.

Malcolm looked puzzled. "Who the hell is Kennedi, and I thought your mother was dead?"

"Dead...shiitttt I'm alive in the flesh, baby." Maricar smiled, exposing her discolored teeth.

"It's a long story, babe," I stated.

"Again, I will introduce myself. I'm Maricar, and you are."

"I'm Malcolm. Now Venus, what the fuck is up?"

"Malcolm? Oh really..." Maricar started before I immediately shut her down.

"I thought she was dead. I hadn't seen this woman in over fifteen years. Now, she's here begging for money, but trust me she's leaving soon. Please take Milan upstairs and let me handle this baby please. I don't want our daughter around this drama."

"You got five minutes, then you need to do some fucking explaining," Malcolm barked.

"Okay, okay."

As Malcolm made his way up the steps with Milan, Maricar started walking around my house making herself at home. As soon as she kicked her filthy ass sandals off and exposed her half polished toes on my marble floor, I was instantly annoyed. Even her faded black skinny jeans and ugly lace top got under my skin. She was in desperate need of a makeover.

"You living large as shit, Vee, that's your new name right? Girl you're good. So I know the kids said you left them for some dude named Malcolm, but they said he was cute and some big famous person. That can't be him right because that nigga look like a burnt piece of bacon." She laughed for a few seconds. "Do you remember when Michael Jackson got burned in that Pepsi commercial? That nigga was running down the steps when his hair caught on fire. Did something like that happen to him? I mean the kids said he was famous or some shit?"

"Next question."

"Well you better start answering them because I got plenty of questions."

"What do you want? How much is it going to cost me to make you disappear, you and those fucking bastard kids? You didn't do right by me ever. Have a conscious for a change. My life is good. Don't come back in it and ruin what I've built."

"What is it all worth to you? How much you think is fair?"

Walking over to my purse on the kitchen island, I grabbed five stacks and gave it to her.

"Look I need you to leave now. I'll be in touch. Just give me twenty-four hours to figure everything out. Now get your shoes and get out."

"Twenty-four hours Kennedi, I mean Vee." Maricar laughed as she finally left.

Anxiety took over as I grabbed my phone to call Sonny. He finally picked up on the second ring.

"Sonny where the hell have you been? I've been calling you forever. I need your help. I need your help now," I whispered before walking into the kitchen.

"First off, what did you need to talk to me about Gianni. That's the only thing I'm interested in hearing right now."

"I saw her at Short Hills Mall the other day. You told me she was dead. What the fuck is going on?"

"Who was she with?"

"Some lady named Karla and a little boy. I think his name was Carter, Cruz, I don't know something. So, is she alive? Was that Gianni?"

"Yes, Kennedi it was."

"What the fuck Sonny?"

"We need to meet. I'll tell you everything."

"Yes, we do need to meet. I can't believe this."

"I've got a job for you. I need you to settle a score that's well overdue. Meet me at the spot in thirty minutes."

"I'll be there."

"You'll be where?" Malcolm interrupted. I quickly pushed end on my phone. I was caught and didn't know what he'd heard.

"I have to go. I'll be back."

"To meet Sonny. Who the fuck is that?"

"It's not what you think. I have something I have to take care of. I will tell you everything trust me."

"Kennedi, that's your name right? You're not going anywhere until you tell me who the fuck you really are?"

16 Charlotte

"Do you like your roses?"

"Yes, I love them! I love you, Malcolm." I said, looking around my bedroom. It was surrounded with white roses. He'd been caught cheating a couple of days ago for the millionth time and was trying to get back in my good graces.

"I love you more, Charlotte."

"Let's stay together forever. I just need you to stop with all the girls. Since you've become famous it's getting worse and worse. I just need you to be faithful to me," I said, staring into his brown eyes. He was so handsome that his smile always made me melt. My husband was a lady's man but I knew I had his heart.

"They mean nothing to me. No matter what, we will always be together, me, you, and Gianni," Malcolm said to me with so much conviction. I believed him this time.

"Let's just go back to old times, like our college days when we were happy. Before all the fame life was great. I'm not always going to be here. I just need you to stop taking me for granted."

"So you're giving me a clean slate?"

"I've forgiven you so many times before and you never change. This time mean what you say." I ran my hands down his cold black wavy hair.

"I promise I'm going to change. We have a family now, a new baby girl. It's all about you, too, I assure you, no more girls, no more drama."

"Well then yes, you're forgiven."

Partially opening my eyes, I looked around my hospital room startled. It didn't take long to realize that I'd been dreaming as my blood pressure machine suddenly cuffed my arm. A sudden sadness came over me as thoughts of being back with Malcolm entered my mind. It was just a dream. However, the weird thing was I dreamed of roses and the more I looked around, I saw that there were at least four dozen red roses spread throughout the room. Malcolm had been in my dreams the past two nights since I'd been in the hospital. Was he sending me some kind of sign, I wondered?

"Good morning sleeping beauty."

I turned to his voice as much as my neck would allow ready to snap.

"What the hell are you doing here?"

"I just wanted to check up on you to make sure that you were okay. If you want me to leave than I will."

"Rafael, answer one question. Did you know that your sister had my daughter?"

"I'm insulted that you would ask me such a question. I had no clue. I've been looking for my sister non-stop since finding this out. My mother and I even had a big blow out. I was livid that they could actually do such a thing. No matter what my job entails, I have a heart and I genuinely care about you," Rafael responded as he got out of the chair as if he was attempting to leave. Deep down I didn't want him to go, I needed him.

"What am I supposed to think Rafael?"

"Maybe I should go."

"No. Please don't go. I need you." I tried to reach for him.

"If I stay, then please let me enjoy this time with you. No fussing, deal."

Through all the pain I was able to expose a small smile. "Deal."

"Cool."

"Rafael. Where did all these flowers come from? I told Sonny I didn't want to see his face back up here. I want them all gone."

"Well, they aren't from Sonny, they're from me," Rafael sat on my bed and then smiled proudly.

"Are you serious? From you. I didn't know you really cared."

"Of course I care Charlotte, it's just that you're married, and I know that's wrong. But no matter how I try to fight my feelings for you, I just can't. My mother cheated on my father for years with random guys and I vowed never to be like her. She was probably the reason why he killed himself. They would argue all the time about her infidelity. My dad was a good guy, and I always wanted to grow up to be a good man like he was. My father raised me with morals and respect. I'm different from my mom and sister. I'm more like my dad."

"It sounds like he was a great man."

"He was," he agreed.

"My circumstances are different though, Rafael. Don't ever feel bad about being with me. Things happen the way they're supposed to," I stated trying to reassure him.

"Well promise me that you will never leave out of the house the way you did. You scared me. Don't ever threaten to hurt yourself for Sonny. He's not worth it."

"Well, thanks for the flowers, and I promise I'll be smarter next time with how I react. So, what are we going to tell your boss about these beautiful flowers? I'm sure Sonny is gonna wonder who got them, so we need to come up with something."

"I know but getting the flowers just felt like the right thing to do at the time. I just wanted you to wake up with some peace, that's all."

"I could use some peace too but it's hard. I feel trapped, Rafael. I find myself wanting to be with you and not knowing if you want the same thing. You've been so distant lately."

"I've been trying to fight it trust me, but when the accident happened I couldn't stand being away from you. I needed to make sure you were okay. To see you all banged up destroyed me."

"What do you mean? I thought this was your first visit." I was confused.

"It is the first time I've been here. I'm talking about at the scene of the accident. When you pulled off I followed, only minutes behind you, trying to find you against Sonny's wishes. I just felt like you needed me. When I saw the truck turned over on the side of the road, my heart stopped. I just wanted you to be alive."

"So *you* found me?"

"Yes, because the weather was so bad, I almost missed seeing you. I called 911 immediately, then Sonny. I just didn't want him to give me an order I would regret."

"What do you mean? Was Sonny upset that you went after me?"

"It doesn't matter. I just did what was best. In his own sick way, he loves you. I told him I was going to the store when I found you."

"Well, I appreciate you. Thanks," I said, staring at Rafael in disbelief that he'd done this for me. *The fact that Rafael thought enough of me to get flowers but not Sonny, is even more confirmation that I needed to leave his ass.*

"What are you day dreaming about?" Rafael asked exposing that sexy grin.

"It's nothing. How long have you been here?"

"A couple hours. How are you feeling?"

"Still really sore. This neck brace is uncomfortable and driving me insane. Besides the whiplash, I have a herniated disc so I guess I have to wear it, but hopefully not for long."

"Well, you look beautiful and it's important that you get better."

I couldn't help but blush. "Stop lying, I feel like shit. This deep laceration on my head definitely will force me to wear bangs for a while. These stitches still hurt," I said, rubbing my index finger against the bandage.

"No matter how you wear your hair, you would still be gorgeous. I would never lie to you."

"That's what all you guys say."

"I'm not all those guys, I'm me."

"You're too good to be true."

"No, you're just not used to a man treating you the way you deserve, that's all."

"Maybe you're right, but how do you think you can keep this up?"

"I'll think of something. Just be patient, if it's meant to be, we will be."

"I'm gonna hold you to that. Ouch!" I said, trying to move my arm. It was in a cast and a sling. I was in terrible pain. The rods in my arm were starting to bother me again.

"Are you okay?" Rafael immediately responded to my moans ready to help.

"I think I need some more pain medication."

"Well, you have a new nurse on duty and she's been in and out. She didn't want to wake you, but I think she needs to check your vitals. Speak of the devil, here she is right now."

"Hi Mrs. Sabatino, I'm Nina."

"Please don't call me that, Nina. Please call me Charlotte."

"Okay, no problem."

"No I'm sorry. I didn't mean to be so rude. I need some more meds. I'm in a lot of pain all of a sudden and I have a terrible headache."

"Umm, I'm gonna let you guys do your thing and I'll be back tomorrow. How's that boss," Rafael interjected. He'd instantly gone back into work mode.

"Sure Rafael. Thanks for stopping by and tell Sonny thanks for the flowers." I laughed.

"No doubt," he said, leaving out of the room.

Rafael was so good to me, and here I was stuck with a man that I hated.

"Alright so your vitals are great," Nina informed with a smile. She was a pretty young girl. She was shapely, with a tiny waist. She looked like one of those Kardashians, like she was Indian or Persian, or something.

"So, does that mean I can still go home tomorrow?"

"Well Charlotte, once the doctor comes in, he'll be able to give you an answer, but I don't see a reason why you can't go home. Missing your family huh?"

"I'm missing my daughter."

"Oh, how old is she?"

"She's six years old," I replied as tears started to fill my eyes.

"Mrs. Sabatino, are you okay?"

"Please don't call me by that last name. My name is Charlotte Fitzgerald, not Sabatino, and I'm fine."

"I apologize, I keep forgetting."

"It's okay, I just need to see her and I can't right now, so I'm a little emotional."

"Well, if it makes you feel any better, your husband has been by your bedside staring at you for hours while you slept. He seems like he loves you very much."

I forced a smile. "Oh, that's not my husband. My husband is actually an asshole."

"I'm sooo sorry, Charlotte, I didn't mean to pry."

"No, it's okay. It's rare that I get to talk to anyone, especially another woman, so it's fine."

"Well, I'm a good listener," Nina said, fooling around with my IV.

"It's not much I really can say, but know that I miss my family. My ex-husband died in a fire, some years back and I ended up marrying a man that my daughter hates, so I always feel alone."

"I'm sorry to hear that Mrs."

"Fitzgerald."

"Mrs. Fitzgerald. It's funny I work part time for a…"

"Well hello, Charlotte." The doctor walked in interrupting us.

"Hello Doctor Gordy. Please tell me you're here with good news."

"I am. You'll be leaving tomorrow as we spoke about earlier. You're going to be a little uncomfortable granted you have a broken right arm and wrist, but things could have definitely been worse."

"How long do I have to keep this neck brace on?"

"Well, you know you need to keep it on because of the whiplash for a couple weeks, but the majority of your pain is coming from your herniated disc. You will probably experience numbness in your leg or foot, even tingling, but you should be able to resume to light activities in six weeks."

"Six weeks? Are you serious…ugh."

"Look at it this way…things could've definitely been worse. You must have a guardian angel," Dr. Gordy replied.

She was right. Malcolm must've been watching over me. Maybe he's watching over Gianni, too.

"You'll be fine. Nina, can you do me a favor, your shift is almost up but I need you take care of something in room 407," Doctor Gordy instructed.

"No problem."

As Nina left the room, the doctor went over with me all of the medication information and all of the things I need to do for a speedy recovery.

Once he left I was relieved and knew that I was blessed to have survived the horrific accident. I really had a reality check. If something were to happen to me who would take care of Gianni. She didn't even have Godparents. I'd be damned if Sonny would raise her. That would've been horrible for her to lose both of her parents. I had to out-smart Sonny at some point. It was important that I came up with an exit plan.

Just as the medication started to kick in, and I began to drift off, I was suddenly awakened by another visitor.

"Well hello Charlotte. Did I wake you up?"

"What the fuck are you doing here Karla, and where is my daughter you sick bitch!" I sat up as much as I could. The nerve of that bitch to show up here and to be without my daughter was even worse. If I had a gun I would've blown her damn brains out. I looked around for something to throw at her.

"Don't worry about Gianni, she's fine. I started to bring her up here, but I'm enjoying her so much that I decided it wouldn't be a good idea." She sashayed into my room closing the door behind her.

"Get the fuck outta my room. I'm calling the police." I picked up the phone off the bed.

"I wouldn't do that if I were you. If you involve the police, you will never see Gianni again," Karla threatened as she walked up closer to my bed. Her bright red lipstick blinded me.

"What did I ever do to you? Why did you take my child?" My tears represented all the pain I was in. I looked at her sling, forgetting that Sonny had shot her in the shoulder.

"You're so fucking weak and pathetic. Bitch if someone

took my son I would be ready to kill their ass, not sitting here crying like some punk. I just don't get it. Why does Sonny love you so much? You're not even all that cute."

"Is this about Sonny? You took my daughter because you feel like I took your place? He's making me be with him! It was either be with him or die. Gianni is all I have Karla. Sonny killed my father and my husband," I stated with all the strength I had.

"What the hell are you talking about?" Karla folded her arms awaiting my response.

"I was married to a big entertainment mogul and Sonny killed him. Gianni is all I have left of my late husband. I don't want to be with him, but I don't have a choice right now. Please bring my daughter back to me. I'm begging you."

"So he forced you to marry him, huh?" Karla asked as if she really didn't want to believe me. As she paced the floor in her ripped G-Star jeans, she seemed to be getting even more upset.

"Karla if I had a choice I would still be in LA. I don't want to be here. You can have him for all I care."

"I don't want him anymore. It's not about that. It's about leverage. Sonny has something I want. When I learned you and Gianni were all he cared about these days, I knew how to get his attention."

"What is it? I'll pay you. I need my…"

"Pay me?" She laughed. "Charlotte I'm good. All of my bank accounts are stacked. My issues are worse."

"Well, what can I do to help you? I'll do anything."

"So you would betray a man that you sleep with every night for a woman who kidnapped your daughter? A woman you don't even know."

"It's about being a mother and doing whatever it takes to protect your child…so yes."

"So you'd die for her?" Karla asked, putting her hand in her cross body Louis Vuitton.

"Of course. Any mother would."

"I doubt mine would," she stated in a low voice.

"Karla, why? What makes you think all this is okay?"

"Look bitch! My mother and Sonny came up with that

dumb ass plan to take your daughter. I did you a favor. Gianni doesn't need to be around that pedophile!"

"Pedophile? What on earth are you talking about?" I asked confused. "Why do you want revenge on Sonny so badly?"

"Why so many questions? What's your point we're not friends?"

"Look Karla. We're both victims here. You're not alone. You can talk to me. I just want to know…"

"You're right. My beef shouldn't be with you but I don't trust you."

"You don't have to trust me, but we both want the same things. I want out."

"Whatever. You're just nosey as fuck. Look, Sonny set me up, so I blame him for everything I've been through. He did things to me that he should've been dead for a long time ago."

"What did he do?" I said continuing to pry.

"The worst thing he could do. Look, I don't really like to talk about it. It's really painful. As a woman, I know me taking your daughter was wrong, but I needed to. It's not personal. He did me wrong and you need to get out as soon as you can. He loves you now, but he will throw you to the wolves as soon as he's done with you."

Karla started to get comfortable, pulling the chair close to my bedside. I felt a little uncomfortable at the way she was just opening up to me. I didn't know how to take her being so vulnerable.

"Charlotte, if I bring Gianni back you have to promise to leave and never come back. You have to get her away from him. I will help you escape from Sonny, It's what's best."

"Why do you want me to leave so bad? What aren't you telling me?"

"Look, he's sick. Sonny needs help."

"Karla, it's hard for me to understand what you're going through if you don't tell me everything."

"Sonny was like a father to me and I really looked up to him. When my dad committed suicide, I was devastated and was missing that father figure. He quickly filled that void. He taught me how to shoot a gun and made me into the woman I am today. I don't know if that was a good thing but I don't know anything else."

"Okay so what does that have to do with him being a pedophile. I'm still confused."

"He took my virginity when I was only sixteen years old that's why he's a pedophile! He made me feel like life was only great with him. I was young and dumb. He took advantage of me and I believed him. I believed him." Now Karla was crying. Her hard shell had suddenly turned into cotton. "I got pregnant at sixteen to fraternal twins that I named Cruz and Karlie. My daughter, Karlie died though." Karla could barely see from all the tears. "He had me arrested for child endangerment. I did an eight year bid for that motherfucker! He set me up."

My mouth fell open. I couldn't believe what I was hearing. I'd known Sonny to be a lot of things but fucking with a young girl and fathering babies wasn't one of them.

"I caught him," Karla repeated.

"I don't understand when you say that."

"I caught him."

"What do you mean by that?" I asked confused.

"It means that she's crazy as a shit house rat," Sonny said, entering my hospital room.

Immediately Karla got up and drew her gun.

"You know what you did. You're going to pay," she said, pointing her .25 caliber pistol in his direction.

"Where is Gianni, Karla? The fucking charade stops now!" Sonny belted.

"Sonny as long as Charlotte stays with you, neither of you will see her," Karla responded.

"Karla, please don't. I need to see my daughter," I begged.

"I'm leaving now. Charlotte trust me, it's better this way. It's for Gianni's best interest." Karla pointed the gun at Sonny as she backed out of the room. My only chance of getting my daughter back was slipping away just like that.

However before she could leave, Sonny's security, Bryan was right behind her with his gun in hand and a silencer attached.

"Where do you think you're going bitch?" Bryan asked, letting off a shot right in her back.

"No Bryan! No! Now I will never get my daughter back!" I cried.

Just like that, my hopes of getting my daughter back fizzled that fast into thin air.

17 Malcolm

After putting Milan in the sunroom and turning on Doc McStuffins I instantly went into attack mode.

"Who the hell are you? Bitch, you got some explaining to do!" I screamed at my wife. For some reason this feeling felt all too familiar. Something felt off. Something just didn't feel right.

"Look Malcolm, I have somewhere to go. We can talk later."

"No the fuck we can't! Who the hell is Kennedi and who is Sonny? So you're cheating on me?"

"Malcolm, it has to wait! Look I cannot miss this meeting. I've been sitting here going back and forth with you for over an hour. I've told you over and over, it's not what you think. I'm not cheating on you," Vee pleaded then backed up. She knew I was ready to snap at any moment and she was right. Within seconds, I'd slapped Vee directly across her face, instantly leaving a red mark."

"Malcolm stop fucking putting your hands on me! I'm sick of this shit! All that I have done for you!" Vee yelled holding her face.

"Tired of what? What could you possibly be tired of?"

"Are you fucking serious? All I do for you. All I put up with. Dealing with your OCD shit. Inhaling bleach all day. Your fucking tantrums and abuse, that's enough in itself. You got nerve to question me." She fumbled through her cell phone as tears strolled down her face.

"That phone gonna get you fucked up."

"Look. You see this man right here. This was you just eighteen months ago." Vee showed a picture of me holding Milan when she was born. My face was even more disfigured. I was even more unrecognizable.

"What's your point?"

"Do you see how fucked up you looked. I loved you at your worst. You barely had a left ear and you only have nine damn fingers! I've paid all of your medical bills that are still rolling in. You think you look fucked up now. When you start thinking about me being such a fucked up woman, think about the person who changes your disgusting ass bandages twice a day! I…"

"Get the fuck out you lying whore. You don't care about me. I'll find out what the fuck you got going on, watch. I'll get Nina to help me."

"Let me tell you one motherfucking thing you burnt up piece of shit! You bring Nina into any of our marital business and I swear to God you'll regret it. Try me," she threatened. I knew I hit a nerve, but not on purpose. I was serious. I was going to find a way to figure out what she was hiding.

"Get the fuck out bitch!"

"Nigga how are you gonna put me out of my shit. I pay the fucking bills up in here. I'm only leaving because I got shit to do.

"Fuck you and take your spoiled ass daughter with you. Shit, you sure she mine?" I asked following behind her. My blood boiled as I shoved her a few times.

"Oh nigga you tried it! Don't be disrespectful. My daughter huh? Hell no. You keep her," Vee said running out of the house as if she was trying to avoid an ass whooping.

I just let her go. It was frustrating to rely on my wife to tell me everything about my life and now it made me wonder what else she could be hiding from me. Was my entire life a lie?

Grabbing my phone I texted Nina.

Hey, you off yet?

Yes, you ok? Nina replied a few seconds later.

I need you

Where's Vee?

She's not here. I need you here ASAP. It's an emergency

On my way!
Don't call her plz.
K. Be there shortly.
Cool.

There was no doubt in my mind that Nina wouldn't drop everything she was doing to come help me. My mind raced and I felt alone. I didn't know what to do. My wife still hadn't given me any answers, even after slapping her in the face. I was so mad. As I sat on the floor of my kitchen, I searched through my mind for answers. My heart ached. Finally, I prayed to God for answers.

Dear God,

I know I don't come to you much, but I'm in need.

I pray that you reveal any secrets my wife is hiding from me. Please reveal to me why she has the need to lie to me. I just don't understand. Please help me get the understanding I need.

Amen

When I felt angry, cleaning gave me a release. I got the plastic Big Gulp cup from under the sink that I used for cleaning and poured bleach in it. Pouring a little at a time, I stared at the sink trying to get this one spot clean that had been bothering me for days. Just as I started scrubbing, the doorbell rang. Quickly, I got up and walked to the door. It was Nina.

"Hey, you got here fast," I said, giving her a hug.

"I was just getting off work and I was nearby anyway. Where's my baby girl?"

"She's in the sunroom on the floor playing with her toys. Look Nina, I'm losing my mind!"

"What's wrong?" she asked putting her handbag on the small table in the foyer.

"I need your help," I said, leading her to the office.

"Sure. What's going on Malcolm? You're scaring me."

"My wife has been lying to me. I think she's having an affair. It's so much going on." I sat down in the oversized office chair behind the desk and put my hands on my head.

"Okay Malcolm slow down. Tell me what happened."

After filling her in on everything from my wife's mother not being dead, her lying about her name, and her going to meet some guy, Nina was in a state of shock.

"What I'm trying to figure out is why would she lie about her name?" Nina asked confused.

"I don't know, but she's cheating on me Nina. She's seeing someone else. With all the shit that's out here, she has the nerve to be having an affair. I could never touch her again. She's tainted."

"Malcolm maybe you're overacting. Do you have proof that she's cheating?"

"No, but I don't need proof I just know. Plus, I heard her on the phone with some dude named Sonny. Every time I ask her what the hell is going on or where she's going all Vee talks about is some investors for that fake ass boutique that she's been talking about for two years. So we can live in a nice house and she can drive a Ferrari, but can't seem to get a boutique." I shook my head. "That shit don't even make sense. Do you know how much I've been fighting my…"

"Fighting what?"

"Never mind. It's…" I stumbled over my words trying to figure out if I wanted to reveal the feelings I'd been fighting with. Before today I never acted on my feelings. I felt that it was wrong, but since my wife was cheating, I no longer had to hold back how I felt.

"What?" Nina hopped up on the desk sitting opposite of me. Trying to be cool I quickly pushed the chair back and almost fell.

"Oh my gosh. Are you okay?" Nina hopped up grabbing for me, catching the chair in time. She tried hard to hold in her laugh but couldn't help herself.

"Are you okay?" she laughed standing between my legs. Right where I wanted her.

I inhaled her sweet fragrance. She smelled so good which instantly made my dick hard. I wanted her. Right here in my wife's office. I was a wreck and was a bit emotional but no longer did I feel alone. Nina was an angel in my eyes. She was pure. Nina always knew how to make me feel better.

"You don't have to stand. Sit right here," I said, pulling her down onto my lap.

"Malcolm, no. I can't."

"You're not attracted to me. I know I'm…"

Before I could say another word, Nina's tongue was down my throat. The kiss we shared was full of passion. It felt like I could feel her soul. She felt right. As she pulled away, she stared at me deeply.

"Don't ever think I'm not attracted to you. You're handsome just the way you are. Your wife doesn't deserve you. You deserve better."

"Like you."

"I'm not saying that." She laughed and looked away shyly. Nina was beautiful and exotic. She was simple, but beautiful, naturally beautiful.

"Can I kiss you again?" I asked.

Before she could answer we were at it again. As we kissed we ended up sprawled across my wife's mirrored desk, kissing and breathing heavily as we were finally getting something we both wanted. I removed her scrubs then kissed her perky full breasts. She was perfect and I needed to feel her. As I pulled off her baggy pants I uncovered a masterpiece. Standing above her I just stared. She looked so innocent. She was all I wanted and needed.

"Malcolm, I have to tell you something."

"Not now. Just, don't say anything."

Kissing Nina again I picked her up and placed her gently on the white oversized rug. Taking off my pants as I laid on top of her so she couldn't see all of my missing pigment. I didn't want to turn her off. Deep down inside I wanted to ask her to go and take a shower since I knew she'd been out all day, but didn't want to ruin the moment. It was killing me that she might not have been clean, but there was also something angelic about Nina that made me trust her.

As my extra hard dick rubbed on her leg she kept flinching, she then started shaking.

"Nina what's wrong? Are you okay?"

"Malcolm, I'm a virgin."

My eyes showed pure shock. "Really?"

"Yes, and I'm scared."

"It's okay. I'll be gentle," I said reassuring, kissing her on her forehead. Just as I thought, she was clean, un-tampered with, and pure. Nina was perfect, she was different from my wife, and I wanted to feel her.

As I entered her slow and steady, I felt a tightness that was a feeling I don't ever remember feeling in my life. As I worked my way inside of her tight, wet pussy she moaned and held on to me as if she was in pain but also felt good at the same time.

"You want me to stop."

"No. Make love to me." Nina looked me deep in my eyes.

Kissing her and sucking her breasts she wound her hips in a circular motion as if she didn't care that it was painful. Unloosening her ponytail I let her hair fall. She looked even more beautiful.

"How does it feel?"

"It hurts."

"I'll stop if you want me to."

"No. Just keep going slow."

"Like this?"

"Oohhh, awww Malcolm. Yes, like that. Oh Malcolm…"

"Go ahead cum for me," I stroked in and out until I could no longer hold back. Moments later, I nutted all up in her pussy. We both climaxed together.

We laid on the floor for a while before either of us said anything. Finally Nina spoke.

"What now?"

"Let's just enjoy this moment. Let's not over think it."

"I just lost my virginity to a married man so that's not quite the plan."

"You never know what the future will bring," I said, getting up handing Nina her clothes.

"Let me get myself cleaned up," she said standing up. However, before Nina could get her clothes on, we heard a gargling sound coming from the kitchen.

"Oh shit Milan!" I quickly jumped up as Nina followed behind.

"Oh my God, Malcolm! She drank the bleach! She's choking!" Nina panicked. "Call 911!"

As I watched Milan's eyes roll to the back of her head I couldn't move. I stood there paralyzcd. When I looked at her I saw my lying cheating wife and deep down inside, I didn't want to help her.

18 Kennedi

God give me strength, I said to myself. My neck was in so much pain. It felt as if I was carrying an elephant on my back or something. I knew it was all from stress. Something really had to give. After going to the spot hoping that Sonny would show up, I finally decided to leave. I was pissed at Malcolm for making me miss my meeting. I'm sure Sonny was pissed as well since I hadn't shown up because once again he wasn't answering my calls. Instead of heading back home though, I hit the highway headed to Camden to approach Maricar for the mess she'd started. I wanted to tell her ass in person that she had to get the fuck out of my life. If she didn't want to comply, then I definitely had plans to get rid of her one way or another. That bitch had to go.

As I drove down the New Jersey turnpike with force I blasted my favorite song, 'Where Ya At' by Future. Grabbing my phone out of the cup holder, I tried Sonny, but it went to voicemail yet again. I'd been blowing his ass up non-stop. I needed answers. He had to have had an explanation for lying to me, and I needed to know why. Was it to protect me? Why would he save my life, all to betray me, it just didn't make sense. I was so confused.

The moment my phone rang seconds later, I immediately grabbed it with hopes that it was Sonny calling back. *What the fuck Malcolm?* I said to myself as I temporarily blocked both him and Nina from my phone. They both had been calling me back to back for the past twenty minutes. I'm sure all they wanted was for me to come back and get Milan since Malcolm had a fucking temper tantrum, but I wasn't doing it this time. Malcolm was just gonna have to work that shit out by himself because I had shit that needed to be taken care of.

Suddenly, my text alert sounded.

Hey you really need to come by the club tonight. It's urgent that I talk to u, Mocha text.

Not sure if tonight is good. Just call me.

NO! I need to see u IN PERSON!!

Not having the energy to go back and forth with her, I ended with a simple, K just to end the conversation.

No sooner than I placed the phone back down, my text alert went off again.

"Look Mocha. I said ok," I stated out loud then grabbed the phone again.

Got your calls. Sorry I didn't make it to the meeting. Something came up. Tomorrow works better. Got some things to take care of. Promise I'll fill you in on every thing. A lot going on.

Sonny had finally hit me back. I was so happy to know that he'd missed the meeting his damn self. I responded immediately.

It's cool but I REALLY need to talk to you. I need answers Sonny!

I know.

Can we talk before I go home tonight? Everything is a mess.

I'll try. Don't tell him about Gianni.

I won't. I wouldn't dare.

Cool. I'll hit you back.

I felt a little better knowing we at least had a tentative conversation scheduled. Tearing the road up, I made it to Camden a few minutes later ready for a war with my egg donor.

As I bent the corner, Brooks was driving by in his Maserati and immediately stopped me by beeping the horn. I knew he probably had just left my grandmother's house taking care of my family's drug needs. I rolled down my window.

"Hey, young lady," he greeted.

"What's up Brooks?"

"Yo, I'm so sorry to hear about Big Mama. You know that was my girl."

"Thank you. I miss her already."

"I bet. Yo, I wouldn't even know what to do if my grand-mother passed away, so I feel yo pain, Ma," Brooks stated in his sexy New York accent.

"Yeah this shit ain't fun."

"Don't worry, Ma. Shit will get better." He smiled exposing a dimple. His diamonds would blind you. He was iced up from his ears, to his neck, to his wrist.

"I know. Thanks for the concern," I responded. "Let me go. I'll holla at you later."

"Bet," he replied before taking off.

Pulling up in front of Big Mama's house I saw my son Chase sitting on a porch a couple of doors down with some smoked out dread wearing thug who had a long, unkempt beard. I caught eye contact with both of them as soon as I got out of the car. Before I made it to the sidewalk Chase and the dude all of a sudden got into a heated argument.

"Get your faggot ass on, nigga," the guy said shooing Chase away like he was all of a sudden embarrassed to have him around.

"It's all good," Chase said as he walked off.

"Chase! Come here!" I yelled. I might not have been around him much, but I also wasn't gonna stand by and watch my son being a sucka.

"What Kennedi? Don't embarrass me out here," Chase warned.

"Look don't let no motherfucking body talk to you side ways!"

"Mind yo' bizness. We good."

"What happened to your eye? How did you get a black eye?" I questioned him. "Did that motherfucka hit you?"

"It's nuffin'. Dang."

"You letting that fake ass thug beat your ass. Do you know your bloodline? Your father, Sharrod ran these streets. Both of us still have mad respect out here because of that. I'ma fuck him up." I started walking the dude's way before Chase grabbed my arm to stop me.

"Kennedi don't come around my neighborhood embarrassing me. Last time I checked, you were the reason I don't have a father. You never cared before so don't care now. You gonna ruin everything," Chase said practically begging.

I instantly got a flashback of me having this same conversation with Maricar. It hurt, because I knew exactly how he felt.

"Just leave me alone!" Chase said as he ran up the street. He was definitely going through some shit and there was nothing I could do about it.

Oh well if you don't want my help, fuck it, I thought to myself as I made my way to my grandmother's house.

When I walked inside, it smelled just like burning plastic. That smell was oh so familiar as I walked into the kitchen. Just like I thought. Aunt Lee-Lee, Maricar, and Earl were all sitting around the table getting high.

"You want some, Vee," Maricar teased when she noticed me. "Did y'all know this bitch was goin' by the name Venus now?"

Lee-Lee shook her head. "Didn't know...don't care."

"Bitch where the fuck is the rest of my money?" Maricar asked before hitting the pipe. "The little bit you gave came in handy like a mutha though!"

"Why the hell are y'all crack-heads disrespecting my grandmother's house?"

"Don't come up in here preachin'. You fuckin' up my high," Maricar said, exposing those fucked up teeth of hers.

I was so pissed. I could've rammed her head straight through the wall.

"Why y'all always doing that shit in here? It stinks. Damn, I got some shit to do and I can't even get a nap around here," China said, coming out of her room irritated. She wore a pair of tight shorts and a workout bra top, exposing her curves and navel piercing. She was so pretty and had no idea her worth. She damn sure looked like a grown ass woman with hair all the way down her back. She was starting to look more like me, and it was scary.

"Girl, go back in that room, this grown folk bizness," Aunt Lee-Lee ordered high as hell.

These motherfuckas were really having a field day off the

five g's I'd sent Maricar by Western Union. My blood boiled.

"You know damn well if my grandmother was still alive, you wouldn't be disrespecting her house like this. That's just like you to come back and fuck everything up, Maricar."

"Look lil' bitch. If you have problem wit what I do, take yo' fuckin' kids to yo' big ass mansion and let grown folk be around here. Your ass never answered my question either. Where my money at?"

"Bitch you lucky you're still breathing. I ain't giving you shit, and if you bring your ass back to my house, I'm gonna kill you," I warned.

"Like you did Aunt Kasey huh?" China instigated as she took a bottle of Bel Air champagne out of the fridge. As she popped the bottle they all started begging China for some. I was in a state of shock.

"Little girl you're not grown! You're only fourteen years old."

"My birthday was yesterday. I'm fifteen now, but I guess you don't like to remember that day huh? Opens up some bad wounds I'm sure," China responded.

Maricar slapped her hand against her right thigh and laughed. "She told your ass."

"You know what? I don't know why I came back down here. It ain't nothing but negative energy in this bitch. I need to go before I catch another charge."

"Come on, Maricar, pass it now," Earl freeloading ass complained. He ignored me as if I didn't exist.

"No bullshit. You givin' that bitch way too much attention," Aunt Lee-Lee chimed in.

"Look, I paid for the shit so I can hit it as long as I want!" Maricar fired back. She took another pull and started talking with smoke coming out her mouth.

"Kennedi, you betta have my money by midnight, or you gonna be sorry. Your little secret life gonna get exposed fuckin' with me."

"Bitch I ain't giving you shit, and if you fuck up what I have then trust me, you will regret it. Don't say I didn't warn you."

"I knew you were gonna pull this bullshit so that's why I got some other shit in motion. You'll know not to fuck wit' me after this. I'm a real OG Kennedi. You think you know these streets. Where you think you get it from? Ain't nobody trippin' off that shit you talkin'. I can reach out and touch yo' ass when I feel like it. Thinkin' I'm a joke," Maricar stated. "And take yo' kids wit you. Shit, if I ain't want yo' ass back in the day, what the fuck makes you think I wanna raise yours," Maricar added.

Her statement stung, but I couldn't expose weakness if front of that bitch.

"You bad teeth having, bitch! Fuck you and those kids. I ain't doing a damn thing for nobody in here. All y'all can burn in hell!" I said turning around and walking out of the door.

I meant what I said. Nobody in that house fucked with me, so I was done. Deep down it hurt that the only family I had didn't care if I lived or died, but I had to be strong. Besides, God had given me a second chance with Milan so I wasn't taking those kids to my new home so they could poison everything I'd built. That would've been a sure way of me losing Malcolm.

"Game on, bitch!" Maricar yelled out.

When I got in my car, a tear escaped my eye. I was in pain even though I tried to fight it. I couldn't leave the neighborhood fast enough as I started up my car and peeled off down the street, leaving tire marks in the payment. I called my family all types of names as I made my way to Philly, headed to see Mocha.

When I arrived at the strip club minutes later, Mocha was waiting for me at the front door.

"Hey boo!" she said super excited to see me. Giving me a kiss on my cheek, she looked super cute in her little Pocahontas costume. "Let's sit back here, we need to talk," she said, pulling me to the back of the club.

"Girl I've had a drama filled day. I need a fucking drink ASAP," I said as we sat down. She motioned to the waitress to bring us some shots.

"Okay, so did you try to set me up or some shit?" Mocha didn't waste any time drilling me.

"What are you talking about?" I certainly wasn't in the

mood for anymore bullshit.

"Don't play dumb. You know what I'm talkin' about. Did you set me up with that car?"

I shook my head. "No, why?"

"Cuz the police were all over that shit the other night, that's why. Luckily I stopped drivin' that shit cuz something didn't feel right but I did go check on it everyday just to make sure nobody fucked wit' it. Can you imagine if they had caught me in that shit! Luckily I parked it blocks away from my crib. Now you need to tell me, what the fuck is up?"

"Mocha, the more you don't know the better."

"No, fuck that. Tell me what's going on now!"

"He's dead Mocha," I blurted out. I didn't have the energy to argue.

"A yooo. I can't get no more charges. I'm on parole. My DNA all in his car, and if they run my shit, they gonna know I was in the car, what the..."

"Calm down Mocha. I got this. You good. No more questions, you just gotta trust me. My partner will handle everything."

"Trust you? You didn't even tell me the truth. I ain't trying to get caught up in no shit."

"I told you I got you. I wasn't trying to set you up or get you in trouble," I said texting Sonny.

Them peoples got it.

He hit me right back.

I know. Already taken care of. Hit me in the morning.

K

To ease her concern, I showed her Sonny's response. "See...no worries. We good. Everything is handled," I said as the waitress came over with a tray full of shots.

"Are you sure?"

"Yes, I'm positive."

"Good, cuz I was about to beat your ass," Mocha stated. "You so damn secretive but I kinda like that shit."

We both couldn't help but laugh. After toasting, we both took our first shot. Four shots later, I was already tipsy.

"Girl I really needed to come out tonight. I have so much

going on. It feels good to be out of that damn house. I mean, I love my husband and all, but I need a break. Shit. I feel like I'm always taking care of everybody else."

"When I'm here in this club, I let all my problems just roll off my back and do me. I just feel free.

"I know that's right." I said, taking another shot. This one burned my mouth a little.

"Look, I gotta get ready to go on stage, but I'll see you when I'm done. Wish me luck. Pray for the rain Gods. I need some paper hurricaning round here." Mocha laughed.

"You got this boo!" I yelled back as I watched her phat ass jiggle. I was definitely feeling my drinks now.

I had the waitress move my drinks to a table closer to the front and as I walked up to my seat, I heard a dude yell, *that is that bitch.*

"A yo' your name Brittney?" some big dude asked walking up on me like he was about to do something.

When I heard the name Brittney, I knew it was from my work with Sonny. With the dude's tone, I knew what time it was.

"Naw, I'm Kennedi."

"Oh, so you don't know my brother Troy?"

"Sorry I don't," I said, unbothered. I might've been drunk but I wasn't stupid. There was no way this nigga was about to catch me slipping.

"Bitch why are you lying? I seen you with him the night he got shot," the dude shot back.

"Aye, Kennedi, you good." a familiar voice called out. It was Brooks. He walked over exposing his .45 on his hip. "We good over here?" he said standing toe to toe with the guy.

"Wassup Brooks? You know her."

"Yeah, why wassup?"

"She look like this chick name Brittney who set my brother up," the guy informed.

"Nigga, her name Kennedi so she good," Brooks replied. He looked so sexy while defending me with his bow-legged ass. I immediately missed when Malcolm took charge of a room like this.

"Oh, my bad, shawty," the guy said backing up like he didn't want any trouble from Brooks.

"You still causing trouble? I guess some things never change." Brooks smiled.

"Whatever. What you doing in here?"

"I came here to meet my man. What are *you* doing in here, Ma? You probably a long way from home."

"I'm not that far away. Besides, I needed to unwind. I came to see one of my friends dance."

Before Brooks could respond, the DJ's voice came through the speakers.

"Coming to the stage, the sexy lady y'all all have been waiting for, Missss...Mocha..."

"Mulla-la Ya-yo...Bitch betta have my money..."

Rihanna blazed from the speakers as Mocha went to work. Immediately I grabbed my red Birkin bag, ran to the stage and start throwing stacks, showing love. It felt good being the old me. Even if it was for one night, it felt so damn good. I was drunk as shit at this point. As I stumbled back to my seat, Brooks gave me that, *it's time for you to go,* look.

"Give your girl your car keys, you going with me."

"Why should I?"

"Because you fucked up, that's why. You in good hands, Ma," he said, licking his bottom lip.

As soon as Mocha got off stage I did as I was told for a change.

"Are you sure you're gonna be okay? I can leave now and take you home. Do you even know this guy? I mean he's cute and all, but that don't mean the nigga ain't crazy," Mocha said with concern.

"I'm good. I've been knowing him for years. He got me," I explained.

"Okay. Text me later," she said before walking off.

Brooks opened the door for me like a gentleman. This was the shit I missed about the old Malcolm. I loved Malcolm, but he wasn't the man I fell in love with anymore. I missed how we used to be, before the accident. I needed that old thing back, even if it was just for tonight.

As I grabbed on the seat of Brooks expensive jeans, his manhood came to immediate attention. He was definitely packing. He was so put together. From his sharp shape up to his well-manicured shadow beard, he was definitely turning me on.

"Cut that shit out Kennedi, you drunk."

"I want you."

"No you don't. I'm just taking you to my spot to sleep that shit off."

"Nigga," ain't nobody drunk," was the last thing I remember saying.

The next morning I woke up with a splitting headache, in an oversized tee, and laying on at least 400 thread count sheets. Looking around, I immediately saw a portion of Philly's beautiful skyline which meant I was in some type of high-rise apartment or condo overlooking the city.

"Good morning drunk ass."

I looked over at Brooks. "Oh shit! What time is it?"

"It's 11:00. Drink this Gatorade so you don't throw up in my bed."

I looked over at his bare chest. "Oh my God. What happened? Did we…"

"Naw man. Your horny ass kept trying to rape me last night until you threw up all over me." He laughed.

"Are you serious?" I was so embarrassed.

"Dead ass serious. Your clothes were a mess so I gave you one of my t-shirts," Brooks said with a smile, exposing his grill, and dimples. He was so damn cute.

"I'm sorry." I drank some Gatorade, then reached over to rub his leg. Even though I was sober for some reason I was horny as shit. I instantly imagined his thick dick inside my walls which made my clitoris throb.

"It's all good. Man don't start nothing girl. I'll have you leaving your husband," he joked.

"You can't make me do anything unless I want to, and this

is what I want to do," I said climbing on him.

"Kiss me," I begged.

"Don't get yourself into nothin' you can't handle, Ma. I'm warnin' you I can be addictive. When you layin' in bed wit' yo' man, the thought of me bein' inside you gonna drive your ass crazy. Look at you, gettin' my shorts all messed up," he whispered as my wetness sat right on his Nike basketball shorts.

"What cologne is that?"

"Chanel Platinum."

"It smells so good."

"Get up and get dressed girl. I know people probably waitin' on you."

Even though my pussy was soaking wet, reality quickly set in. I'd stayed out all night and hadn't been home so I knew that Malcolm was beating my ass on sight when I arrived. I had no idea how I was gonna get out of this shit. For some reason, I knew my business with Brooks was far from over, but right now wasn't a good time. I had more important shit to take care of.

19 Charlotte

"Please hurry and get me out of here. He shot her! He shot her!" I yelled.

"Charlotte please calm down. Who are you talking about?" Rafael inquired.

"Bryan…he shot Karla!"

"What? Are you serious?"

"Yes!"

"I'ma kill that muthafucka. When did this happen? Did you actually see this?"

Just like Rafael, I was also in shock. "Right in my hospital room. He shot her in the back after she pulled a gun out on Sonny. How am I gonna get Gianni back now?"

"Oh my God is she alive?"

"When Sonny didn't see any blood, after Bryan shot her, he lifted up her shirt. She was wearing a bulletproof vest. But Rafael, I could still tell she was hurt."

"Where are Sonny and Bryan now? Where's Karla? Where's my fucking sister?" I could tell there was a bit of relief in Rafael's voice but he was still mad.

"I don't know. They rushed her out of here fast. Sonny's gonna come back to get me tomorrow once I'm released so you gotta get here before he does. Karla was gonna tell me where Gianni was. She was gonna help me Rafael, I just know it. Please come and get me!" I yelled in a panic.

"Charlotte, listen to me. I need you to calm down! Did any hospital personnel come in? Do they know anything?"

"No, Bryan used a silencer, so I don't think they heard the gunshot."

"Look, if someone comes in, don't answer any questions and play it cool. Karla texted me an encrypted message a few hours ago, so I need to check something out. I'll be there as soon as I can."

"Rafael please hurry."

"I will."

"I love you."

"I love you, too."

Just like that those words fell out of my mouth. It had been a long time before I used those three words outside of Gianni. Rafael was special and I was falling for him deep. How the hell could we escape this world without being killed? I was so confused yet frustrated. It felt as if a 300 lb. man was sitting on my chest. I didn't know if I was coming or going. I needed air. Grabbing for the remote I requested my nurse. I hoped Nina was on duty. For some reason, she was easy to talk to.

"Hi, Mrs. Sabatino. How can I help you?" a young white nurse with red hair walked in.

"My name is Mrs. Fitzgerald…"

"Charlotte right? Your paperwork says…"

"Look, my name is Charlotte Fitzgerald. Where's Nina? Is she working today?"

"No. She had a family emergency. I'm filling in. Now, what can I help you with?"

"I need to go home."

"Actually you're in luck. Before you buzzed me I was just wrapping up your discharge papers. Your doctor is actually releasing you tonight."

"My husband did this, didn't he?"

"Umm…I don't know what you're talking about ma'am. It could be that we need the bed. You should be out of here in a couple of hours."

I missed my daughter so much and I could feel myself starting to lose it. Just that quick, Sonny had ruined my chances of getting Gianni back. For all I knew, Karla could be dead by now.

Still in pain, I carefully made my way out of bed. Going over to the closet, someone already had a brand new Pink outfit and a bra and panty set as well, from Victoria Secret in the small closet. I'd already taken a shower earlier so I decided to take off my gown and slip on the clothes so I would be ready when Rafael came to pick me up.

Two hours went by and Rafael still hadn't shown up. I was starting to become anxious.

*Where are you?*I texted him

I waited five minutes before texting him again when he didn't respond. *Rafael, answer me. You need to hurry and pick me up.*

Again...no response.

I was worried, sick. Did Sonny and Rafael go to blows? I was in the dark and had no idea what was going on. *Maybe he was on his way?* I thought to myself trying to stay calm.

I started to doze off, when a middle-aged nurse walked in the room pushing a wheelchair.

"Are you ready to go home?" she asked in a familiar tone.

As soon as she looked up over her glasses at me, I got a better view and immediately panicked.

"What the fuck are you doing here? Get out of my room! I'm not going anywhere with you!"

"Oh you better, if you want to stay alive," Ernestine said dressed in blue scrubs as if she was really a part of the staff.

"I'm calling security," I said, reaching for the hospital phone on the bed.

"Put the damn phone down. I'm here to help you. My son told me what happened. I'm not going to hurt you."

"Ernestine. Why should I trust you? You helped kidnap my daughter."

"And I've regretted it ever since. I know the reason why Karla took your daughter now. It was to protect her from Sonny and me. She really is fond of Gianni."

"If Karla was trying to protect my daughter from you and Sonny, then why should I go with you?"

"Charlotte what other choices do you have?" she asked.

"Rafael will come help me. I'm going to call him."

"Look girl! He's downstairs waiting. Now you can stay here and fuss with me and get us both killed by Sonny, or you can trust me."

She can tell I was hesitant.

"Look, I know this seems crazy but I really am here to help you. Sonny is a maniac and needs to be stopped once and for all."

Not going with my gut instinct and stepping out on faith, I willingly allowed Ernestine to push me through the hall right past the nurse's station as if she was a real RN.

"Where are you taking me? You're going the wrong way," I stated.

"Look, it's best that we go this way by the ER. They have part of the lot blocked off in the front. Plus, I can't risk running into Sonny. Who knows where he is?"

"Okay," I whispered, nervous as hell.

When Ernestine and I finally made it down to the ER, I immediately spotted Nina who was in tears and a deep conversation with some woman. She was also trying to calm this guy down.

"Hold on, Ernestine."

"We gotta go," she replied even though I ignored her.

Nina!" I called out. "Is everything okay?"

"Look we don't have time for this," Ernestine warned, but it was too late, Nina was already approaching us.

"Hold on, that's one of my patients," Nina said to the guy as she walked over.

"Hey Charlotte. Are you getting out?" she questioned.

I nodded. "Yeah, I am."

"Then why are you going this way? All patients are discharged in front of the hospital," Nina informed. She looked at Ernestine confused. "Are you new?"

"Yes, I am," Ernestine replied with confidence.

"I was looking for you this morning, but they said you had a family emergency," I said, directing the attention off of Ernestine.

"Yes. The little girl that I watch drank some bleach, and now we're dealing with CPS and their BS."

I covered my mouth. "Oh my goodness, is she going to be

okay?"

"It's not looking good right now. The doctors and CPS won't let her father see her."

"Where's her mother?" I questioned.

Nina shook her head. "Who knows? We've been calling her forever."

"Well, I'll definitely keep you in my prayers," I said.

"Thanks. Charlotte, I hope everything works out for you. You are really a good person," Nina replied.

"Mommy, Mommy!"

The sound of someone calling for their mother made my heart sink, and instantly caught my attention. As I turned around to see where the voice was coming from, tears instantly filled my eyes. I thought I was dreaming as my daughter ran up to me with a huge smile.

"Mommy, I missed you!" Gianni said hugging me tight.

Even though I was in pain I didn't care.

"Be careful, you don't want to hurt Mommy's bruises," Rafael said, running in behind her.

I couldn't hold back the tears as I kissed my daughter all over her face, then gave her a massive bear hug. "Baby. I missed you, too. Are you okay? Let me look at you," I said, inspecting my baby girl for bruises or scars.

"She's fine, Charlotte," Rafael assured.

"Where was she? How did you get her?" I asked in a panic.

"Let's discuss that part later." Rafael stated in return.

"What are you doing in here? You're supposed to be out-side waiting for us?" Ernestine looked pissed.

"Gianni couldn't wait, so she jumped out of the car and ran inside once I told her who we were picking up. I told Gianni you were in a car accident but that you were going to be okay," Rafael informed me.

"Look, we gotta get out of here now," Ernestine added.

"Mommy! Mommy! Auntie Karla said you wanted me to spend time with her and my cousin Cruz. We had fun Mommy!" Gianni yelled.

I kissed her once again. "You did?" *Cousin Cruz*, I thought.

Who is that? It was odd to see how happy she was. I just knew that when we were reunited that she would be traumatized and distant. Instead, she seemed happier now than before.

"Where is Cruz?" Ernestine asked.

"He's fine. He's with family." Rafael looked at Ernestine like she should know what that meant without going into details.

"Well it looks like someone is happy to see you, so let me get back over here before my boss hurts somebody," Nina said as we all looked over there at the guy she was referring to. He was going off on all of the hospital personnel.

I was so happy to finally see my daughter that I'd totally forgot that she was still standing there.

"Mommy, that's the nice man I met!" Gianni yelled as she took off running towards him.

"Gianni!" I yelled but she was already over there hugging this strange man. He was disfigured, and looked a bit scary. I didn't know where the hell, Gianni could've possibly know this man from. "Gianni! Get over here now!" I could already tell that I was going to be even more overprotective of her.

Rafael instantly ran over and got Gianni then apologized to the man. If I could've gotten out of my wheelchair fast enough, I would've snatched her up. I couldn't risk losing her again. As Rafael and Gianni walked towards me, the guy waved and nodded his head. I mouthed, sorry, and for some reason we locked eyes for a quick second right before Nina joined him back at the registration desk.

"Gianni you can't run away like that. You scare Mommy when you do that okay?"

"Okay Mommy, but I met the man at the restaurant with Auntie Karla. He has a baby."

"He does," I said as Rafael and Ernestine ushered us out of the ER.

"That was weird. Gianni is never that open to strangers," I whispered to Rafael as he helped me into the car.

"I know right. Be gentle with her. She has no clue what she's been through," he responded.

"Does Sonny know you have her?"

"No, and he won't," Ernestine interjected. She helped Gianni in the backseat, as I sat up front to get details from Rafael without Gianni hearing us.

As we pulled off, I looked back at my baby and smiled. I couldn't believe I had her back. She must've really been exhausted because she was sleep within five minutes. Reaching for the volume, I turned up the music so she couldn't hear me.

"So, where was Gianni?"

"At my cousin's house. I got a text from an unknown number, 1026. That's my cousin's address."

"Oh my goodness, so is Karla okay?"

"I don't know. When I got there I realized my cousin sent the text. Karla told her if she didn't hear from her by a certain time to text me. That was always our code. We always met up there in case of an emergency."

"Why didn't you check there before? Did you know she was there the whole time? Were you in on it, too?" I whispered pissed off.

"Are you crazy? Do you think I would enjoy watching you suffer? I would do anything to see you smile. Is that what you think of me?" Rafael whispered back with disappointment.

"No, I just don't know what to think."

"I went to my mom for help because she was the only person who could help you at this point."

"You really trust her?" I mouthed in a deep whisper.

"Yes, of course. She's my mom," he whispered back annoyed and looked up at his rearview mirror. "So Ma, have you heard anything about Karla yet?" Rafael asked looking at Ernestine.

"Sonny isn't answering my calls, but I know how to get his attention. He's fucked with my daughter for the last time."

"Oh now you want to stand up for Karla? Ma, this is nothing new. What did Sonny do to you that now all of a sudden you want to get his attention?"

"He killed my granddaughter. That sick bastard killed her."

Rafael seemed shocked. "What? Who are you talking about...Karlie?"

"Yes. He's sick and I hate him now more than ever," Ernestine added.

"Ma, what are you talking about? I thought…"

"Well, you thought wrong, Rafael. Sonny admitted it out of anger this morning. He set Karla up to take the fall. He did it all on purpose."

"Wait…so who's coke did Karlie overdose on? Was it Sonny's?" Rafael asked.

Ernestine nodded. "Yes, he told her it was candy. That sick fuck killed his own daughter, just to get rid of Karla. All this time I resented Karla for wanting to have his baby, but when Karlie died I hated her even more. I always wondered how she could be so careless and allow Karlie to get into her drugs. But come to find out Sonny was the mastermind behind this whole shit. He knew that would be the wedge between me and Karla. He knew how I felt about my granddaughter. He knew that would make me hate Karla for sure."

I could hear Ernestine's voice shaking as if she was trying to fight back her tears, trying to stay strong. I couldn't believe what I was hearing. Sonny was sicker than I thought.

After listening to Ernestine go into further detail on how Sonny set Karla up for the murder of her own child it all made sense. Karla had caught Sonny feeding her daughter cocaine and with his power he penned it all on her. He not only took Karla's daughter away, but he also took eight years of her life when she went to prison. Having my new alliance with Rafael and Ernestine made me feel a little safe, but my nerves were still all over the place.

"What the fuck Ma! Why are you just telling me this after all these years? Sonny needs to die. I'm going to fucking kill him!" Rafael spat.

"Son. Be patient. He's gonna regret the day he ever met me. I know that man very well. I know where he's weak. Trust me he's going to pay," Ernestine boasted.

"Sonny's calling me now Ma, should I answer?"

Ernestine shook her head. "No, don't answer. Let him sweat a bit."

"So, where are we going? Rafael, we can't go back there. Let's run away together. Me, you, and Gianni," I finally said.

"Run away together? Wait…son are you fucking this girl? Are you fucking Sonny's wife?" Ernestine questioned.

"Ma, have some respect," Rafael responded.

"That was never part of the plan. Your dick is going to ruin everything. What the hell have you done?" Ernestine shouted.

"What plan?" I asked as Rafael lower his head ashamed. Suddenly, something didn't feel right. "Rafael, where the hell are you taking me?"

20 Malcolm

"What the hell is wrong with you people? My daughter could be dying in there. She needs me!" I yelled.

"Sir, if you don't calm down we're gonna have security escort you out of the building. You're disturbing the other patients," a nurse warned.

"Fuck that! I'm not gonna calm down. I don't even know if my daughter is okay. Why am I still down here in the ER when my daughter has been moved to another floor? This is not right! I deserve to know what's going on! I'm her father!"

Nina ran up to me, trying to calm me down again. We'd been in the emergency room all night. When we first arrived, the doctors were updating me on Milan's status but about two hours later I was approached by CPS on some bullshit about child endangerment. I wasn't able to see Milan since. Nina had already schooled me on how to handle the CPS bitch by not answering any questions until I had a lawyer who specialized in this type of shit. If it wasn't for Nina I probably would've said some shit to incriminate myself, so I thanked God that she'd been by my side the entire time.

"Malcolm, please calm down and listen to me. I know you're upset but you've gotta get it together. For one, this is my job so you can't be disrespectful to my co-workers. Hell, I just got this job so I can't fuck up. However, the bigger issue is that you don't have an ID or any insurance information for Milan, so you can't even prove that you're her father, so we gotta stay cool. The staff calling CPS is protocol due to the circumstances of Milan drinking the bleach. Under normal circumstances, security would've been put us out but because I work here they're looking out for us. We really need to get in touch with Vee. She needs to let them know that you really are her father," Nina informed.

"Fucking bitch! Why hasn't she called us back? What mother would leave their fucking child all this time?" I yelled then threw a chair across the waiting room.

"Okay sir, you have to leave…now!" the same nurse stated with authority.

"Malcolm we need to go. I've tried to pull as many strings as possible, but you're not making things easy for me," Nina said.

"Fuck that. I'm not going anywhere!"

Suddenly, a heavy, balding security guard appeared. "Sir, if you don't leave the premises, we will call the police," he threatened.

"No need sir. We're leaving," Nina responded as she pulled me toward the door. She looked at on older lady who seemed offended. "I'm so sorry ma'am."

I desperately wanted to kick the out of shape security guards ass but knew that wasn't a good idea. Nina managed to pull me outside, then finally convinced me that it was best for Milan if we left and tried to get in touch with Vee. I hoped she'd be home by the time I got there even though I wasn't looking forward to the brawl I'm sure we were going to have. She was definitely gonna get in my shit about me leaving Milan alone to get hurt but I was furious at her as well for blatantly not answering my calls. Both Nina and I were quiet the entire ride to my house.

When we arrived, my eyes widened when I didn't see Kennedi's car in the garage. I still couldn't believe she wasn't at home. I quickly pulled out my phone to dial her number. This time instead it went straight to voicemail. I was furious. Instead of venting to Nina though, I decided to go inside and take a much needed shower. I hoped that would calm me down because it certainly felt like I was about to go fucking postal.

"I'm going upstairs to take a shower. Why don't you use the guest bathroom and do the same?" I suggested. "We've been out forever."

"I do need to take a shower, but I'll wait until I get home."

"Are you sure?"

"Yeah. I just don't feel comfortable doing that here after what happened."

"I understand."

"I can tell you something else that's not comfortable."

"What?" I asked.

"The fact that I still don't have any panties on."

A few dirty images raced through mind. "Are you serious?"

"Yeah, after we heard Milan choking and ran into the kitchen. I panicked so badly that I put my clothes back on but obviously forgot my panties."

"So, you've been like that all day. Eww…that's nasty," I joked.

"Well, it wouldn't be the first I went without any," Nina enlightened.

The thought of her tight pussy on my dick again instantly made me hard. I slowly slid my hand down her ass.

She moved away. "I can't Malcolm."

"Yeah, I know," I said, suddenly thinking of my baby girl. "I'm gonna go shower now."

"I'm hungry so I'll go try to find my panties then fix us something to eat while you shower."

"Cool. Just make sure you wash your hands," I responded. She might've thought I was joking but I was dead serious.

Twenty minutes later, I walked back downstairs feeling refreshed. Nina had prepared a fruit salad for me. However, when I sat down at the breakfast bar I noticed that she was crying.

"What's wrong Nina? Why are you crying?" I quickly jumped up to console her.

"Malcolm. Everything is wrong. I lost my virginity to a married man, and his child drunk bleach while I committed the ultimate sin. It's all my fault. I love Milan. I feel horrible. What are we going to tell Vee?"

"She's going to blame me. With my OCD, she's going to know this was all my fault not yours."

"But I was supposed to be watching her."

I rubbed her back in a circular motion. "No, you weren't. You were off. I called you over. She can't blame you. I will not let her."

"Okay."

"Do you trust me?" I asked.

Nina nodded. "Yes."

"Don't worry, Milan is gonna be fine."

"I love that little girl so much Malcolm," Nina said, bursting into tears again.

"Come on stop crying. Let's go in the family room and sit down. Did you find your underwear?"

"No, I didn't which is strange because they were right on the floor in the office."

"Don't worry, I'll help you look. Maybe they're under the rug."

Nina sniffed. "Oh, by the way, I called the hospital and asked one of the other nurses that I'm cool with to go check on Milan. She's gonna call me back as soon as she knows something."

"Man, I don't know what I would do without you. That fucking wife of mine, man, I'm ready to call it quits. Her not coming home again and not even answering the phone, I know for a fact she's cheating now," I laid across the couch, pulled Nina down with me and held her close.

She wiped her remaining tears away. "Malcolm, things are starting to get weird. Why is it that you don't have an ID? What grown man walks around without a driver's license?"

"To be honest, I'm the one who has a fear of driving now so I didn't want one. I was hit by a drunk driver Nina, so getting behind the wheel is just something I don't like to do anymore. I wouldn't look like this if it wasn't for that awful day."

"I understand, but things are just starting to seem off. Where is your other family? Do you not have contact with any of them?"

"I mean the crazy thing is I can't remember what might've happened two or three years ago but I remember my mother dying. She died of AIDS. She was on drugs, but I don't really like to talk about it."

"Malcolm I just gotta feeling that something isn't right and we need to get to the bottom of this. After we deal with Milan, we really need to figure out the missing pieces. I just can't believe that you have no one but your wife. That seems odd. Are you sure you have no other family?"

I was starting to get irritated but knew Nina was only trying to help.

"No."

"Oh my God, Malcolm. Did you see the lady at the hospital in the wheelchair?"

"The lady you were talking to, with the little girl?"

"Yes. That's one of my patients. Her name is Charlotte Fitzgerald. Does that name ring a bell?"

"Not really."

"Malcolm, her daughter hugged you like she knew you. Are you sure you just don't remember?"

"Well, the little girl I met at the restaurant, remember I was telling you about a cute little girl that spilled juice all over me. That was her."

"Fitzgerald isn't a common last name especially for black people so it's funny how you both share that," she continued to badger.

"Nope…I've never seen that lady in my life," I replied. "Look, I'm starting to get a headache and…"

"Okay. I'll take care of it."

Just like that, Nina grabbed a bottle of Advil next to the microwave, placed two in her hand then grabbed some Fiji water out of the refrigerator. This girl was definitely wife material. She'd been there for me and did everything that my wife should've been doing. It hurt that Vee wasn't here by my side, or answering my calls, at a time like this. I mean, this was her daughter, not Nina's. Where the hell could she be that was more important, than being here with me?

"Nina, I appreciate you."

"Malcolm, where else should I be? I care about you guys."

Giving her a passionate kiss, we laid on the couch and fell asleep minutes later.

The smell of gasoline got stronger. My daughter was reaching out for me, but I couldn't save her.

"Daddy help me, please help me!" she cried.

I couldn't get to her. The fire was too hot. I couldn't reach her.

"Sonny, please save my daughter and my wife. I can't live without them."

"Your family is dead. I didn't get a chance to get to your mistress, but your wife and daughter are dead."

"No. I'll get you your money. Please let them live."

"It's too late. They're gone."

"Noooooooo!"

"Motherfucka are you fucking this bitch in my house?" Vee yelled as she started throwing blows waking me up out my sleep and from the weird dream I had. I didn't know anyone named Sonny so I wondered what the dream was about or meant.

"Bitch are these yours?" Vee said as she tried to stuff the pink thong down Nina's throat. My reaction was delayed. I was still out of it and it took several more seconds to realize what was going on.

"Vee, stop it!" I yelled as she tried to beat Nina to a pulp. Nina screamed and cried. I honestly didn't want to take the 'I can explain' route because I honestly couldn't. How the hell was I going to explain a pair of panties on the floor? I had to face it...I was caught.

"Malcolm, how could you do this? How could you cheat on me? How could you fuck this bitch in my house? I can't believe I came home earlier and found those nasty ass panties on my office floor!" I could tell from her expression that she was hurt.

"So what time did you get home?" I asked trying to turn the tables.

"Don't fucking question me. You have no right to question me after this shit," Vee fired back. "Nina, get the fuck out of my house now!"

"She's not going anywhere," I replied.

"What do you mean, Malcolm?" Vee asked in shock.

"She's not going anywhere! Where the fuck, have you been? You have some fucking nerve!"

"I've been working. She's getting the fuck out of here and you can go with her!" Vee belted then looked at Nina with disgust. "Bitch I trusted you!"

"It's not what you think, Vee," Nina held her nose as it bled.

"Not what I think…what the fuck am I supposed to think. Those panties aren't mine. I shop at La Perla bitch, not Target. Besides, I know I just saw you hugged up with *my* husband on *my* fucking leather couch that *I* bought."

"So, you're worried about me fucking Nina, but not your daughter!"

"Why would I be worried about Milan?"

I quickly realized that I hadn't told Vee about the accident yet.

"Where is Milan?" Vee suddenly asked.

I didn't respond. It was difficult to let the words escape my mouth.

"You know what…since you don't want Nina to leave, I'm packing up my daughter and we're getting the fuck out of here," Vee informed in a matter of fact tone.

I tried my best to choose my words carefully but they just blurted out.

"Milan is in the hospital!"

"In the hospital? What the fuck are you talking about? Stop bullshitting," Vee responded.

"It's not a joke."

"Why the hell is she in the hospital?" Vee asked with tears in her eyes. Suddenly, my wife charged at me like a raging bull. "Why the fuck didn't you tell me?"

"Look, I left you multiple messages, texts, and you never responded."

"Why the fuck is my daughter at the hospital alone while you're in here fucking this bitch? Why is she there?" Vee screamed.

I lowered my head for a moment. "She drank some bleach."

I could tell Vee was furious and scared at the same time.

"I was asleep. I didn't realize I left the bleach for her to reach it. Now the CPS…" I tried to say.

"CPS? Nobody is taking my daughter because of your dumb, burnt up ass!"

"Look, we called your phone several times and you never called back! If your whore ass wasn't out fucking someone else and would've called back, then you would've known."

"Malcolm I'm gonna go. I'll call you if I hear anything," Nina stated.

"No, don't go."

"So you're really fucking this slut, huh? I mean why are you begging her not to leave?" Vee looked at Nina with an evil scowl. "Bitch I'll make sure you never work in this town again. You let my daughter drink bleach while you were fucking my husband? You're finished!" Vee screamed as she searched for her phone inside of her purse. It had been ringing non-stop.

"What the hell do you want Lee-Lee?" Vee asked just before screaming into the phone. "What? Noooooo, Lee-Lee nooooo!" she screamed as she fell to the floor in tears.

Her screams were painful. Whatever she had going on revoked emotions I didn't even know she had.

21 Kennedi

"Was that the hospital? Is that about Milan?" Malcolm asked repeatedly as I ignored him.

He knew nothing about my former life so there was no need to tell him anything now. My heart felt like it had split in a million pieces as I rushed toward the door and left. I was in so much pain and had to get to the hospital fast. As I drove towards the freeway, Lee-Lee's words played continuously in my head. *"Chase dumb ass done killed hisself ova that damn down low thug. He so damn stupid."*

I couldn't believe that my only son was dead. This couldn't be true. As sick as it might've sound, I used to pray for this day, that I no longer had to worry about Chase and China haunting my new life, but not like this. I never would've wanted Chase to commit suicide. He was still my son. I couldn't help but to think if this was karma for me being such a horrible mother? *Did my absence play a part in him killing himself?* My world was falling apart and I felt alone. No matter how much money I had, I still wasn't happy. It felt as if my life was becoming unglued by the second, and there was nothing I could do about it. Could things get any worse? My daughter was in the hospital, my husband was fucking around on me, and now my son was dead. Everything was going wrong all at once. However, there was nothing I could do about Chase before I went to check on my baby first.

As I pulled into the parking lot everything was blocked off due to the construction. I turned towards the ER and parked in the lot. Pulling right into a handicap space I jumped out and ran inside. After getting Milan's room number from the information desk, I quickly made my way upstairs.

"Hi, My name is Kennedi Fitzgerald and my daughter Milan Fitzgerald was admitted yesterday. Can you tell me which direction her room is in?" I asked the young black nurse at the desk. "I have the room number, but I'm so nervous I can't even think straight."

As she typed in all the information I gave her from Milan's date of birth to this and that, she finally looked up from the screen.

"Yes, Mrs. Fitzgerald, we still need someone to fill out Milan's paperwork. I also need your ID and an insurance card to give to patient registration."

"Excuse me lady, I need to know where my daughter is and if she's okay. I don't have time to go thru a whole bunch of bullshit paperwork! I need answers!"

"Look, all I'm trying to do is help you. Your husband got put out of the hospital last night for being completely disruptive and I don't want that to happen again. Your daughter needs you. I'm a mother myself and I understand how you feel."

"If you understand, then you should know that I need to be with my baby."

"I realize that and it's one of the reasons why I'm trying to help. At least give me your ID and insurance card and we'll start from there. The paperwork is necessary so we're aware of any allergies as well as family medical history. This can make a difference in the way that the doctors treat her."

"Fine." I went into my handbag and pulled out my wallet to give the nurse all she needed.

She looked at the ID. "Oh, I thought your name was Venus. Your husband kept saying that name."

Luckily Maricar's lazy, trifffling ass hadn't given me a middle name. "Oh, that's my middle name. I go by that mostly."

"Oh, that's understandable."

After calling down to patient registration to let them know all my information had been photocopied, she handed me several papers to fill out. Once that was done, she looked up with a smile. "Okay Mrs. Fitzgerald, let me get you to your daughter. Right this way. Also I wanted to give you a heads up, CPS has gotten involved. It's hospital protocol to report to poison control as well as CPS when cases dealing with neglect are presented. Mother to mother, I'm just letting you know what you're up against. Your husband put on a show last night and the CPS representative wasn't happy at all. They've been trying to contact you."

"I was out of town on business," I said as we got on the elevator. I was a nervous wreck. Once we got to the room there was a guard standing outside.

"Hey, Travis, this is Mrs. Fitzgerald. She's here to see her daughter," the nurse informed. I could tell she was trying to help.

"I've been given strict orders that this patient is not able to have any visitors," he stated.

"Please sir, that's my daughter. I've been out of town and I need to know if she's okay."

He shook his head. "I'm sorry ma'am…"

"Well, who can I talk to? I know there's someone here that can help me," I pleaded.

"Let me call my supervisor and see what I can do," the nurse replied.

"Yes, please thank you. She needs me."

As I waited for the nurse to call, I looked at the guard in a desperate plea. "Can I just peek inside until this gets resolved?"

He sighed then looked around. "I guess."

"Thank you sir," I said, before pushing the cracked door opened a bit. The minute I saw my baby hooked up to so many tubes, I instantly broke down.

"Nooooo. I can't lose another child. I can't." I fell to the floor in tears.

"Ma'am, let me help you up. It's going to be okay, the young Hispanic security guard said, offering his compassion.

"What would be okay is if I could go inside."

"I'm sorry. I'm just trying to do my job. I would help you if I could, but I need my job."

"Whatever." I brushed him off between sobs before the nurse returned with her supervisor. I got up off the floor and tried to get myself together.

"Hi, Mrs. Fitzgerald, I'm the Hospital Administrator, Zoey

Bradshaw. I'm aware of what's going on with your daughter. Let's get into a private area so we can fill you in. Call the doctor." She looked up at the nurse as she led me to a conference room not far from Milan's room.

"Ma'am, I just need to see my daughter. I know my husband was upset last night, but that shouldn't have anything to do with me!" I followed her into the room and took a seat.

"Mrs. Fitzgerald, we have protocols that we have to adhere to at the hospital. Your daughter's situation is severe. Now I've been informed that you still need to fill out the paperwork and that we have all of your insurance info," She said sliding a clipboard across the table. As I listened to her talk a hole in my head, I quickly filled out the paperwork needed and minutes later, an older white woman dressed in a cheap looking thrift store suit walked in.

"Hello, I'm Dr. Walker, and this is Erin Freeman, from Child Protective Services."

"Glad to meet you both," I said as proper as I could. I didn't want them to think I was some ignorant young black girl.

"Mrs. Fitzgerald, your daughter ingested a large amount of bleach, and quite honestly she's fighting for her life. We have her heavily sedated right now to give the medicine a chance to work, but things don't look that well."

"What do you mean? Is my daughter is going to die?"

"We're not saying that Mrs. Fitzgerald, but still want you to know how sick your daughter is," the doctor stated. "Actually your nurse and nanny, Nina informed us that she administered Milan milk to dilute the bleach in her system while the ambulance was on the way so thank God for that. Things may have been fatal if that hadn't taken place. We believe that she swallowed way too much. There is major damage in her gastrointestinal tract. In addition to that, Milan was choking and began to vomit while Nina was trying to administer the fluids, which caused an acid that damaged a lot of internal tissue and her esophagus. Another major concern is the amount of fluid on her lungs."

"So are you saying that there's nothing you can do? Is she going to survive this?" My hands shook as I waited for the doctor's response.

"We're doing the best that we can."

"Please help my baby! I need to see my baby!" I screamed as the doctor's words fell on deaf ears.

"Mrs. Fitzgerald, I have a couple of questions for you, I am..."

"Ms. Bradshaw, let's let her see her daughter first and then we can handle all of the other protocols. I think both she and her baby need each other right now," Zoey suggested.

"No problem. I'll wait in here," Erin replied.

"Let's go," Dr. Walker said.

"Thank you," I said, gathering my belongings. As we walked back to the room my text alerted. It was Brooks.

Wassup Ma? I just heard about Chase. You good?

No...I need you. I'm in Jersey at the hospital

Yo, you a'ight Ma?

It's my baby!

After getting the address from the doctor, I asked Brooks to meet me here. I didn't want to be alone. As we approached Milan's room I closed my eyes and took a deep breath.

"We'll give you some time alone," the doctor said, as she and Ms. Bradshaw closed the door.

"Hi baby girl, it's Mommy." My eyes were flooded with tears. I cried like someone was beating me.

"Why God? Why my baby?"

She was too young to be going through this. She was just a baby. There were tubes in her mouth and connected through her stomach. She was also hooked up to a breathing machine and there were all type of machines going.

How the hell did Malcolm allow this to happen? While he was busy up Nina's ass my daughter was put in danger. This was both of their faults, but Nina had to go. As my blood boiled, I cried with so much anger. I kissed her forehead, rubbed her arm, and stared at her for what seemed like forever until Brooks texted informing me that he'd arrived.

"Sir, I'll be back," I said to the security officer as I made my way down to the lobby. As I turned the corner there Brooks stood, concerned, dressed in an all white linen outfit and some

Louis Vuitton sneakers. Taking off his shades, he walked in my direction.

"Ma, what the hell is going on?" He hugged me as we walked over to the couches by the entrance. After filling him on everything, from catching Malcolm with Nina, to CPS, Chase, everything, he continued to hug me as I cried on his chest like a newborn baby.

"Look I know your situation, but you need a real man by your side, Ma. I'm gonna be here for whatever you need. You feel me?"

"That means a lot," I said, looking up at him. He was exactly what I needed. Suddenly, my phone alerted me that I had a text. It was Sonny.

Hey, is this your car here at the hospital?

Yes, you here too?

Yeah. I'm beside your car. Come outside. We need to talk!

I jumped up abruptly. As long as I'd waited to talk to Sonny, my meeting with Brooks would have to end. "Brooks, thanks so much for listening. I have something I have to take care of. I will call you later okay." I said as I jumped up abruptly.

"It's all good. You comin' round the way later?"

"Yeah, I have to deal with everything with Chase next."

"I'm sorry you goin' through all this shit. But you not alone, aight?"

"Okay. I'll call you when I'm on my way down. Thanks again for coming."

"Anything for you," Brooks said as he walked off.

I let him walk ahead of me. Moments later, I spotted the blacked out SUV right beside my car. Once the window rolled down, I could see Sonny sitting in the backseat as he motioned me to the car.

I walked to the truck and got in.

"Wow Kennedi, you look like hell!"

"I feel like it. Sonny, my life is a mess." I started crying again.

"What the hell is going on?"

"My son committed suicide last night, and my baby Milan

is upstairs fighting for her life."

After letting Sonny in on everything that I'd gone through in the past twenty-four hours he was in a state of shock.

"Sweetheart, I know what I have to tell you isn't going to make you feel any better."

"What's going on? Why did you lie to me about Gianni?"

"Okay, I'm a man, and I respect you a great deal so I think now it's time for me to tell you everything. Gianni and Charlotte are both alive."

My body immediately went numb. I stared at him for at least a minute. "What! Sonny how could you do this to me? I trusted you."

"The more you knew, the more you..."

"I would what? You told me I could trust you and you betrayed me Sonny. If I'd never seen Gianni for myself, you would've never told me."

"That's not true. It's all about timing."

"So what does that bitch Charlotte know?"

"Now don't be disrespectful, Kennedi. That's my wife. We're married now."

"What?"

"Yes. We both got what we wanted. I have Malcolm's life, and you have Charlotte's."

"I didn't want Charlotte's life, I wanted my own. So now what? I'm just supposed to go on with my life living this fake marriage? He's not my husband and Charlotte is not your wife if everyone that we thought were dead are still alive."

"Everything is fine. He doesn't even remember who you are," Sonny tried to convince me.

"Well, my mother resurfaced after being gone out of my life for fifteen years and told Malcolm my real name."

"She did what?" Sonny asked as she sat up.

"Sonny, I need you to kill her. She needs to die. Her and that bitch, Nina."

"Why do you want to kill the nanny?"

"Were you listening? She's responsible for my daughter being at this hospital. Her and that damn Malcolm."

"So you want Malcolm dead, too?" Sonny asked with a devilish grin.

"No. I don't like him right now, but I still love him. But I'm also not sure if I even want to be with Malcolm anymore. Shit is bad."

"What happened?"

"He cheated on me with that bitch! I thought having her around would help, but it's actually ruined everything that I fought so hard for."

"Well, consider it all taken care of. Send me a picture of them and their addresses and I'll make sure they both don't make it to next week."

It was the first time I smiled. "Okay, so what's the plan about Gianni and Charlotte? How did you even pull all this off Sonny? I need details," I said, grilling him.

"You don't need to know specifics, you just need to know that they don't know anything about you and they think Malcolm is dead like the rest of the world," he assured.

"Sonny, this is dangerous. Why do you have us so close?"

"I love being close to you." He rubbed my leg as an over-sized guy walked to the truck.

"Sonny, you need to move us again. You have to," I damn near begged.

"No, you're staying right here in Jersey," Sonny ordered.

"Boss," the man interrupted.

"Yes Bryan," Sonny answered.

"Charlotte is gone. They said she checked out of her room last night."

"What! That fucking bitch! That fucking bitch! I'm going to kill that whore! Contact the head of hospital security. I need them to check the fucking cameras! I need to know how this happened! Now Bryan!" Sonny yelled.

What the hell was going on? I wondered.

22 Charlotte

The next morning I woke up in better spirits. I have to admit, being held hostage with Ernestine definitely felt better than being with Sonny. As I opened my eyes to the beautiful bedroom with all of the gold trimmings on the furniture and champagne colored drapes of the two level penthouse suite at the Trump Towers, I definitely couldn't complain about the accommodations. Ernestine had brought us to New York thinking that this was the best place for Sonny not to find us. I was still angry and wasn't speaking to Ernestine or Rafael. Rafael was frustrated that I was giving him the silent treatment.

"Mommy, can I go downstairs and watch cartoons?" Gianni said running out of the bathroom from brushing her teeth. It was so good to see my daughter finally in good spirits.

"No. I want you to stay up here with me."

"But why Mommy? You don't have the TV on. Grandma E says it was okay."

"That's not your grandmother," I quickly snapped.

"She's Auntie Karla's mommy and she's really nice. She got us away from Sonny."

"Go ahead Gianni, but only in the living room. Do not...I repeat do not leave out the door. Do you hear me?"
"I won't Mommy."

"Who the hell does that bitch Ernestine think she is, having my daughter call her Grandma," I mumbled.

After eating a lobster omelet and drinking my mimosa, I carefully laid back on the bed and stared at the paintings on the ceiling. My mind began to wander, just a couple years ago when I was going through my shit with Malcolm, I thought my life was so hard. However, the shit I was going through now, made my life with Malcolm look like a walk in the park.

"So, are you still going to just ignore me?"

"What do you want Rafael?"

"I told you I had nothing to do with my mother bringing you to this hotel. The plan was supposed to be to help you escape, not hold you hostage."

"I don't believe you."

"Why not?" he asked.

"I don't know who to trust anymore."

"That hurts. I risked my life to help you Charlotte and that's what you think of me? You think I'm a liar. That really hurts," Rafael said as he walked out of the room.

A part of me wanted to believe him, but I just didn't know what to think anymore. My heart hurt, because I really felt like the day I was able to get rid of Sonny, that Rafael and I could really have something. He just seemed perfect. As bad as I wanted to make love to him I tried to fight it.

There was a knock at the door.

"Yes," I said as Ernestine pranced her way into my room with a satin robe on like she was trying to be sexy.

"Look sweetheart, I don't know what Sonny, nor my son, sees in you but it's my duty to come clean and let you know that my son had nothing to do with me holding you here. You're a mother, and I hope you would understand that I needed you to get Karla back, the same way you needed Rafael to help you escape from Sonny. I mean darling, what were your options?"

"It could've been just me and Rafael, with my daughter."

"Well, I'm the piece of the puzzle that keeps you both alive. See, now that I know my son really cares for you, I might have to give him what he wants, and erase Sonny out of your lives for good."

"How?"

"By killing him," she blurted out.

Her words were chilling as she turned around and walked out of the room not bothering to close the door. She was serious and I now understood how I needed her. Rafael was telling the truth and now I felt bad. I slowly got up out of the bed to go use the bathroom. As soon as I sat down on the toilet, I could hear Ernestine in a full on argument with someone in the next room. I listened closely so I could hear her conversation.

"Where's my fucking daughter, Sonny?"

"She's around here somewhere. Maybe Marty had her for breakfast, who knows?"

I was so glad the phone was on speaker.

"I'm telling you now, if you hurt my daughter again, Charlotte is dead."

"You bitter old bitch, bring my wife home now."

"You mean your wife and your precious Gianni?"

"You have Gianni?"

"I have them both. Now return Karla unharmed, and you can have your precious family back. Oh and after this I want nothing else to do with you."

"Ernestine, I'm Sonny Sabatino, it's only a matter of time before I reach out and touch you. I have eyes everywhere. Believe that bitch!"

"Hello…hello!" Ernestine said moments later.

Sonny had obviously hung up. His words were chilling. Moments later, Ernestine let out a loud scream of frustration. After hearing that I didn't know if it was all a part of the act or if she really meant what she'd said. All I could do was hope that Ernestine had a plan and that I would be on the winning side. After attempting to use the bathroom I decided to have a talk with Rafael. I walked out of my room and called for him.

"Rafael!"

"Yeah?" he replied in an unenthused tone.

"Where are you?"

"Downstairs."

"Can you come upstairs for a minute?"

"Alright. Let me just finish this last game with Gianni."

Returning back to my room I decided to take a shower. As I entered the bathroom I walked to the shower and turned the water on. After taking off my clothes, I looked at myself in the mirror.

How did I become a mob wife? This was never part of the plan. The first chance I got, this awful weave was coming out and I was going back to the old me. There wasn't much I could do about removing these new breasts and tummy tuck that Sonny paid for, but I did like my new body, minus the cast on my arm.

As I got in the shower I let the water run through my hair and all over my body, I poured body gel in my hand and rubbed it all over me. I felt a sigh of relief. Maybe things would work out in the end, I kept trying to convince myself. Breaking me from my daze Rafael walked in.

"Can I join you? I'm dirty."

"No, I don't want you to come in here," I lied.

"Well I'm coming in anyway," he said as he started taking off his clothes exposing his six-pack. He was so sexy and so hard to resist.

As soon as he got in the shower he started kissing the back of my neck. "So, you don't miss me?"

"Yes, I miss you," I said, turning around and indulging in a passionate kiss.

He rubbed his hands all over my body. As soon as he got to my wet box, his finger slowly entered me. As I moaned he kissed my neck while fucking me with his fingers. First one, then two, and then with no warning, not caring about my injuries, he lifted me off the floor and plastered me against the wall of the shower. As his large dick entered my body, Rafael made love to me as if he meant every stroke. He was perfect. As bad as my body was in pain, I yearned for Rafael like an addicting drug.

"Rafael, you feel so good. Make love to me."

"Shit. I'm about to cum."

"Don't take it out. I want you to cum inside of me."

"You do?"

"Yes."

"You want to have my baby?"

"Yes. Cum in *your* pussy."

Just like that, he did as he was told.

After watching a couple of movies and having dinner, we were all tired and were ready for bed. The more time I spent with

Ernestine I realized she was actually a pretty cool lady. During the last movie, Gianni fell asleep so Rafael carried her upstairs for me and I followed behind.

"Goodnight Ernestine."

"Goodnight Charlotte. Now I see why my son is fond of you. You're a good woman."

"Thank you. That means a lot."

Rafael looked at me with so much hope. He was smiling from ear to ear. As he laid Gianni down in the other bed, he joined me in mine.

"So now what?" I asked as Rafael held me close.

"You're going to be mine. I promise you that."

"That sounds good. Goodnight babe."

"Goodnight sweetheart," Rafael replied.

We both were sleep within minutes.

"Wake the fuck up!" I heard someone say just before being nudged.

Opening up my eyes, I was awakened with the shock of my life.

"Oh my God! What are you doing here?" I screamed. Rafael laid in the bed lifeless as Sonny's nickel plated .45 Magnum was placed in his mouth.

"So, were you being held prisoner or were you in here fucking this traitor?"

"Sonny, where's my daughter?" I asked glancing over at the empty bed.

"I'm like a thief in the night, Charlotte. Now answer me you black bitch!" Sonny yelled right before Ernestine came in the room with Bryan holding a gun to the back of her head.

"Sonny, get that fucking gun out of my son's mouth!" Ernestine ordered with authority as I watched Sonny huddle over top of the man I'd fallen for. I wouldn't be able to live with myself if he killed him.

Sonny gritted his teeth. "Do you think it's okay to fuck

your boss' wife? Huh? I can't hear you…you fucking bastard." He lifted Rafael's wife beater. "Gotta make sure you're not wearing a vest. Your sister got me with that but it will not happen again."

"Sonny please don't, there's nothing going on between us," I pleaded.

"Pull your panties down now!" Sonny demanded. As I pulled my panties down he ordered me to lay back. "Put your finger in that pussy!" I did as he ordered. "Now sit up!"

As I tried to maneuver and sit up he grabbed my wrist then smelled my hand.

"I can smell him all over you…you bitch! You black nigger bitch!" Sonny said as he shoved my head back.

"Sonny, I just got off of my period. I didn't sleep with Rafael. He was just holding me because I was having nightmares again. I don't have my medicine here."

I could only hope that the lie would work.

"So, you're going to kill your son, over a bitch!" Ernestine yelled.

As Sonny took the gun out of Rafael's mouth he got up and pointed the gun at Ernestine.

"Ma, what are you talking about?" Rafael asked confused.

Both Ernestine and Sonny stared at each other in silence like two pit bulls.

"Ma, what the fuck are you talking about?" Rafael questioned again.

"Rafael, Sonny is your father," Ernestine finally replied.

Rafael let out a nervous laugh. "No he's not. I'm a Jr."

"So, Ernestine since you're in the mood to reveal all these secrets then tell it all! Tell it all bitch!" Sonny yelled.

"Tell me what? What the hell is going on?" Rafael jumped off the bed, but Bryan was right there ready to shoot as he and Sonny switched targets.

"Tell you that your precious, whore of a mother, killed your father to be with me," Sonny revealed.

You could hear a pin drop for at least thirty seconds.

"No fucking way. She would never do such a thing!" Rafael said in denial.

"Sonny, stop it!" I yelled.

Sonny looked at me with disgust. "Mind your business bitch! Tell him Ernestine, tell your son what you did you evil bitch! Tell your son what you did when your husband found out about the affair."

It looked like Ernestine wanted to cry. "He was going to tell you Rafael! He was going to tell you he wasn't your father and I didn't want that to happen, so I had to kill him." She pointed at Sonny. "But he's not innocent in all this when he helped me cover it up."

"You lying bitch. I don't know who's worst, you or Sonny," Rafael said, as tears escaped his eyes. "That was my hero. You killed a part of me, Ma. He was my world."

"Blah, blah, blah. I don't want to hear that shit. No time for this weak ass crying shit," Sonny chimed in.

"Fuck you Sonny! You're going straight to hell for what you did! You just want to ruin my kids' lives," Ernestine replied.

"No *you* ruined our lives! You slept with him. It was your choice," Rafael stated with so much pain in his voice.

I wished I could help him. My heart continued to pound as I wondered where Gianni was. I couldn't lose her again.

"Sonny, where's my baby? Please don't hurt her. She's been through enough," I begged.

"Shut your mouth you black bitch before I send you to your maker," Sonny responded.

"Where's my daughter you bastard?" Ernestine yelled.

"In hell with your husband, want to join them?" Sonny asked right before letting off a shot right in the middle of her head.

"Noooooooooo! You fucking bastard!" Rafael jumped up and rushed Sonny as Bryan tried to shoot but couldn't get a good aim. As soon as I could, I made a run for the door in pain and all, but didn't get far. There was a guy waiting right outside the door who grabbed me. Seconds later, all I heard was the sound of someone's silencer going off.

My heart stopped.

23 Malcolm

"Malcolm, I can't believe, Vee!" Nina said as she stormed in my house brushing past me straight into the office.

"What happened?"

"She went to my Dad's pharmacy and lied on me. She told him that she'd fired me because I was caught using drugs in the bathroom. She also told him that I'd been fired from my job at the hospital for stealing drugs. He is furious with me and says if I don't prove that she's lying he will disown me. Malcolm, do you think it's smart for me to be here? Suppose Vee comes back? She's out for blood. I shouldn't even be here. She probably wants to kill me."

"Calm down Nina. I haven't seen her in days so I doubt if she'll be back anytime soon."

"Are you serious?"

"Anyway, why are you worried about any of that stuff if you know it isn't true? It's not true, right?" I asked as Nina lowered her head.

"It's true that I got fired, but it's not the reason. Vee got me fired from the hospital. I was on probation with me being new, and because Milan was in my care at the time of her accident, instead of suspending me, they fired me," Nina cried.

"That bitch. I'm so sorry, Nina. This is all my fault. All of it! If I never had sex with you, none of this would be happening."

"So now you regret being with me?" she asked sitting behind the desk.

"No, I don't regret being with you. I just wish we would've

been smarter. That's all."

"So now what? What happens with us now?" Nina questioned.

"Well, that's up to you."

"How is it up to me? You're the one who's married."

"Well, if it's meant to be it will be, right?"

"Right, and honestly I shouldn't even be focused on that right now. Milan is way more important. I hope the new lawyer I found can at least get you a visit with her because the one we spoke to yesterday sounded like he'd just gotten out of school."

"I agree. Have you heard anything about her condition? Vee won't answer my text messages or phone calls," I asked.

"I spoke with one of my friends, and she said nothing has changed. It doesn't look good though, Malcolm. She did say that Vee has been at the hospital by Milan's side everyday. I gotta get the new lawyer's number because I lost the paper I wrote it down on.

As Nina turned on the computer, a tear escaped my eye. I wouldn't be able to forgive myself if Milan's condition took a nose dive

"Everything is going to be okay sweetheart. Don't cry," Nina said. She held my hand right before going to town on the keyboard.

How did we get here? I stared at Nina. She was beautiful. She was all I needed.

"I heard this guy is one of the top lawyers in New Jersey, Malcolm," Nina replied while looking at the screen.

"I like that. Get me somebody worth calling."

"What's your budget?"

"Vee controls all the money so I don't really…"

"Well no worries. I have savings. The way she was paying me, I should have enough for a lawyer for you for sure."

I looked at her strangely. "You would really do that for me?"

"Of course I would. Why not?"

"Wow." I stared at her again in awe.

"Why are you looking at me like that?" Nina questioned.

"I don't know I just appreciate you so much. Vee, she's just so secretive and so sneaky. But you…you're perfect."

"I'm not perfect."

"You're perfect for me," I added.

Nina blushed. "Have you always been so charming?"

"Who knows? All I know about myself is what my wife has told me."

"Have you ever thought of Googling yourself?"

"No, for what? It wasn't like I was some big celebrity before the accident. I'm a nobody."

"How about we see who you really are sir?"

I laughed. "If you say so."

"Where's the iPad? Let's sit on the floor and have some fun with it."

Grabbing the iPad from the top drawer, we sat on the floor as Nina went to town. I normally only used the iPad to play games. This was going to be interesting.

Sitting on the floor next to me, Nina went to Google and typed in my name and just like that an image of a dapper guy popped up. He was quite flashy. There were so many stories but there was one that made my heart stop instantly. The title read, *The Music World Mourns the Death of Malcolm Fitzgerald.*

"Hold up…could this be me?" I asked looking at Nina. As we both read my heart sunk.

Malcolm Fitzgerald fights for his life after being abducted by unidentified men dressed as police officers. His assistant reported him missing…Firefighters were able to rescue Fitzgerald from the burning vehicle he was abducted in…

"I can't believe this," Nina said as she scrolled down the article.

There were pages and pages of other articles. We then came across another article on a gossip sight, and there she was, my wife, coming out of a building with the guy that I knew now was me. The title read, *Malcolm Fitzgerald and his Latest Mistress Kennedi Kramer Leaving his Downtown Condo.*

"What the hell? What does this mean? Why is she titled my mistress in that picture?"

"Oh my goodness Malcolm. If she is your mistress then who is your wife?" Nina asked as she typed, *images of Malcolm Fitzgerald's family* in the search engine.

Just like that family photos popped up.

"Nina! Nina no!" I yelled.

"That's Charlotte, my patient, that's her! Remember, I asked you did you know her. She said her husband died in a fire. Look here in this picture. His finger is cut off just like yours. Malcolm, this is you."

As Nina continued to search, another article popped up. As I read the article I was sick to my stomach.

Charlotte and Gianni Fitzgerald Best Dressed at the BET Awards.

"That's her. That's the little girl from the restaurant and the hospital. Now I get why Vee was rushing me out of the restaurant. She knew Nina. She knew that was my daughter."

"Malcolm, I can't believe this, your family thinks you're dead."

I was furious. "A lady came to my door not long ago and called that bitch Kennedi but as usual she tried to weasel her way out of it. She's been lying to me about who she was the whole time. "I'm going to kill that bitch."

"You can't tell her anything. We have to come up with a plan. I will help you," Nina suggested.

As my blood boiled and my heart raced I couldn't believe what I was hearing. "Why…why did she do this? Why did she keep me away from my family? Are we even legally married?" Thousands of questions filled my head. "If she changed her name then why not change mine?"

Nina shrugged her shoulders. "I wish I knew. None of this makes sense."

"The only thing she didn't lie about was me being in a car fire."

Just as I got up off the floor the doorbell rang. In a rage, I went to the door hoping that it was Kennedi. I knew it was a stretch but I hoped that she'd accidently left her key and garage door opener somewhere."

"Who is it?" I yelled with anger.

"It's your mother-in-law and your step-daughter!" a lady replied in a deep voice.

When I opened the door, I was mad as hell, but I knew that this troublemaking lady could give me the answers I needed.

"Hi son, where's your wife?" she asked walking into my house without my approval. She immediately tossed off her dirty sandals as if she lived there which made my skin crawl.

"She's not here. Who are you?" I asked the teenage girl who was with her.

"China. I'm Kennedi's daughter."

My eyes widened. "Daughter?"

"She never told me she had a daughter. Damn, you look like her. How old are you?" I asked.

"I'm fifteen. She had a son too, but he died the other day. That's why we need to talk to her. She hasn't been answering our calls," China said with so much pain in her eyes. I could tell that she was deeply hurt.

"He died? How? How old was he?"

"He was only twelve years. He kilt hisself," China replied.

"Wow...this is a lot to take in right now." I looked at the older lady. "And what was your name and relation again?"

"I'm her mother, Maricar," she responded.

Nina ran out of the office after overhearing my conversation with the iPad.

"Sweetheart I'm sorry." Nina said coming out of the office.

"Who is you?" China asked mugging on Nina. She looked just like her mother.

"I'm Nina, Milan's nanny."

"Malcolm? I thought you was dead?" China asked confused.

I watched as the older lady walked away but was so interested in China's comment, that I didn't bother to ask where she was going.

"So, if you the nanny, then why you call him sweetheart?" China questioned aggressively.

"Don't worry about that. Tell me what you know about

me?" I asked right before I heard a bunch of pans fall in the kitchen.

"What's going on in here?" I asked running into the kitchen to see what was going on.

"Y'all got some oodles-n-noodles?" Maricar asked running water in one of my pans.

"Look lady, you've gotta go and please put your shoes back on!" I spat.

"Well shit I'm hungry. I can't be telling you all I got to tell you on an empty stomach," Maricar replied.

"Maricar, come on. Uhh…you so embarrassing," China said in a typical aggravated teenage tone.

"Why are you all here?" I asked.

"Well Mister Malcolm, I sent you a letter and you never called me, so I thought I'd pay you a visit."

"Well, Vee handles the mail so…"

Maricar chuckled. "Look boy I dun told you that daughter of mines name is Kennedi. Kennedi Kramer. Google the bitch I'm sure her mug shot will pop right up."

"Maricar, you told me that we was coming up here because of Chase. Why you lie? I'm not in the mood for all this drama," China said irritated. I could tell she was advanced for her age. Her clothes were way too revealing.

In the corner of my eye, I could see Nina doing just that. Googling Kennedi. Just like that she turned the iPad around displaying a mug shot of my wife.

"So what y'all got to eat in this piece?" Maricar asked as she opened the refrigerator with her dirty ass nails.

"Look lady stop opening my shit, with your dirty ass hands. You need to wash your fucking hands!" I yelled.

"Damn, my bad. It ain't that serious," Maricar said getting a bottle of water before closing the refrigerator door.

"What was she in jail for?" I asked.

"So you really don't know shit about the bitch you married, huh?" Maricar answered. "Well you got you a live one Malcolm. She fucks up everything she touch. I mean she dun ruined, these kid's lives and disowned them, for some other guy named Malcolm over in LA. Shit he died now she back on this side with your ass."

"What did you know about this Malcolm guy?" I asked as Nina stood in a state of shock in the doorway of the kitchen.

"China tell 'em. You know more bout that shit than me," Maricar advised.

China frowned. "I'm not telling him shit. Kennedi is still family. I don't owe this man nuffin'."

"And what the hell you owe Kennedi. She ain't never gave a fuck 'bout you," Maricar shot back.

"The same way you ain't never give a fuck about her! You ruined her life, and she ruined ours. You fucked up Maricar. I'm ready to go. She ain't here so I'm ready." China placed her hands on her hips.

"Well since my granddaughter wanna be disrespectful, I'll tell you what I know. She was a twin. She said the guy Malcolm fucked her sister Kasey, and he was married wit a family and she messed that up. Guess he was pussy whipt or sumthin…Umm what else? She sent Chase's father to prison. She somehow managed to get her twin sister killed and got away wit it. Oh and…"

"What the hell are you saying? This all can't be true," I said in disbelief.

"Boy, you surprised. These days you gotta check the internet to see what you gettin'. So where the hell is that gorgeous grandbaby of mines at? She need to meet her big sister. Shit, I'm back now, so I need to make sure we keep this family unit thing strong," Maricar stated.

"She's in the hospital," I replied.

Maricar looked at me. "What the hell dun happened to her?"

"Look that's probably where your daughter is so maybe you should go there and find her," I said.

"You puttin' us out?" Maricar asked.

I nodded. "Yes, I think you should get your shoes, and get out of my house."

"Well you know my granddaughter China is entitled to stay in this house. Shit this her mama's house. China you ain't got to go. You can move up in here, too. Shit they got enough space."

"Come on Maricar. Let's go," China replied.

Before I could get them to the foyer, suddenly that lying slut who I now knew as Kennedi walked in. Nina was scared to death. I could see it in her eyes.

"What the hell are you all doing in my house?" Kennedi said as she walked into the kitchen, pulled out a gun and cocked it back.

24 Kennedi

"What the hell are you doing in my house bitch?" I asked, pointing my 9mm Luger right at Nina. "Didn't I tell you to never step foot in here again, huh?"

"Please don't shoot me, I'll leave, just please don't shoot," Nina pleaded.

"You think you gonna fuck my husband in my house and then come back in here like it's all good. Bitch you got me fucked up."

"Kennedi, that's your name right, put the fucking gun down," Malcolm stated with authority.

"You damn right nigga, that's my name. Now what?" I was tired of Malcom's ass taking up for this bitch.

"Look I don't want any trouble, I just want to leave," Nina said trying to inch her way towards the door.

"Bitch, now you want to leave. Fuck that!"

"You've already ruined my life! You told my father lies, you got me fired!" Nina belted.

"Oh bitch, don't play innocent. I might've lied about you stealing drugs from the hospital but you've been lying to your father about all those drugs you were getting to help me drug my pathetic husband. That's right Malcolm, your little precious Nina was in on everything. She helped me drug you, to keep your crazy ass on an invisible shock collar."

Both Maricar and China's head moved back and forth between Nina and I like they were at a tennis match.

"Nina, what is she talking about?" Malcolm asked.

Nina shook her head. "Babe, she's lying."

"Babe. Bitch did you just call him babe?" I dropped my handbag and got closer.

"Those weren't drugs, it was all a lie," Nina informed.

"What are you talking about?" I questioned.

"Those pills I gave you. They were never Benztropine. They were only over the counter Naproxen pills to help with some of his pain."

I was enraged. "Bitch, so you took my money all this time for some fake ass pills?"

"You're right I took your money, because I needed it. In return I put Naproxen in the prescription bottles to make your conniving ass think you were drugging Malcolm. That's the only thing I'm guilty of. I would never hurt Malcolm. He's a good man and you don't deserve him."

"Oh yeah bitch?" I said ready to fire before Malcolm jumped in front of her.

"If you shoot her, then you're going to have to shoot me."

"Malcolm, are you serious right now?"

"Yes, I am. Let her leave. She's innocent in all this. We have bigger shit to discuss."

"Goddamn Kennedi. You got some real live problems. Your damn nurse-nanny done fucked your husband, huh." Maricar laughed before I aimed and shot right past her head hitting the picture right by her head.

"You crazy bitch!" she spat, holding her head.

I looked at Malcolm who stood firm. He wasn't going to move until I let Nina go. "Malcolm you're right. Nina, get the fuck out my house. And if you come back here again, you die."

Running through the foyer and out the door Nina yelled, "Malcolm, I promise you I'm going to bring her to you! I promise!"

"You're gonna regret choosing a bitch you hardly know over your wife. Here I was coming home to talk about how I was gonna forgive you for not being there for Milan. How I still wanted us to be a family despite the fact that she's in the hospital because of some shit you and your little bitch caused. But here you are plotting with that whore," I said.

"My wife, huh? You sure you don't have nothing to tell me, because last time I checked, your name wasn't Charlotte Fitzgerald. That's my fucking wife's name."

I stood frozen not knowing what to say as Malcolm continued.

"Bitch you were my mistress. You stole my life from me! Were you that desperate?"

"I fucking loved you, took care of you. Wiped your burnt up ass when you couldn't even cough without crying and this is how you repay me? You would be dead if it wasn't for me nigga. Desperate…are you serious? Never have I ever had low self-esteem motherfucka. Niggas been checking for me since I came out the womb. I ain't never had a hard time getting a man. You got me fucked up!"

"Well, you wanted me bad enough to lie to me so none of that shit you just spit must be true. Are you sure that Milan is even my daughter?" he asked.

Maricar laughed but I ignored her.

"Really? You gonna go there." I leaned against the wall with my gun by my side and suddenly glanced over at my daughter, China. She was a nervous wreck. "China, I'm sorry you always have to see me at my worst. I know what you're thinking about and I'm sorry, baby. I love you."

"You don't love nobody, but yourself," Malcolm added.

"Nigga, have you looked in the mirror lately? You think you're the only nigga I can get? I was with you because I loved you. Yes, I went to extremes to be with you, but it was either me, or death. Do you not understand that I saved your life?"

"Do you understand what you sound like?"

"A dumb bitch in love. Don't forget that you cheated on me in my house with that bitch first."

"Yes! I was in her tight virgin pussy fucking the shit out of her while your daughter almost choked to death and died."

"You evil fuckin' bastard." China said and gave Malcolm the look of death. "She's a baby."

"Who knows if Milan is my baby? I bet she don't even

know who your daddy is?" Malcolm shot back.

"He was my foster father who molested me and got me pregnant, that's who her sperm donor is." I pointed to Maricar. "You know why Malcolm, because that bitch was trying to extort me for money…someone who was supposed to be my mother, left me, and my twin sister in a bus station, when we were little girls. Malcolm I was abandoned as a child by this bitch and you're looking at me like I'm scum. I'm a fucking survivor. Milan was my second chance at doing the right thing and being a good mother and you and Nina almost fucked that up."

"It was an accident damn it!" he screamed.

"Motherfucka do you know all I've been through! You don't know my life. I lost my son and my daughter almost died all in one week, but I'm still here. No matter how many names you call me Malcolm, you can't tear me down." I yelled as tears streamed from my face. My pain was heavy.

"You stole my life! My family is still alive, and you knew it!" Malcolm yelled back.

"Malcolm, I just found out! I thought they were dead. I tried to replace what you lost. All I tried to do was love you."

"Damn, Kennedi, I didn't realize I fucked you up so much," Maricar instigated as if she got pleasure out of seeing me in pain.

"Maricar shut the fuck up," China defended. It felt good to see that she understood my struggle.

Maricar looked at China. "Now you being disrespectful? You defending the same mother who never even mentioned she had kids to her supposed to be husband?"

I ignored both of them. "Malcolm so now what? What you want me to do?"

"Nothing because if my wife is still alive, then this marriage, this life, was all lie and I don't want any part of it."

It felt like I'd been kicked in the chest. The fact that Malcolm was easily willing to give up his life with me was an indescribable pain. I made sure to aim the gun directly at his head. It was the only way to show him how hurt I was. Reacting quickly, Malcolm charged at me knocking me to the floor as the gun fell out of my hand.

As we rolled around on the floor fighting, Malcolm was starting to get the best of me. However, as he gave me a blow straight to the face, suddenly my Williams Sonoma cast iron frying pan came across the back of his baldhead. He was out cold. It was China. She helped me. She helped her mother.

"Ma, you okay," she asked.

"Aww isn't that cute. China to the rescue saving her mother," Maricar mocked.

"Why are you so angry towards her when you're the one who fucked up her life? She couldn't be a mother to us, because she never had a chance from day one. Ma, we're more alike than we want to admit. I know your pain," China said as she cried, hugging me tight.

"I'm sorry, China. I promise, we're going to live right. I'm going to be better for you and Milan," I said.

Maricar laughed. "You two are too much. Kennedi you're never gonna be a good mother. You gonna be just like me."

"I will never be like you bitch!" I shouted.

"Why are you such a hater? You came here to ruin what my muva got goin'. You lied to me and told me we were coming here to talk to her about Chase, when the whole time you wanted to tell Malcolm about her past," China admitted.

"So you're the one who told Malcolm everything." Jumping up I grabbed my gun and pointed.

"Kennedi you really need to stop all of this nonsense. You know you're not about to use that thing," Maricar stated with confidence.

Maricar talked a lot of shit, but the closer I moved toward her, the more she walked backwards. This continued until she was up against the refrigerator.

"Bitch you better use…" was the last thing Maricar said before I slapped her straight against the face with the butt of the gun. As soon as her frail body hit the floor, without thinking, I snatched a knife out of the butcher block and started stabbing her. I just couldn't stop. As blood gushed everywhere I cried, as I watched all of the life leave my mother's body.

"Ma! Ma! Stop it!" China screamed. "Stop it!"

It was a bloody massacre. Dropping the knife on the floor, I went over to my bag and pulled my cell phone out.

"Wassup Ma."

"Brooks, I need your help. I need you now!"

25 Charlotte

"Gianni! Gianni! What did you do to my daughter? Why isn't she moving? Gianni!" I yelled as I shook my daughter once Bryan threw me into the backseat of the black Suburban.

"Mommy, I'm sleepy," she said in a groggy tone as she fell back asleep as if she'd been drugged.

That feeling of thinking my daughter was dead once again took me back a couple of years to the night Sonny took us away from Malcolm. It was all so traumatizing that I hoped Gianni wasn't gonna be fucked up in the head when she got older. Once I knew Gianni was okay I prayed that those two shots I heard where meant for Sonny and that he'd be erased out of my life forever. I prayed that Rafael made it out alive. As I held Gianni's limp sedated body close, I watched the back hotel door to see who made it out alive. Suddenly, my heart sunk.

"Come on boss, we gotta get out of here!" Bryan said as Sonny jumped in the passenger side. All of a sudden I started to feel woozy and the more I tried to open my mouth the more I couldn't talk. Nothing would come out and then suddenly everything went dark.

~

Whether you're a brother or whether you're a mother, you're stayin' alive, stayin' alive. Feel the city breakin' and everybody shakin' and we're stayin' alive...stayin' alive, aha, aha, stayin' alive...

As I opened my eyes to Sonny jumping all over the bed singing along to the Bee-Gees, I prayed that everything that happened last night was a nightmare.

"Top of the morning to you Blackie. Sleep well?"

"You crazy bastard, what did you do to me? Where's my daughter?" I asked trying to open my heavy eyelids.

"She's fine. You know how she loves those animals so Francesca took her to her petting zoo down on the grounds. You've been sleeping a long time. Rough night, huh? Wild sex with my son, Rafael? God rest his soul. Too bad I had to kill him and that old hag of a mother of his, Ernestine." Sonny let out an eerie laugh. "I kind of feel like I should've shot him in the head, too. What do you think? Shooting him in the chest might not have been enough, but if the bullets didn't kill him right away, then the internal bleeding will." He laughed again.

"I didn't sleep with him. You're sick," I lied.

"No, I'm love...sick. So how did you like my theme music? You know I love you. That's why I couldn't kill you. I've sacrificed and gone through a lot to be with you so that would've been stupid. Besides, I can't give up that sweet pudding between your legs," Sonny boasted as he put on a black Prada t-shirt to compliment his black jeans. That usually meant he was about to be up to no good.

"Go to hell."

"Not quite ready to go, but I've done some bad shit so I'm sure when it's my time that's where I'll be. For now though I'm gonna enjoy heaven on earth with my black Barbie," he answered. "However...if you ever think about leaving me again, I promise that not only will I kill you, but I'll make you watch Marty fuck Gianni in her mouth before I kill you both." As Sonny got close in my face, his spit flickered in my eye.

"I hate you!" I turned over as tears started to form in the corner of my eyes. The first chance I got, I was going to kill him. I knew that was the only way to escape this nightmare.

"You might hate me now, but one day we'll look back on this moment and laugh. Charlotte, you're special. Usually when the women in my life get to your age, I have no more use for them, but you're different."

"Bring me my child. I don't want her to be away from me another second."

"You'll see Gianni when I see fit. For now get up and get dressed its three o'clock in the afternoon. I have to run out, but I have a great night planned for us. We need to have a fresh start. I forgive you for your wrongs."

"My wrongs are you..."

"Ah-ah-ah. Don't say another word. You don't want to make me upset," Sonny warned. "Now, I have to settle a debt for a friend of mine, so I'll see you soon." He left out of the room humming tunes.

As I sat up in the bed with my sore body, I let out a loud scream and started crying. Rafael was my ticket out of this hellhole. He'd been so good to me and just like that he was dead. I felt like it was my fault. Getting out of the bed, I started throwing shit everywhere. Shoes, frames, vases, whatever I could get my hands on went against the wall. Glass shattered everywhere. Finally Alfred, the doorman, ran upstairs and burst through the door.

"Madame, are you okay?"

"No! Do I look like I am okay?"

"Well your nurse has arrived. Would you like for me to have her come back another time?"

"Nurse? I don't need a nurse. Who sent her here?"

"I'm not sure Madame, but if she's here then I'm sure Mr. Sabatino agreed to it. I honestly don't think you should send her away. A follow up could be needed," Alfred advised.

"Fine. Give me a minute to get myself together," I said, wiping my eyes.

"I'll also send someone to clean up in here," Alfred said as he walked out of the door.

I tiptoed around the glass and slipped on a pair of black leggings, a tank top and some Puma tennis shoes. Walking out of the room, I stopped when I got to the top of the stairs once I saw Nina sitting on the couch in the formal living room. She looked comfortable as she sipped freshly squeezed lemonade that I'm sure Alfred brought her. He was a sucker for a pretty woman.

What is she doing *here and how did she find me?* I thought. *Did Sonny hire her?*

I pulled my hair back into a ponytail and started down the stairs. As soon as I walked into the living room Nina's nervousness startled me. Usually she was more pulled together, but she looked very disheveled as if she hadn't been home in days.

"Hi Nina, what are you doing here? Is everything okay?"

"Is your husband around?" Nina whispered as if she was about to unleash some major news.

All types of negative thoughts flashed through my mind. I prayed to God there was nothing wrong with my blood work after being so promiscuous with Sonny over the past few years.

"No, he's not. What's wrong? How did you find out where I live?"

"From your hospital records. I was able to get it from someone at the hospital."

"What? That's not right. What the fuck happened to patient confidentiality?

"No, it's not right but trust me, it's necessary. Can we go talk somewhere private?"

"More private than this, what's going on?"

Nina looked over at Alfred. "I just don't want anyone to overhear what I'm about to tell you."

"Okay, let's go on the terrace."

"Madame, Mr. Sabatino has ordered that you do not leave the house. He told me to call him if you do so."

"Alfred, I'm going on the terrace to have a confidential conversation with my nurse. Is that okay with you? I mean you've gone from being the sweet doorman to the watchdog, I mean really?"

"I'm sorry Madame, I just don't want any trouble."

"It's fine. I'm just going to get some fresh air." I rolled my eyes as Nina and I made our way to the gazebo on the terrace to chat.

"Before I say anything, I need you to take this address and phone number and put it in a safe place," Nina said handing me a napkin with some handwriting on it.

"Done. What's up? You're making me nervous." I stuffed the napkin in my bra as we sat down at the table.

"I know this is going to come as a shocker to you, but you have to believe what I tell you. Malcolm is alive."

"What are you talking about? Nina, are you okay?" I asked. I was really nervous at the fact that she was in my house at this point. Maybe she was on drugs or something. I mean did she think I had money. Is that why she was here?

"His wife is probably going to kill me for telling you this but I had to."

"Okay Nina, you might need to leave. You're making me upset. Now…"

"No, seriously Charlotte. Malcolm is alive."

"What type of sick game are you playing? Get the hell out of my house!" I yelled.

"Sweetheart didn't Alfred tell you that you were not to leave out of the house," Sonny said as he appeared in the doorway.

"I just came out to get fresh air," I said not knowing how much he'd heard.

"So, who do we have here?" Sonny asked as he entered the gazebo. Once he took a seat beside me. Nina jumped up.

"I'm gonna go now," Nina said nervously as she tried to exit the gazebo.

"Nina right?" Sonny inquired.

"Yes. Yes. How do…"

"From the hospital right?"

"Yes," she quickly answered in a fearful tone.

"You work for a friend of mine, Vee, right."

Suddenly she started shaking. "Not anymore."

"So, what are you talking to my wife about? Who invited you to my home?"

"Nothing. I was just coming to check on her…to see how she was recovering."

Sonny looked at me. "Is that right Charlotte?"

I honestly didn't know what to say so I chose not to say anything.

"It's so odd that you're here because I've actually been

looking for you. I mean I can't help but think that things happen the way they're supposed to because I actually just left my house to find you and then my doorman called to tell me that my wife had a visitor, and here you are." Sonny smiled. "Wow, it's my lucky day."

"Charlotte, you…" Before Nina could say another word, Sonny pulled out his gun and shot her. As her body fell to the ground he stood over top of her and emptied the clip.

"Sonny!" I yelled in a panic. What was she going to tell me? Was what she was telling me the truth? Was she talking about Malcolm? My mind raced as I tried to suppress my feelings, so that Sonny couldn't detect my feelings.

"That whore slept with a friend of mine's husband so I promised to kill her." He picked up his phone and called Bryan to come and get her body and placed his gun on the table.

"I can't believe you!" I cried then tried to get up.

"Sit your ass down! I'm not done!" Sonny said. "Why was she here? What were you talking about?"

"She didn't get a chance to tell me anything before you killed her."

Sonny walked up to me. "Are you sure?"

I swallowed a lump that formed in my throat. "Yes."

"Mommy! Mommy! Look, I found Auntie Karla where the goats sleep," Gianni said as she suddenly ran from inside the house excitedly. "She was all tied up!"

As soon as I looked up, there Karla stood, aiming a gun, right at Sonny. I jumped up immediately and grabbed Gianni. Trying to avoid her from seeing Nina's dead body I immediately went into mommy mode.

I jumped up. "Gianni find a hiding space, run quick!" I said as she ran, terrified back into the house.

"Put your hands where I can see them." Karla ordered as we both put our hands up. "So glad I remembered all your hiding spots for your guns. You would've thought that after all this time you would've changed it up a bit. Oh and by the way I just wiped away most of your staff," she continued.

Sonny stared at her. "Be careful and that's my one and only

warning."

"I love Gianni. As soon as she freed me from that cage you locked me in, she did such a great job with not letting anyone know that she came to my rescue. I liked Alfred, and Francesca, but they didn't help me when they could, so they're dead." Karla didn't seem the least bit affected by Sonny's threats.

Karla's clothes were completely soiled and her face seemed to be healing from some type of bruise on her left cheek.

He laughed. "They were old anyway."

"Bryan, he's dead, too. Just caught him running up here to your beck and call. Gotta love silencers," Karla said pleased with herself.

"No sentiment to him either. Everyone can be replaced," Sonny replied with no remorse. "But Karla, I can top all of your bodies with two words. Mama and Brother."

"What the fuck are you talking about?" Karla asked as she now aimed the gun directly at Sonny. I tried to inch away from him to give Karla a clear shot.

"Karla, my darling, so have you not heard the news? I killed your mother and that sweet brother of yours last night."

Her face was filled with concern. "You better not have touched my brother."

"He's dead. Your mama too," Sonny added with a devious smirk.

"You son of a bitch! Keep your fucking hands up!"

Sonny laughed. "Okay, gangster."

She looked at me. "Is it true? Did he really kill my mother and Rafael?"

I lowered my head for a quick second. "Yes."

Instead of bursting into tears, Karla smiled.

"Take a look at the bottom of the terrace. Got a nice surprise for you. Go ahead get up and look," She ordered as Sonny followed directions.

As soon as Sonny turned around I could see his rage as his face turned beet red. "You killed him! You killed him! You fuck bitch!"

"Damn, if I would've known I would get this type of r

sponse, I would've killed Marty a long time ago." Karla let out a loud laugh then pulled the trigger, hitting Sonny right in the chest.

"Karla nooooo...don't kill him. Not yet. I need to know," I said as I watched Sonny hold his chest. Blood oozed through his fingers. "Tell me Sonny! Is what Nina said true? Is my husband alive?"

"Aighhhh. You bitch. You shot me."

"Sonny, tell me! Is Malcolm alive?"

He smiled. "Bitch, you'll never know the truth."

Quickly, I grabbed Sonny's gun off of the table in a rage and started firing off shots.

Blop, blop, blop.

The last shot sent him off the terrace, 30 feet.

26 Kennedi

"Hey Ma, how you feelin'?" Brooks asked while looking sexy as ever.

"I have a major headache. What the hell did you give me to help me sleep?'

"Just a little something, something."

"Well, I needed it. Thank you."

"You ain't gotta thank me."

"Yes, I do. I mean you helped me clean up then dispose of my mother's body with no questions asked. On top of that you opened up your home to me and my daughter so I really appreciate you. A lot of people wouldn't have done that."

"Look I'm tryin' to get brownie points," he said smiling.

"No Brooks, seriously, thank you. You didn't have to come to my rescue last night. Without both you and China, I might be in jail right now."

"Well, I'm glad your husband was knocked out cold so he has no idea what happened."

"Fuck him."

"So are you ready to tell me what happened now? What would make you snap like that? I mean look at your hand. You damn near severed your finger stabbing your mother."

"Brooks, I don't want you to think bad of me…."

"Look I'ma stop you right there. I smoked my pops when I was twelve years old, so trust me, I get it."

"Guess we have more in common than I thought. You crazy huh?" I said, trying to make light of the situation. I wanted to hide my emotions.

"That's why you need to stop fakin' on me. Now what the lady do?"

"Just put it like this, she's tortured me and is responsible for everything that has gone wrong in my life. She deserved every fucking slice that I gave that bitch."

I could feel myself getting worked up, so I got off of the bed and went into the bathroom. Closing the door, I locked the door and turned on the water in the sink. As soon as I sat on the floor, I cried like a baby as quietly as I could. I'd lost my grandmother, my son, and killed my mother in less than a month. My daughter was in the hospital fighting for her life, my husband didn't want to be with me, and I was in pain. The only family I had to lean on was my daughter China, who was a constant reminder of my childhood molestation. I didn't know what to do. I was at a loss.

Knock, knock.

"Yes," I said trying to hold in my tears.

"Open the door," China said.

Getting up on my knees I unlocked the door. As she walked in with Brooks' t-shirt and boxers on I laughed. We damn near looked like twins dressed alike.

"What you laughing at?" she asked taking a seat on the toilet.

"Nothing much. You just remind me so much of myself," I said, trying to wipe my face quickly.

"You been cryin', huh?"

"I'm just scared. For the first time in my life, I'm really scared."

"I ain't no snitch. You know I ain't gonna tell on you."

"No, I'm not scared about that. I'm scared about what's next?"

"What do you mean?" she asked fidgeting with her nose ring.

"With us, China I'm so sorry. I'm sorry for how I left you and Chase. I just never knew how to be a mother. I never knew how."

"Look Kennedi, since Maricar came around, I kinda understood you more. I didn't realize how messed up she was. The way she shitted on you everyday while she was at Big Mama's house, you would've thought you really did something to her. She hated you with all she had."

"I know she did. Everybody always hated me. That's why I stayed away. You hated me. Chase hated me. So I just wanted to start over with Milan and do the right thing for once. I didn't know what I was doing with Chase. I didn't want any kids. I mean, I had Chase for all the wrong reasons. I was young."

"I know, but what did I ever do to you? Why didn't you want me?" China questioned.

"I know I'm wrong...do you want to hear the truth?"

China nodded. "Yes."

"Every time I looked at you. I saw the man that molested me and took my virginity. I saw him. You used to look exactly like him. He raped me almost every night for years. I didn't want to be a mother at fourteen, especially having a baby by someone who raped me. His wife even raped me. China, I've been through hell. That's why I never judge anybody. You never know what people have been through and why they are the way they are. I'm in pain. I have flaws. I've been betrayed. I have betrayed my husband. I've done a lot of bad shit. But know that, I never mean to hurt anybody. I'm human and everybody always expects me to be strong. They expect me to just get up, and keep pushing. Well right now I feel weak." I cried uncontrollably.

"It's okay to be weak sometimes," China said as she put her hand on my shoulder. It was if she didn't know if it was okay to touch me.

"I can't remember the last time I hugged my son and now he's gone. Look China. I know I've been a horrible mother to you, but I promise that you don't ever have to go back to that house. Whatever you got at the house you can leave it there. I can't risk losing another child. We're all we got." I got off the floor and held my daughter in my arms, for the first time in the fifteen years of her life, as she cried. We cried together and I felt a weight lifted.

As soon as I looked up, Brooks was standing in the doorway with tears in his eyes.

"Get up and get dressed you cry babies. Let's go see Milan," he said as he shook his head pleased.

"I ain't no cry baby," China said, as she got up and left out of the room. We all laughed.

Grabbing Kleenex from the tissue box on the counter Brooks wiped the tears from my face and gave me a kiss. As I closed my eyes, I kissed him back. Passionately he sucked my neck and kissed all over my face the blood rushed to my clit. Still kissing me, Brooks picked me up and placed me gently across his satin sheets and closed the door.

"So now you want me. Suppose I don't want you," I teased. I leaned back and watched him quickly take off his shorts as he exposed his Ethika boxers.

"This is how I want you, vulnerable. No guards up. Trusting. No mask on. Just me and you."

"Make love to me Brooks." That's all I could say, as he took his boxers off of me and started up my leg kissing my inner thigh. As soon as he opened the lips to my pussy and flicked his tongue against my clit back and forth, I squirmed and held the back of his head for dear life.

"Yes, Brooks yes. Just like that. Oh shit. Yes just like that," I moaned as he sucked my lips and licked my sugar walls.

"You like that."

"Yes. Don't stop I'm about to…ahhhh!" I said as he sucked all of the juices out of my box. As my body laid limp, he got up and put his shorts back on.

"Now get up and get in the shower so we can go. I don't want us to be late seeing baby girl. Visiting hours are over at eight."

"I want you, come here."

"Yo come on. We ain't got time for all that. I just wanted to give you a sample. Shit, I ain't goin' no where." He gave me one final kiss before walking out of the bathroom.

Damn, was he too good to be true? Was this really going to be my life? Things were really looking like they may fall into place. As far as I was concerned whatever Malcolm and I had was over. He'd made his choice so I didn't feel an ounce of remorse for him. He was dead to me and hopefully so was his little mistress, Nina, by now. I was a little concerned that I hadn't heard from Sonny yet, but hopefully he'd taken care of her for me once I sent that picture. She had to go, and Sonny promised me that he would see to it that it was handled. Sonny had the family that he wanted, and now that Malcolm knew the truth, Sonny would probably kill him, too. All I sacrificed for the past couple of years I no longer had a desire for. There was no longer any space in my life for Malcolm and it was now going to be all about my daughters, from this day forward.

The ride to the hospital was a long one. Brooks, China, and I had a good time singing and laughing. I didn't know that China was so cool. She was so much like me it was scary. I was looking forward to getting to know her as her mother. After 45 minutes into the car ride China dozed off. It seemed like Brooks was waiting for that moment because he immediately went in with the questions. As he grilled me on all things Malcolm, I was very open and honest with him about everything that I did. It felt good that he didn't judge me and just listened. For some reason it was easy to talk to him.

"So, has he tried to call you yet?"

"No, and for all I know he could still be knocked out or bled to death. I don't care." I lied.

"You do care. Yo you ain't gotta fake for me, Ma. I understand that you hurt, but don't lie. Look, we go way back man, I mean, how real you are is what attracts me to you. I ain't never gonna judge you." Brooks looked over at me exposing that beautiful smile I loved.

"I just want out. We're going to have to get a divorce. I mean, maybe our marriage will not be valid anyway since his fucking first wife is still alive. Who knows? At this point, all I wanna do is be a mom to my girls."

Brooks laughed. "Well damn, what about me?"

"Well, after the sample you gave me today of what you have to offer, shit I ain't going nowhere." I laughed just before turning the radio up, closing my eyes and enjoying the calming voice of Sade.

Once we got to the hospital and signed in it felt good to see China so excited about meeting her little sister. As we approached the elevator my heart dropped to my stomach when I saw Erin from CPS walking in my direction. I didn't have time for the bullshit. I just needed to see my daughter.

"Hello Mrs. Fitzgerald…"

"You can call me Kennedi," I responded with an exhausted tone. I wasn't in the mood for anymore bad news.

"Well Kennedi, I've been trying to get in touch with you in regards to…"

"Erin, I'm sorry but I've been through a lot these past couple of days and I just want to see my daughter."

"Well I just wanted to let you know that Child Protective Services will not be pursuing a case against you. Milan's nurses as well as her doctor have been advocating for you and feel that you're not a threat to your child. We also thought long and hard about all parents being capable of making a mistake and don't think Milan should be removed from your home. However, this decision is contingent on your husband going to parenting and anger management classes. I'll also be assigned to your case and will make unannounced visits for a while just to make sure Milan is in a safe environment."

"Trust me, you don't have to worry about my husband being around Milan anymore. I'm gonna go to court to get full custody of her."

"Oh really? Well, we can discuss that at a later time. For now, I will let you guys get to your visit."

"Erin, thank you so much! You really made my day with this news. Thanks again!" I reached out and gave her a huge hug.

Could this be a sign that God knew I was trying to do better? Quickly, we all got on the elevator as tears of joy strolled down my face. Once we passed the nurse's station and were approached by the same black nurse who'd helped me before.

"Mrs. Fitzgerald, oh my goodness, where have you been? I've been calling you since yesterday." She looked frantic.

"What's going on?" My heart started to pound.

"It's Milan."

"What about her? Oh my God, what is it?"

Brooks immediately jumped into support mode by rubbing my back in a circular motion.

"I'm not gonna ruin it for you. Since you're here, you can just see for yourself," the nurse replied as we all quickly walked behind her.

Even though the nurse finally smiled, I still prepared myself for the worst.

As soon as we walked in her room, I cried. "Milan. It's Mommy."

"Mommy," she said with a huge smile. She was no longer hooked up to the machine, and was breathing on her own.

"Ma, she's so pretty," China said.

I looked at her. "Did you say, Ma?"

"Yeah, is that okay?"

"Yes, that's perfect." I said with tears of joy.

As Brooks stood between us and hugged both China and I he smiled. Maybe I could be a good mother. Maybe it's a possibility that I can be a better person. Only time will tell, but right now, life felt a lot better.

27 Malcolm

"Daddy help me! Help me Daddy!"
As soon as I got to the car it burst into flames.
"Noooooo!" I screamed as my body caught fire. I could see
my daughter's body melt as we both screamed in pain.

Waking up again in a deep sweat my head was pounding. I
could barely walk. I'd been going in and out all day and hadn't had
the strength to get up off the floor. My head hadn't stopped bleeding and my phone only had 20% battery life left. Picking up my
phone, I tried calling Nina again for the millionth time.

"Nina call me back. Call me back please. I need you," I
said leaving her another message. I'd been calling her phone since
I came to. I was starting to feel faint.

As I laid on the floor I stared at the picture on the wall of
me, Kennedi, and Milan Looking at the image that now represented a lie, I became infuriated all over again. This bitch had
stolen my life and identity from me. All this time I'd been having
flickers of a brown-skinned woman in my dreams but I thought it
might've been my mother. I knew I felt love for the woman, but I
could never see her face. I prayed that Nina found Charlotte and
my daughter, my real family. I wanted out of this house and wanted
to be as far away from Kennedi as I could be. I hated that bitch and
only God knew what I would do if I ever saw her again. I wanted
no parts of her or Milan. I couldn't bare to raise a child that I
wasn't even sure was mine anymore.

Picking up the iPad off the floor beside me, I stared at the photos again of the old me. I was so frustrated because I couldn't remember anything about this guy. I was mad that I just let Kennedi dictate my life. I allowed her to tell me lies without questioning her at all. I had nobody to blame but myself.

How could I be so stupid! I yelled as I threw the iPad into the wall causing the glass to shatter.

With all the energy I had left I got up, picked up the fireplace poker and began to destroy everything in sight. From the ceramic statues to the glass vases I wanted to break everything I could get my hands on. The angrier I became, the weaker my body felt. As I fell to the floor I cried like the first day of kindergarten.

My body felt weak. I was losing too much blood perhaps. I didn't know what was going on. Was that the doorbell I heard, or was I hallucinating? *Maybe it was Nina,* I thought to myself. *Maybe I was hearing things,* I thought again as I fell to the floor. My eyes were getting heavy. All of a sudden I could hear footsteps walking toward me. I tried to get up, but my body felt heavy and it didn't allow me to. I could hear voices.

Oh no. I can't lose him. I just got him back. Should I call 911?

No, don't call the police! We don't know what happened here.

We need to get him to the hospital.

Malcolm it's me. It's your wife. Open your eyes.

Come on. Let's get him in the car.

There was nothing I could do, even though I had so much to say. My body felt weaker and weaker as I was being pulled and dragged. I couldn't open my eyes to see her face as bad as I wanted to.

"Daddy, is that my daddy."

"Gian…" I couldn't say it. Everything went dark.

Get caught up on Kennedi, Malcolm &
Charlotte's lives before A Wife's Betrayal!!!!
Get Your Copy of

Paparazzi

Today!!!!

See More LCB Titles at
www.lifechangingbooks.net

CHECK OUT THESE LCB SEQUELS